THE
HOSTESS

THE
HOSTESS

Diary of a female vampire

MICHELLE F. SANTOS

authorHOUSE®

AuthorHouse™
1663 Liberty Drive
Bloomington, IN 47403
www.authorhouse.com
Phone: 1-800-839-8640

This is a work of fiction. All of the characters, names, incidents,
organizations, and dialogue in this novel are either the products
of the author's imagination or are used fictitiously.

Published by AuthorHouse   01/12/2015

ISBN: 978-1-4918-7396-0 (sc)
ISBN: 978-1-4918-7378-6 (e)

Library of Congress Control Number: 2014905140

Provided by Dreamstime / imagery by Dreamstime

This book is printed on acid-free paper.

Book Two
The Hostess;
Diary of a Female Vampire

We have drunk the Soma

We have become immortal

We have gone to the light

We have found the gods

The Rig-Veda

Chloe

Wow! What an ending to the first diary. I can't wait to settle down and begin the second one. It's about 8:15 in the morning and the sun is shining pretty bright. It looks like it's going to be a beautiful day so I should get a lot of reading done. I learned the hard way I had to have more than a pillow to sit on if I was going to read for a couple of hours. I decided to steal a couch cushion from the garage. I've stretch out, poured myself a cup of coffee from my thermos and I'm ready to go.

I'm Chloe. I just realized I read the entire first diary and never said who I was. I kind of feel I need an identity, like Nicci.

It's the beginning of summer, again. I'm out of school with no job lined up for the summer. I think I will read the second diary as my summer job. There were three diaries that I found, when I was snooping through the houses, in my neighborhood , that were either foreclosed or just abandoned. The housing market is still in a slump in my neighborhood.

They are perfect for me to hone my investigating skills (snooping) in case I ever want to become a detective or something. I'm extremely nosy and like to see how other people live.

Anyhow, I was walking through, examining old trunks, and my foot fell through an old floorboard. While trying to pull it out, I found three old books. On closer inspection, I discovered they were diaries written by a woman. After flipping through the pages, I noticed it was written in both Italian and English. The writer was a woman that looked like she was saying she was a female vampire. (How cool was that?) The first one told of her change in 1834, her first love and roughly the first one hundred years of her love life.

I've just started the second book. It seems to pick up near the end of WWI. Dominique Santa Maria, Nicci, is the hostess of a popular club in Harlem, called the Savoy. It had the reputation of being one of the hottest clubs in Harlem. It had live music and dance shows. No, it wasn't an exotic dance club. I don't think they even knew what a strip club was in the early 20th Century. Dance music was just being born. No one was waltzing anymore. Women were flashing more skin; boobs, thighs, even ankles.

Thank god—they had electricity, phones, and even the radio. The big band sound was the dance music craze. Women had even started cutting their hair. The rich were extremely rich and the poor were extremely poor. Prohibition had been made into law, which meant Organized Crime (the Mob or Mafia) had come into being and was involved in everything. Lucky Luciano was in New York City and Chicago. People were going to silent movies, Broadway and the Ziegfeld Follies. Cole Porter's love songs were constantly playing on the radio.

That's enough history. Back to Nicci's second diary.

The Savoy

Chapter 1

It was 1918 and I'm still at the Waldorf-Astoria in my suite. It was June and I heard a knock at my door. It was early evening, so I had been up for at least an hour, but Maria answered the door. A young man in an Army uniform was standing at the door.

"I have a telegram for a Dominique Santa Maria. Are you her?" He said.

Maria answered. "No, she's in her bedroom dressing for the evening."

I heard the voices so I came out of my room to see what was going on. "What's going on, Maria? Who's this at the door?"

The soldier spoke up."Ma'am, I have a telegram from the War Department. You are listed as a Mr. Jack Smith's next-of-kin. No one else was listed. May I give it to you?"

I took the telegram from the soldier and slowly opened it. I had heard about women receiving telegrams from the War Department. It was always bad news, usually death. I knew Jack was a vampire and couldn't die so I couldn't think what it could possibly say. As I began to read it, I could feel the tears beginning to form. I couldn't let them spill over and fall because they would have been bloody. As I read the letter, I let it flutter to the floor. Maria picked it up and read it. I was frozen from shock.

"Oh my God! Ma'am? How could this happen?"

The soldier interrupted. I felt his hand grab mine, steering me to a chair before I fainted. "I hear he died a hero. They were in a minefield in Germany and he stepped on one. I don't think he suffered. He died immediately."

I looked up at the soldier, not believing what he had just said. I took the telegram from Maria and read it again.

Dear Miss Santa Maria,
This telegram is to inform you that Mr. Jack Smith was reported
"killed in action".
He was reported to have died a hero saving his platoon.
He will be awarded the Purple Heart for his bravery.
His body will be shipped home to have a military burial.
Please accept our sorrow at your time of loss.
Sincerely,
The War Department

"Thank you." I whispered as I stood and closed the door, pushing the soldier out. I could hear the muffled sounds of the soldier's feet as he walked away from my door. I broke down into big heaving sobs. "Maria, he was a vampire. He wasn't supposed to die. The only way he could have died was to be decapitated or severely dismembered. I can't believe he was killed."

"Nicci, I've never lost anyone special so I don't really know what to say. I know your sad and heartbroken but pull yourself together. I don't like to see you so sad. Hold onto your good memories. You have to figure out what to do about the Savoy."

After a few minutes of sniffing, I said. "Oh my gosh, you're right. Call Samuel! I've got to get to the Savoy and break it to the staff that Jack won't be back. We have to make plans and business decisions. There's so much to think about. I guess this means I'll officially take over the Savoy."

I went back into the bedroom to finish getting dressed for the evening. I had never mourned for anyone before because basically vampires don't die. What to wear! I don't own anything black but navy blue was close enough. I needed to look both sad and businesslike. I wanted the staff to take me seriously if I was going to take over the Savoy. Jack had left me in charge when he left for the war. I had been running it with assistance from Harry and Ricardo since Michael was dead. They were the male dancers. We still hadn't replaced him since his death last year from a freak accident. (I had killed him because he knew I was a mulatto and had nerve to try and blackmail me.

(For those who don't know me, my name is Dominique Santa Maria. My friends call me Nicci. I was turned in 1818 by Jack's competitor, my first love, Heinrich. My darkest secret is that I'm a mulatto. In America, mulattoes are considered Negroes and have very little power in 1918. They definitely couldn't mix with whites in clubs unless they were performers. I am Italian with a thick accent, so no one ever questions my color. I'm considered exotic. To bring you up to date, I came to America and met Jack Smith. He was the host of the Savoy. It turned out he also owned half of it. Jack and I fell in love but Heinrich, my maker, reappeared after nearly 100 years, to try and rekindle our relationship. Jack didn't agree or appreciate Heinrich's advances but WWI started. Heinrich naturally returned to Austria, where he joined the Austrian Army. Jack joined the American Army when the USA joined the war. Heinrich hasn't returned yet and now Jack is dead. I killed Michael because he was going to expose me as a mulatto. That would have destroyed my life.)

I quickly dressed in a navy blue pinstripe suit. I had Maria call Samuel, my chauffeur, to come get me. We needed to get to the Savoy as soon as possible. I need to make some sort of plan for the future of the Savoy. It looks like since I'm Jack next-of-kin, the Savoy will be mine. The men weren't going to like it. I'll have to take a low profile if I expect to own half of the Savoy.

****

Samuel drove me directly to the Savoy. I planned to break the news to the staff, immediately. It was 8p.m. and the club had just opened for the night.

Chapter 2

Upon arrival at the Savoy, I gathered the staff around the bar.

I dramatically waved my hands. "Listen, everyone quiet down! I have an announcement to make. Jack is dead! He died in a German minefield. Evidently he stepped on a mine and that was it."

Tracy said. "Are you sure?"

"Yes." I sighed, trying to hold the tears back."I received a telegram this evening from the War Department saying that Jack had been reported killed in action. He is to be awarded the Purple Heart." The more I talked the more I cried. I didn't care if they saw my bloody tears. Everyone at the staff meeting knew I was a vampire. I think I really loved him.

Harry put his arm around my shoulder and said. "Nicci, be strong. I know how much you loved him but we'll get through this. What are we going to do about the club? Are you going to continue to run it or will you encourage the other owners to sell it or close it down? Have you noticed the Temperance workers have been picketing outside the club because we serve alcohol? That just adds to our problems."

"I think, if the partners will have me, I'll buy up Jack's share of the club. (I hadn't let anyone know that Jack had left the club to me and named me his next-of-kin.) I definitely want us to stay open. We'll have to keep it quiet about my ownership, for now. No one can find out that a woman is involved in the ownership of the Savoy."

Martha sniffled and wiping her nose added. "I'm going to miss him, though. I think that's a great idea, Nicci. You've been running the club since Jack left for the war. You might as well be partial owner. Plus, we need to replace Michael. He's been dead for almost a year, too."

Ricardo offered Martha and me red, silk hankies and I wiped my bloody eyes. Martha blew her nose. At least I didn't ruin his hanky. "Thanks for your support. I'll talk to the owners tomorrow. For tonight, it would be nice if we dedicate the evening to the memory of Jack. Let's pull ourselves together and have a great show. We need to open the doors."

****

The club hadn't changed since Jack left. Vampires still poured into the club for our famous Bloody Marys and humans came for the alcohol and dancing. The club has a fabulous floorshow. Since they were short a male dancer everyone got to do more solos instead of all couples. I don't think the audience even noticed we were down a man. We were going to have to start holding auditions soon. First, though, I had to meet with the other partners of the club. I needed to own the club, officially. I didn't even know who the partners were.

I played hostess and greeted most of the guest when they came to the door. We had our first floor show at 10 p.m. Harry and Ricardo opened with a tap number, next, the girls came out in their skimpy, white, satin shorts with white feathered boas wrapped around their necks. It was amazing to see Harry and Ricardo flip the girls across the stage.

I, personally, went from table to table greeting all the guests. I carried my own personal Bloody Mary with me. (Naturally, it was real blood.) I thought once I took over the Savoy we would start serving dinner. I had kept up my correspondence with Sally and now that the war was over I was going to invite him to work as head chef at the Savoy. He had promised me he would come to America at the end of the war. I knew if I brought Sally on board the food would be exciting for both humans and vampires.

(Salvatore Regnosco was the last vampire I had loved in Italy. He let his friends call him Sally. He had promised me, before I left

Europe, he would keep in contact with me, even during the war. He was not your typical vampire. I loved him for his laugh. Sally was short and a little on the chunky side. He had been a baker when he was human and consumed a lot of bread. He had a long blond ponytail and blue eyes that sparkled when he laughed. As an aside, he was good in bed, too. He generated so much heat when we made love that he could steam up a window. Sally even made sparks of electricity appear when we kissed.

I could hear myself sighing every time I thought of him and our many escapades we had been involved in. Sorry, I got a little reminiscent)

****

The club, usually, does two shows a night and the bar closes at 1 a.m. The privacy rooms for the vampires and their partners, for blood, also closed at 1 a.m. All the guests had trickled out by 2 a.m., and then we had to clean up. I didn't have a regular cleaning staff so everyone pitched in. WuYi, the waiter/busboy and SuChi, the waitress/bus girl did most of the clean up. I usually locked up by 3 a.m. This allowed Harry and Ricardo, both vampires, and Linda and Tracy, also vampires, time to get home to their coffins.

Chapter 3

Tonight, I was to meet the real owners. Jack had neglected to tell me he worked with the Mob, (Organized crime). I didn't feel threatened, like I suppose I should have, but I am over *one hundred years old.* It takes a lot to scare me. In my long life, I've pretty much seen or done everything. They definitely couldn't threaten my life. I was meeting with two lower Mob members that worked for Lucky Luciano. They weren't important. *That's when I met Johnny!*

"Hi, I'm Johnny Vittini. I work for Mr. Luciano. My partner's name is Vito Soloni. Who are you? We're looking for the new potential owner."

"That, would be me, gentlemen. I am Dominique Santa Maria. My friends call me Nicci. I think we are going to be friends, so call me Nicci. Please to meet you Johnny, Vito." Johnny was something to look at. He was a very dark, Italian man with long, wavy, black hair that was pulled back into a ponytail with a small leather string. He had to be at least 6'1", extremely muscular with blue eyes that looked like the ocean. His smile was big enough for all thirty-two teeth to show and cause his eyes to twinkle. If I hadn't heard his heart beating I would have sworn he was a vampire. Vito was a little shorter but just as well built. They both wore black jackets, long sleeve white shirts with black bowties. I couldn't tell if he had a hairy chest. I would have loved to know. Vampires have a tendency to have smooth skin.

"It's a pleasure to meet you gentlemen. I have some business I'd like to talk to you about. I assume you are representing Mr. Luciano."

They both nodded yes.

"I was notified, as Jack's next-of-kin, he had died in Germany. He's going to receive the Purple Heart and his body will be sent home to be buried in the National Memorial Cemetery, with full military honors. He left me in charge of the club. Once he's buried, I'd like to completely take over the club and become partners with Mr. Luciano."

Johnny started laughing. *"Are you serious? Why would Lucky Luciano want to have a dame for a partner?"*

"First of all, gentleman, *I am not a dame! Second, I am a young lady or woman and I do not appreciate being called a dame. Nor do I appreciate your laughter."*

"I apologize, ma'am. What makes you think Mr. Luciano would want a female partner?"

"Well, I am Jack Smith's next-of-kin. He legally left his next-of-kin the Savoy or at least his part of the Savoy. *That next-of-kin is me! I'll give you a minute to let that sink in before we discuss what's going to happen next!* I am willing to pay my share."

You could tell they were both furious. Both Johnny and Vito were changing colors and sweating. They knew they had no choice but to accept my offer. Naturally, I kept getting a little distracted by Johnny's good looks. He probably would have convinced me to let it go if he had offered to have sex with me. Business was business, though. I was hoping he would say Mr. Luciano would be glad to be my partner and he would be Lucky's representative.

Instead he said. "I think he'll do it, but you have to put in $20,000 like Jack did. That's the only way Lucky will be happy. We'll let you run the club but were going to take 20% off the top of the weekly receipts. You can hire your own staff but we decide who can come and who cannot come to your club. You've had some unexplained deaths here in the past few years and the police had to be called. We can't have the cops here unless you let us buy off some cops. You know, for security."

I was worried he might have known about the vampires coming and feeding off some of the guests. I never knew how Jack kept the presence of vampires away from the public or his partners. I was never privy to that information. I got the feeling that he didn't know anything about them. I knew he was talking about Michael's death and the few hosts that had gotten over drained. I was glad that he offered to buy off some cops for me. I had no idea or desire to talk to the police force. Between the Temperance women and me having to fine illegal sources for alcohol, I needed the protection. The Prohibition Act was bound to pass and the club was going to need protection.

"Sure, you can buy off as many cops and judges, as you want. Whatever it takes. Just let me know who I have to pay and how much."

"We'll let you know who's on the payroll. It's Tuesday night. We expect the $20,000 by close of business on next Tuesday night. That gives you a week to gather the money, receipts, and the books together. There will be no extensions."

I smiled. No one knew what kind of money I had. Plus, Jack had left me more than enough money to pay these guys. That will be my little secret. I'm finally going to own something in America. I was so excited.

"Okay, gentlemen, we have a deal. Will Mr. Luciano draw up the contract or should I have my attorney do it? You can get back to me. But for now, let's drink on it to seal the deal. WuYi, could you get three glasses of champagne for us?"

Upon WuYi's return with the glasses, we tapped glasses and toasted. *"To the Savoy!"*

I thought to myself, once this deal is sealed Johnny can be a potential lover. Too bad he's human but who knows maybe I can legitimately change that. I escorted them out and called another meeting of the staff. *We needed a new dancer!*

Chloe's thoughts

Since I was out for the summer, I would have plenty of time to read this second diary. It picks up right were the first one left off. Without trying to make a bad joke, Nicci didn't even skip a heartbeat about killing Michael. It's too bad that Jack got killed. I really liked him. I thought he was a great replacement for that Heinrich she keeps dreaming about. She spent half of the first diary talking about how much she missed him or how good he was in bed. I mean, really! She is over one hundred years, had multiple partners and is still pining over her first love. This Johnny character has potential. He sounds like he may be a vampire before this diary is complete.

I still wish I could take these diaries home and read them in the comfort of my own home. At least my house has air conditioning. These foreclosed houses don't even have electricity. You can imagine how hot it is up in this attic. I thought about moving to another room in the house and opening a window but I'm afraid someone from the street will notice the window was open. I'd be busted. I can't even bring ice cream into the house. I mean, who reads a good book without a bowl of banana split ice cream? I have to settle for a couple of bottles of frozen water and a semi frozen Coke. At least I have two packs of Twinkies, a Twix, chips and a roast beef sandwich. I learned, after reading, the first diary to be better prepared. One never knows when they are going to get to a good spot and not be able to put the book down.

I can't wait to see who is going to take Michael's place. I wonder if she is going to get another vampire or a human. I wonder what she is going to do with Sally if she decides to sleep with Johnny. This is started to get juicy.

Before I start, I need a quick bathroom break. I'll just readjust these pillows, a quick stretch and start reading again.

Chapter 4

I wasn't involved in the auditions. I'd let Harry and Ricardo choose their own new partner. It didn't take long to find out who the vampires were and who was human. I was told that being a dancer at the Savoy was considered a top job. Every man that could dance had turned out, including a few boys that we had to send away. The vampires seem to learn the audition routine within the first five minutes. Some could even anticipate Harry or Ricardo's next dance move. Most of the humans struggled with the choreography because their bodies didn't seem to be as flexible as the vampires.

They ended up choosing a dancer from Harlem. (Surprise, he was a vampire!) He was originally from New Orleans. He had studied tap as a little boy. Harry thought since he was a vampire he could easily teach him the rest of the routines. His name was Robert Manchester. I don't think it was his real name but it made a great stage name.

Naturally, he was a beautiful specimen of a Black man. He was only 5'9' but he had muscles everywhere. Even his thighs look sculpted. His skin tone was chocolate and he had the most amazing, dark, brown eyes. They looked like muddy pools of water. They were edged in gold. They were almost cat-like in appearance. He constantly grinned and seemed to have an easy going personality. He would fit in perfectly. (Or so I thought. I didn't know yet that he was involved in voodoo, much less a voodoo priest.)

****

I had informed the staff that I was taking over the Savoy. They didn't need to know all the details. As far as the guests were concerned the club was still run by Jack. I hadn't announced his death yet. I was going to continue to play hostess. I knew most of the guests would stop coming if they thought the club was owned by a woman. I would use Johnny's name if I absolutely had to have a front man. The only change I had in mind was to find Sally and begin to serve meals. Sally could provide those exciting vampire dishes and regular meals. I knew that would increase business, especially if we had a difficult time getting alcohol.

Now that the dance troupe was complete, we could put my changes in place. Since Robert was a vampire, he only needed a week to learn the routines. That Friday night we introduced him at the first show. The dancers had used this as an excuse to get a whole new wardrobe. The men had gotten gold satin tuxedos for the opening number. They would change clothes for the second half. The women were going to wear a gold bra and short shorts. They were very skimpy outfits but they had fans of gold feathers. I could hardly wait to see the new show. They tapped and flipped across the stage and the audience hooted and hollered throughout the show.

After the applause, from the first show, Harry introduced Robert as the new dancer. No one seemed to care that Michael was no longer part of the troupe. The audience went wild, so of course, Robert gave them a sample of what he could do. Someone threw some salt on the stage and he began to do a soft shoe step across the salt. It was incredible and the audience went wild.

I could see Tracy smiling behind the backstage curtain. The look on her face said he was a definite replacement for Michael. I just hoped he wasn't like the previous Michael.

****

While the audience was in such a frenzy, I thought it would be a good time to make the announcement.

I cleared my throat, loudly, and began. "I'd like to announce the club is going to be making a few changes. You know, with Prohibition right around the corner, we're going to have to control the flow of alcohol here. (The audience began groaning, laughing and booing, all from different parts of the room.) You can drink it but we can't sell it to you. Now, this doesn't mean you can bring your own bottle. (I laughed.) We may have to change the name of a few drinks we serve. So, to compensate for those losses, we are going to start serving meals. Naturally, they will be the finest meals that New York has to offer. You may only drink *soda water*. (I could hear sniggling in the background from a few people.) We may be able to develop tea, lemonade, and our trusty Bloody Marys for those of you that must have a drink. This plan will start in a few months. As soon as I find a chef, we can implement these changes."

I got a round of applause, so I felt like this was a secure idea. I hadn't told anyone I had received a letter from Sally. The letter was written a couple months ago but it finally found me at the Waldorf-Astoria. It was just a note:

Dear Nicci,
I finally found you. I hope you are as good as I am.
I didn't get hurt. I've had plenty of time to create a few new dishes.
Can't wait to see you and have you taste them.
I'm coming to New York City.
I hope you can find me a job and a place to stay.
I hope we can pick our relationship up were we left it.
You have no idea how much I have missed you.
I'll be in New York in July.
Love,
Salvatore *(Sally)* Regnosco

It was already near the end of June and Sally was coming sometime in July. I didn't have much time to prepare for him. He wasn't going to have a hard time getting a job since I wanted him to cook for me at the Savoy. He'd just have to stay at the Waldorf-Astoria until the disposition of Jack's house was settled. In the back of my mind I was hoping we could live together. I realize it's not socially acceptable but I was still having strong feelings for him. Anyway, he's exceptional in bed.

I was sure Jack left it to me but it had to be settled in Probate court. We hadn't been legally married and a complete will hadn't been found. Once that was settled, Sally and I could move in together. It was definitely large enough for Sally, Maria, Samuel, his family and I. His downstairs tenants may have to move. I would give them plenty of notice, though, if need be.

I don't know how Sally found me but I'm glad he did. I had to get into Jack's house and do some cleaning. It needed some redecorating and modernizing. It needed an icebox. (I heard about them on the radio.) I also wanted to add a wood burning stove and some electric lamps. I had so many plans. Maria and Samuel would have to do furniture hunting for me. I had heard about a book called the Sear's catalog. One could order just about anything from it. Both the Savoy and Jack's home needed cooking equipment.

Our period of mourning would be the perfect excuse to close the Savoy and redecorate. I mean really, it's 1918 and we still looked as if we were stuck at the turn of the century. The tables needed white linen tablecloths, white drip candles in the center and small glass ash trays. The ash trays would have to be constantly emptied but I think they gave the club a touch of class. We would use black linen napkins with Savoy embroidered on each one. The Savoy was going to be a class act. The dishes will have a large S on the platters and the silverware will have an S on the handle. I was having a menu printed as soon as Sally created one. We're going to be the classiest club in New York City and Harlem.

I also had to remind the guys to restock our bottled blood supply. We seemed to running low. I wonder if our vampire clientele had increased. I, personally, was down to my last case. I knew Sally loved to drink. We'd have to keep an extra case in the kitchen just to keep Sally happy.

The staff was excited about the changes happening to the club. Everyone knew Sally was coming. They were looking forward to Sally running the kitchen. The entire staff was in on the planning, the redecorating and the big celebration for the re-opening of the Savoy. The dancers were practicing new routines every night. I had hired a new jazz quartet. Music was changing and we didn't want to get left behind. Times were changing and so were dances. Clothing had changed. Women were wearing much shorter dresses with shorter hair.

Chapter 5

We had made it through 1918 and 1919 without being shut down once. On Jan. 16, 1920, The Prohibition Act was passed. It was the 18th Amendment which prohibited the sale and manufacturing of alcohol. A new breed of gangster was born. Special Prohibition agents were hired. They were responsible for raiding the clubs now called speakeasies. Rumors said they could be easily bribed. I was going to have to contact Johnny to get more protection. We hadn't been busted yet but I was having a hard time getting alcohol. My customers expected quality liquor, not that bathtub moonshine. I had enough money flowing around to the local cops that the alcohol should have been flowing a lot more easily.

I also needed Harry and Ricardo to find another mortician to supply us with more bottled blood. At this point, I could not keep up with the demand. The vampires coming to the club seemed to be guzzling the blood. One can't just walk into a funeral home and ask for bottled blood. A lot of hands had to be paid. Plus, as far as the mob knew only humans came to the club. I had to keep it that way.

I needed at least two morticians working for me. Now that Sally was cooking for me, he used a lot of blood in his specialty dishes. We were the only club in the New York City area that served blood to vampires. All his blood dishes had become quite popular.

The club was packed every night. Sometimes we had to send people away because there was no room. Both the human and vampire clientele had grown.

Even though Sally was present every night, he was working so hard, we hadn't had time to resume our relationship. I wasn't going to give up. I figured I'd let him settle in then I'd work on starting our sexual relationship again. But I noticed Johnny had started coming around more often. He seemed to be coming more than once a week and was lingering around the bar, after he picked up his receipts. Receipts weren't due until Friday, yet here he was on a Wednesday night.

In between shows, Martha came over to the bar where I was standing, watching the evening crowd. "Have you noticed how often that Johnny character comes to the club? He claims he's here to pick up receipts. I never saw him coming twice a week to pick up receipts when Jack was here. I think he likes you. I get the impression you like Sally, though."

"I hadn't noticed Johnny. (I couldn't tell Martha I had dreamed about Johnny, just last night.) I really do care for Sally. We used to be lovers in Italy but I feel as if the war has changed him. He doesn't seem to want to renew our sexual relationship. I get the impression he only wants to be friends. Sally was a great lover and I really hate to lose that. All he ever talks about is food and how to prepare it. He wrote to me saying he wanted to pick up our relationship where we left off. I think that was just a ruse to have me help him get in the United States. He's not really interested in having sex with me. That really hurts. I don't know what's wrong."

Martha placed her hand on my shoulder. She sighed and said. "Give him time. He probably saw a lot of horrible things in Europe and has to get used to normal life again. That would change any man."

"You're right." Just as I spoke about Sally, he came from the kitchen wiping his hands.

He reached for my hand. "Nicci, I know I've been rude by not talking to you. I've been so preoccupied with returning from the war and getting used to my new job. I really need to say thank you in a more personal way. Would you have dinner with me after the Savoy closes? I'll make something very special for you. Please say yes."

Martha gave me a look that said 'see, you just needed to give him time.'

I smiled my best smile and said. "Are you psychic? I'd love to have dinner with you. May be you can make that Crème Brule` that you made for Puccini?"

"I'd love to. Anything else special that you'd like for me to make?"

"I would like something else but I have to save that for when we're alone."

Sally was smiling as he returned to the kitchen. He was unconsciously wiping his hands on his apron again.

As the kitchen door swung close behind Sally, Johnny walked through the front door. (What timing!) He had an overconfident smirk on his face as he strolled over to the bar where I was standing with Martha.

"Evening, ladies! I was in the neighborhood and I thought I would stop in to say hello. How ya doing? Nicci, you don't usually stand around the bar smiling. You look like the cat that swallowed the canary. Care to share your thoughts?"

Martha laughed. "We were just talking to Sally, our new chef. I don't think you've met him yet. What do you want?"

"I came to talk to Nicci, not you, Martha. I was wondering if you would have dinner with me this evening."

Martha could barely contain herself with laughter. She gave me that look that said 'what are you going to do now?'

"I'd love to go to dinner with you. I'm sorry, though. I have plans for this evening. How about tomorrow?

Johnny blushed first then his ears slowly turned red with anger. I could feel the heat radiating from the red glow his face was giving off. He looked at me and calmly said. "Well, I don't know about tomorrow night. I may have plans."

(This was interesting. I'd never had two men, at the same time asking me for a date. One was human. One was a vampire. This could be fun.)

I replied. "Well, if you can't do tomorrow, you choose the night and I'll try and keep it available." I laughed and asked. "Why are you so red? Did I embarrass you or something?"

"No. I just thought of something and it was an embarrassing thought. I'm sorry."

"What did you think of?"

"Well, it's kind of rude, but if you must know, I thought, how you would look without that dress on. Again I'm sorry."

I should have been embarrassed but I felt a giggle escape. I haven't giggled in years. "That's okay. It *is* kind of rude but I've thought some pretty rude things about you. I'm looking forward to going out with you."

"I'll be back next Saturday. Don't make any plans. We'll go out after closing." He leaned over and suddenly kissed me on the corner of my mouth and cheek. I wanted to blush. Since I can't blush, I plastered a huge smile on my face. He turned and walked out the front door.

I attempted to go back to work. I could barely think straight much less walk. As I floated from table to table, visiting the guests, I felt a large grin forming on my face.

Chapter 6

Sally had already been at the Savoy for nearly a year before he got around to asking me out. He came to America in 1919, it was now 1920. Since alcohol wasn't readily available it made it tough to serve drinks but we could still serve Bloody Marys. With the talent of Sally's cooking most people didn't seem to notice that they weren't getting real whiskey or scotch. Sally still made that wonderful bread that everyone in Rome had raved about. The Americans' loved it. His specialty was Beef Wellington. His seafood dishes weren't far behind. Being so close to Boston allowed him to get all types of seafood. He also made a variety of desserts for the after dinner crowd. Cream puffs were his specialty. People came from all over New York to get his cream puffs. For the vampires he whipped the cream with blood. They looked a little pink but no one seemed to care or notice.

I sat near the stage eating a cream puff and drinking a goblet of blood while waiting for Sally. I was licking the cream off my fingertips, one by one with a naughty smile. The last show had ended and the guests were milling around and straggling out the front door.

Sally slinked over to my table and began licking the last of the whipped cream off my fingertips. I could feel my blood rising and my lust for him increasing. It was the first time in a long time that I had really looked at him. Lately, he seemed to be always covered with flour or bits of food. As I took a closer look, it was the first time I noticed the army had made him cut his ponytail off. He liked being without it. This meant he had to cut his hair every morning to keep people from asking questions about his hair. Since his body was frozen in time, he still had his pouty tummy. I had forgotten how short he was, with all the tall vampires hanging around the club. He was still terribly cute with that smile that made his eyes twinkle.

I grinned, "Sally, we haven't spent time together in almost a year." The thought of us making hot steamy love on the train when we first met flashed by in my mind. "What happened? I thought we were going to pick up our relationship where we left off."

"Finish that cream puff and lock up. I'll explain while I make you a great dinner at Jack's house. I'm still living there and I hope I can convince you to move in with me. It's time you left that hotel. The people in the lower apartment will be moving out the first of the year. Then we'll have the entire house to ourselves. I want to get them out so that nothing can interfere with our relationship. Speaking of interfering, have you heard from Heinrich? Do I have to worry that he is going to pop back into the picture?

****

I should take a minute here to explain who Heinrich is. He was the vampire that turned Nicci. He was supposedly the love of her life. She was virgin when she was turned so naturally he would be the one she compares all men to. He has a bad habit of turning up, just like a dirty penny, when Nicci is beginning to enjoy her life.

I've now met Johnny and been reintroduced to Sally.

I think I'll stop here for lunch before I get to deep into this dairy and can't stop. Plus I'm getting hungry. Her licking whipped cream off her fingers, got my stomach rumbling.

I had packed a breakfast and lunch; a thermos of coffee, four bottles of frozen water, donuts, bagels with cream cheese, and a baloney sandwich for lunch. Mom had just gone grocery shopping so I got to eat a feast. A person tends to get hungry when they just sit around reading.

My cushions and pillows were already in place with a couple of flashlights and spare batteries, in case it got dark. There was no electricity in the house. Even if there was, I couldn't be caught reading in the attic. A light would be seen from the street. I rarely stayed past dark but every now and then I would hit a juicy part and not want to put the diary down, 'til I had finished what I was reading that section.

At least once a week, I found myself waking up wet and sweaty from dreaming about making love to one of her lovers. It never failed, on one of those mornings, my mother would notice how flushed I was and felt my forehead.

"Are you okay? You look so flushed." She'd touch my cheeks in a couple of places and add. "You don't feel feverish, just sweaty. Are you sure you're not coming down with something?"

Then I would have to say. "Aw, mom, I'm fine. Do you realize you say the same thing at least once a week?"

I finally had to start avoiding her. I'd try to get out before she got up but of course some mornings I just couldn't get up. I mean, after all, it was summer. When I did make it, I'd grab my cooler and head for 1224 Jackson St.

I was ready to settle in and read about Sally and Nicci. In Book One, when they made love, they could fog up the windows. I wonder if they still do that. Also, I can't wait to see what she says about Heinrich. I wonder if he will show up again.

****

She laughed. "Sally, you worry too much. I really doubt Heinrich will reappear. Last I heard he was still in Austria and had a new partner. He was quite content in Europe."

"I'm sorry." He said. "I didn't mean to bring up a sore subject. I just don't want to have to worry about competing for you. I've heard the stories about the fight he got into with Jack, over you. I don't trust him at all."

I laughed again. "That's the least of your problems." (He didn't know Johnny was trying to move in on the picture.)

"After you've closed up, we can get a ride with Samuel. I know he's outside waiting to drive you home. We might as well have him drive us to the house unless you want to go to the Waldorf-Astoria. We won't have any real privacy at your suite so I suggest we go to the house. I still have the coffin Jack bought you. I moved it to the master bedroom. Please, come to the house."

I stood up and brushed the crumbs from my dress and grabbed his hand. "WuYi can you sweep up and get SuChi to help you set the cream colored tablecloths out for tomorrow? Ricardo will do a final check then you can leave. I'm leaving a little early with Mr. Regnosco to discuss tomorrow's dinner menu. We're having a special crowd. Mr. Luciano is coming to see the opening number and eat dinner. He's coming to evaluate the club since I've taken over for Jack. We have to be on our toes. I want this place to be spotless. Please make sure the back guest rooms don't have a drop of blood on the floor. I'll be in to investigate before we open. Good night, everyone!"

Sally hung his apron on a hook by the large stove in the kitchen. He gulped down a goblet of blood, grabbed my hand, and we headed out the front door with the rest of the crowd. He was right; Samuel had the car ready and running right outside the door.

"It's good to see you and Mr. Sally together again, ma'am. May I ask are you spending the evening together?"

We both nodded yes and I said. "Take us to Jack's old house in Harlem. I'm sure you remember where it is."

Samuel had been to Jack's house quite a few times before he left for the war. He knew the quickest way there. Since it was summer, all the automobiles windows were open. I had to put a silk scarf over my hair to hold it in place. The night was beautiful, with a full moon and a light breeze. I could smell all the odors of Harlem, from bar-b-queue ribs to fried chicken. Sally grabbed my shoulders and pulled me close. He began kissing me down the neckline of the red strapless gown I was wearing.

"Sally, this isn't Rome. We can't be so open with our kissing. We're not married. I can't afford to have people talking about me."

"You're being silly, Nicci. You are a grown woman with sexual needs. Who cares who sees us."

"Sally, I'm a business woman now and therefore must conduct myself with a certain air of class. I'm not some cheap floozy. Plus, Samuel is looking dead at me. I must maintain his respect. I can tell you are just warming up. We're almost at the house. I'll tear your clothes off as soon as we hit the door." I whispered in his ear. (Model T's aren't the most comfortable automobiles to be trying to make love in or grope in.)

"I can hardly wait, Nicci. It's been a long time since I've been with a woman as exciting as you."

Samuel interrupted Sally's train of thought and conversation. "Shall I come at sunset, Ma'am? I noticed you don't have a change of clothes. I can have Maria get a set for me to bring to you or I can return a little earlier and you can return to your suite and change clothes. Ma'am?" He smiled. He knew I was spending the night. He had finally gotten used to this part of my behavior.

We pulled up in front of the house. The entire house was pitch black. Sally climbed out of the Ford and Samuel came around to open my door. You could see the excitement on Sally's face as he ran up the steps, two at a time, unlocking the door. As he did this, he reached into the foyer and turned on a small lamp. It illuminated just the front hall but with vampire eyesight that was all we needed.

I turned and said. "Tell Maria to send a change of clothes at 7 p.m. tomorrow. They need to be something extremely special, like my silver gown, because a bigwig will be coming from New York City. Make sure she sends my ruby choker. I also want her to be ready to do my hair. I'll meet her at the club. We can do it at the Savoy, depending on the time. You got all that, Samuel?"

"Yes, ma'am. I'll be here at 7 p.m. with your clothes and hair items. Have a good night."

Sally and I waved and went into the house. As I stood in the foyer, I turned around slowly to see if Sally had made any changes. The house looked exactly the same as when Jack lived there. The same gold Victorian furniture and the gold brocade curtains. He hadn't started redecorating the lower level yet. It had modern American furniture, lots of flowers and an overstuffed sofa. The lower level appeared to be empty, even with the furniture in it. I didn't even hear the sounds of breathing. The family must have finally moved out. We went directly to the upper level, like old times with Jack. I realized Sally had never asked me over to his new home even though it belonged to me. Since he'd arrived in New York, I had been declared Jack's next-of-kin, therefore, the house had been left to me.

When we got upstairs, he offered me a goblet of blood. I took my goblet with me as I lounged in my favorite gold settee near a blacked out window.

Sally went into the kitchen and shouted. "Would you like something to eat before dinner? You know, like an appetizer. How hungry are you? I'd like to try this new dish out before I make it at the club. The Americans call it chili. It's ground meat mixed with beans and tomatoes sauce. It gives you the opportunity to have meat. I bet you haven't had a piece of meat since you were turned. Vampires don't need meat but its fun to eat something different. Julie, my new housekeeper, has been simmering this all day. If you like it I'll make it at the club tomorrow."

I answered back. "I'd love to try your chili. I won't get indigestion will I? It's been almost a hundred years since I last had meat. Do you think I will be able to even digest it? I'm willing to give anything a try at least once."

The chili was interesting. I *did* get indigestion. I had totally forgotten how that felt. I told Sally only humans and very new vampires could eat that stuff. I didn't like getting indigestion. It was like drinking bad blood.

"Enough talk about food. Let's move on! I've other things on my mind besides new dishes." I stretched my arms out for him to join me at the settee and kissed him. I'd forgotten how electricity shot through the two of us when we kissed. "Do you remember that feeling? It's been a long time, Sally. You went to war. I lost Jack in that same war. Now, I have you back." I kissed him again and I could've sworn I saw fireworks.

"Nicci, I had forgotten how you always talk too much, prior to us having sex. Can you just kiss me and enjoy the moment? I forgot you also talk too much when you're nervous. You shouldn't even be nervous. It's just me, Sally. Our love is just being reignited."

As he kissed me on the neck, I felt his fangs graze my throat. I heard myself moan as a smile grew on my face. I returned the kiss to his shoulder and my fangs appeared. I felt myself nibbling on his chest and he moaned, as the skin broke. His hands moved slowly across my body, undressing me. Kneading my skin with the same gentleness he used to make his famous pastries. I stroked him, while removing his clothes,

I felt my thoughts drifting to the memories of how we always generated heat between the two of us when we made love. The windows usually steamed up from all the heat two cold blooded people could create. Suddenly, we became one. I felt his power as he came. With the explosion of his power, my thoughts drifted, again, but this time I was wondering if making love to Johnny would be as wonderful. At least, I didn't scream out Johnny's name.

"Nicci!" I heard Sally say as he shook my shoulder. "What in the world are you thinking about so intently? Usually you call out my name when you come. Your thoughts seem to be drifting. You're not listening to anything I say."

"I'm sorry, Sally. I really *was* focused on our making love. Yet, I do have a lot on my mind and I haven't been able to share the pressure with anyone. Now that I own the Savoy, I have to pay part of the receipts to the mob so that I can get alcohol and protection from the police. I get so frustrated. I don't mind sharing the receipts with the mob because they are partial owners but I hate having to pay for protection all the way from the police, the district attorney and to a judge."

"Nicci, what have you gotten yourself into?"

"Sally, with the Prohibition laws, I have to get alcohol wherever I can get it. That means I have to get into bed, so to speak, with the mob. We still have some quality champagne left over from Jack's days, but it won't last forever. Naturally, the Bloody Marys taste the same but I have to be careful with them because the mob doesn't know the club is also a hangout for vampires. The Vamps don't know the mob is involved. I want to keep it that way. I really did enjoy making love to you but as you can see I *do* have a lot on my mind. (*Plus, Johnny keeps floating through my thoughts. There was no way I could share that with Sally.)*"

"Sweetheart, let's make love again and relieve some of that pressure. You can't change anything right now, so have a glass of 'wine' and kiss me again."

"Oh Sally, you know how to make a woman feel good, especially if she is a vampire." I gulped a glass of blood and kissed him. We started again. This time we slowed the pace and took our time. For some reason, when he entered me, my mind drifted again. I just couldn't stop wondering, what if when I had sex with Johnny, would we have the same passion? I was careful not to call out his name. I don't think Sally noticed my lack of attention, this time.

Sally had kept the extra coffin, just like he said. It was the coffin Jack had bought me so that I wouldn't always have to rush back to the hotel. It was full of good memories of Jack and I. Now, I added new memories of Sally and my fantasies about Johnny. Dawn was coming. I was looking forward to today's rest.

Chapter 7

Samuel was there at sunset with my change of clothing and to pick us up. Maria was waiting at the Savoy, to do my hair. We had to get back to the Savoy to greet the Saturday night crowd. I knew Johnny would be there to pick up the night's receipts and for the date I had sort of promised him. It seemed since Prohibition started we were packed every night. It looked like everyone was also smoking more than usual. There looked like a cloud had settled over the club. The smoke was so dense you could barely see the stage. The new wooden ceiling fans were barely moving the smoke. I had to open the back door to move some of the smoke so that people could enjoy the 10:00 show. The new dancer was a great tapper and I wanted people to be able to see his feet.

Johnny was early. He said he came for the 10:00 show. He took a seat in the back of the club. He sent WuYi to me to invite me over for a drink at his table.

"Hi, Johnny! WuYi said you wanted to share a drink with me. I have some real champagne from Jack's stash. Would you like a glass of that? I'll have my usual. I try not to drink alcohol until the club is closed."

WuYi had followed me back to the table, took our orders and left.

Johnny laughed. "How in the world did you manage to hang on to Jack's champagne?"

"Well, I charge $100 dollars a bottle. Not many people can afford it. Most of our drinks only cost 50 cents-$1 dollar a glass. We stay packed so I sell a lot of the regular drinks. I even have what they call "ice cubes".

"What are ice cubes?"

"It's frozen chunks of water. Ice cubes come from the ice I keep in the new refrigerator I have. I replaced the old icebox Jack used. It keeps your drinks cold. People love the treat." I called WuYi back, to bring a glass of ice water over for Johnny."

"This is the cat's meow." Taking a big sip, then crunching a piece of ice. "It's still cold!"

I started laughing. "What's a cat's meow?"

"It means something is wonderful or excellent."

"Well, how's the champagne? And speaking of the cat's meow, I think you are the cat's meow."

Johnny blushed. It was hard to see in the smoky darkness but I could feel the heat rising in his body.

"What are you doing after the show tonight? Are you still interested in that date?"

"Are you flirting with me? Women don't usually ask a man what they are doing for the evening."

I smiled with a wicked curve to my lips. "Of course, I'm flirting with you. I'm trying to get a date. Has your brain gone soft from too much counterfeit liquor? You can't tell when a woman is trying to get a date?"

"No woman has ever *tried* to get a date with me. That is usually my job. Men usually ask women out not the other way around. Okay, I'll go out with you, but I have to drop the receipts off first. Nothing will be open when we leave after the last show and dropping the receipts off. What we will we do?"

I put a very naughty look on my face and I'm sure my eyes twinkled. "We can go to my apartment. I have a suite at the Waldorf-Astoria. It's quite nice. We can have drinks and get to know each other better."

He grinned and I could see a flash of naughty thoughts in his eyes. "That could be interesting. I would love to get to know you better."

WuYi finally returned with our drinks. We sat and watched the next show. The new show had the latest dance moves in it, to show off how talented the dance troupe was. Naturally, the women were wearing skimpy outfits with plenty of leg showing. Styles had changed dramatically with the turn of the century. Almost, all women were showing their knees and men were wearing baggy pants. Women were cutting their hair to wear bobs and were even smoking in public. Between the smoking and drinking in public, nothing was considered irreverent for women.

I noticed, at some of the tables, groups of women were drinking and smoking without any male companionship. I had even seen women dancing with each other, which was never heard of the year before. This was the early years of the flappers. Women seemed to be doing all kinds of wild dances. You could hear giggling throughout the club.

****

Johnny and I chatted through the whole show. At the end of the show, we finally got down to business about what we were going to do after we left the club.

I had definite plans, regarding things I wanted to try on him. I hadn't been with a human lover since the days of Rudy. That was a long time ago. I was looking forward to the evening. I didn't think closing time would ever come. We'd had a good night, making nearly $5000 dollars.

I had to give Johnny $1000 dollars—20% off the top. Because of Prohibition, a lot of hands were extended for payments, besides the Mob and their protectors. I had the local cops and the doorman that had to be paid, too. I even had to pay the brewers, extra, so that I could get quality alcohol. I didn't want bathtub gin or cheap grain alcohol that some of the speakeasies were serving. The Savoy was known for having the best alcohol in the New York area.

"Johnny, who gets all this money I make? They must be quite comfortable because the Savoy makes at least ten grand a week. And that's after we pay all the people on the take."

"*Don't you worry your pretty little head over who gets the money!* I'll drive to the drop house and you sit out in the car and wait for me. If you don't see who's getting the money you don't have to worry about knowing anything. That way the police can't ask you any questions. Soon as we make the drop we'll head to your apartment."

I wanted to discuss it further but I kept my mouth shut. We gathered all the money and receipts, then he stuffed them into a brown paper bag. When we went out to his car, I noticed he was driving the latest Model T. I wonder why he didn't have any bodyguards or where his partner was. The more I thought about it, I realized I hadn't seen Vito, in quite a while. I decided it was none of my business so I chose to stay quiet and not ask questions. We drove to another club on 121st Street. Johnny went around to the back entrance carrying the brown bag. I assumed he was making another pick up. He couldn't have been gone any more than five minutes when he returned empty handed.

"I'm finally finished for the night. Let's go to your apartment now."

He headed back downtown. I had no idea what part of New York City we were in. I still only knew the areas of downtown, Broadway and Harlem.

He'd been pretty quiet most of the trip. Since I love to talk, I just wanted to hear his voice. "When we get to the Waldorf-Astoria, we can call room service and get some breakfast, if you'd like? I also have some real whiskey and wine hidden in my room. I've been saving it for a special occasion. I think this could be considered a special occasion."

"Where did you get real whiskey and wine from? Did you bring it home from the club before Prohibition started?"

I laughed. "Are you trying to accuse me of stealing?"

"No, it's just that I haven't tasted real liquor since Prohibition. While we're on the topic of drinking and food, I would love some breakfast. By the way, I hear the Waldorf-Astoria is a pretty fancy hotel. How can you afford to stay there? Are you making money at the Savoy that you're not reporting?"

"There you go again, accusing me of stealing. I have my own money, I brought from Italy. We do well at the Savoy but by the time I pay everyone on staff, there isn't a lot of money left. Especially, not enough to pay for my suite."

He raised his eyebrows and said. "Are you some wealthy widow from Europe? How come a woman as beautiful as you isn't married or doesn't have a steady boyfriend?"

I looked down at my feet so he wouldn't see the bloody tears trying to form in my eyes. My thoughts flashed to the memory of Franco and all his wealthy widows, he had killed. Then Jack's unquestioning love warmed my heart. "I had someone but the war took him. So I'm alone again. Thank you for thinking I'm beautiful. I'll find a new love."

He pulled up to the hotel and that cut off the conversation. The doorman came up to my door and opened it. Johnny came around the vehicle and like a perfect gentleman took my hand to help me out of the automobile. I stepped down and walked into the hotel. We headed toward the elevator and the metal gates clanked open.

"You know, we don't have elevators in Italy. You have to climb stairs, but our buildings aren't nearly as tall as the buildings in New York City. I've been at this hotel for four years. Off and on I go and stay at Jack's home in Harlem, when I get tired of staying here. When I lived in Italy, I had a home in Siena and an apartment in Rome. When I was bored with them I stayed in Venice. I love to move around so I changed suites last year."

Johnny interrupted laughing. "Wow, you can really talk once you get started."

"I'm sorry. I tend to talk too much when I get nervous. I'm slightly nervous." I picked up the conversation as if I hadn't even been interrupted. "I now live on the 12th floor. It's what they call a penthouse. It's so much bigger than my old suite. It has three bedrooms plus a sitting room. It even has a wine cabinet. That's where I keep my wine and whiskey. I even have some old scotch. I brought some furniture and art from Italy to make it feel more like home. I have both Van Gogh and di Vinci on my walls. Those are two of my favorite artists."

"Wow!" He said, as we stepped towards the elevators. When the doors clanked close, he began to sweat. "I don't really care for elevators. They make me feel like I'm trapped in a box. I'm always scared they'll break down and I'll really be trapped." Before he stepped in he added. "Who are Van Gogh and Vinci?"

I laughed. "They are great painters. And it is Leonardo di Vinci.

The elevator began jerking from floor to floor. I could see his face turning white and beads of sweat appear on his forehead as we clanked towards the 12th floor.

"What floor did you say you lived on?"

I was trying to keep a straight face when the elevator porter said. "Sir, don't worry. I've been here eighteen years and the elevator has only broken down eighteen times." The porter winked at me. "We were only trapped for ten hours. After we ate my dinner, we did begin to discuss what and who we would have to eat if we stayed trapped much longer."

Jonny stuttered. I thought he was going to faint. "That's not very reassuring. Eighteen times is once a year. That means it could easily happen again and then we would be trapped. Are we due to get stuck this year? Just get us to the twelfth floor and let us out!"

"Miss Nicci, you're not worried are you?' He started laughing.

"Of course not, Jimmy. I know I'm safe with you. Even if it did break down, it wouldn't be so bad spending an hour stuck in a box with two good looking men like you. I bet your wife packed you a good dinner, too."

"Stop it, you two! That's not funny. I'm going to be sick."

Suddenly, Jimmy jerked and the elevator came to a stop.

Johnny screamed. "I knew it! That's it. We're stuck! We're going to die!"

Jimmy and I both looked at each other and broke up laughing. "Johnny, relax! We've just come to my floor. You didn't even notice how fast we were moving. As I just said, we've reached my floor. My goodness, for such a big man, you wouldn't think you'd be afraid of a lift."

He looked like he was going to explode. "I'm not afraid! I just don't like being in boxes. I knew we were at the twelfth floor. I was just playing. Come on Nicci, let's get out of this box."

As we stepped out, I could hear Jimmy laughing to himself. "Crazy white folks."

Chapter 8

My doorway was to the right of the elevator. It was a short distance down the hallway.

"Come on Johnny, you look like you could use a stiff drink more than breakfast. Let me get you that shot of whiskey that I promised you."

"Nicci, you have to promise me you won't tell anyone, I got scared in the elevator. I'm supposed to be a big tough gangster. I'd be a laughing stock amongst the fellas. Promise me you won't tell!"

"I promise! Johnny, everyone is afraid of something so don't worry, your secret is safe with me. Let's get that drink."

As we approached Room 121, I got my keys out of my purse. When I put the key in the lock, Maria opened the door. "I heard someone at the door. I figured it was you at this time of night."

"Maria, this is Johnny. He is a partner from the club. I'm sure I've spoken of him."

They shook hands. "Please to meet you, Johnny."

"And you, Maria." He said.

Johnny had a quizzical look on his face. "Maria is my assistant. She came with me from Rome. We've been together for twenty years."

"Was she your Nanny? You can't be any older than 25. She must have grown up with you."

"Something like that." It was the first time, I really noticed that Maria was aging. I was going to have to turn her soon or get another assistant. "Maria can you get our guest a tumbler of whiskey and pour a glass of 'wine' for me." I was getting thirsty. I could hear the blood coursing through his body and I was fighting the urge to drink from him. "Johnny, come into the sitting room and make yourself comfortable. Did you want something to eat or is a drink enough for now?"

"A drink is really enough for now but I would love some dessert." He said with a wicked grin.

"That can be arranged. Let me drink my 'wine' and change into something more comfortable." I changed into a silk camisole with matching panties and a satin mini robe over it. I had let my hair down.

I heard him catch his breath when I walked into the room, holding my empty wine goblet. "Is your whiskey too strong? It's from Scotland. It's not the cheap stuff, you get most of the time, from the speakeasies around town."

"No, I was just amazed at how beautiful you are. I mean you were beautiful when I met you but dressed like that, your beauty breath away."

"Well, thank you. I just wanted to look nice for your dessert. I would like some dessert too. Don't you want to get more comfortable? At least remove your jacket."

He took off his suit jacket and loosened his tie. He unbuttoned the top two buttons of his white shirt. I could see a white tee shirt on under the shirt. Maria had left the bottle of whiskey on the small table near the sofa, so I refilled his glass.

"Thanks. What kind of wine is that? It looks awfully red and looks kind of thick."

"It's a red wine I brought from Italy. It's very difficult to find. It's a type of red burgundy, mixed with herbs."

"May I taste it? I haven't had any good wine since the beginning of Prohibition."

I couldn't let him taste it. I didn't know if he knew what blood tasted like but I couldn't take any chances. I also didn't have any answers for why I would be drinking blood. I wasn't ready to turn him. I didn't even know if I *wanted* to turn him.

After much thought, I decided, what could it hurt? One sip wouldn't turn him. I let him sip it and tried to enthrall him. For some odd reason it didn't work.

I was surprised. Before I could figure out why it didn't work he said. "That's good wine, a little on the thick side, for me. It reminds me of blood. I'll stick to my whiskey if you don't mind."

"No, not at all. I have plenty of whiskey stashed away in the third bedroom. I keep it for special occasions like this." The whiskey was hidden in the room with my coffin. We kept the room locked to keep housekeeping out when they cleaned. I couldn't have people seeing my coffin. There was just no answer for why I had one. Plus, I didn't want my whiskey to disappear.

After Jonny's third glass of whiskey, he had become extremely relaxed, almost drunk. His words were beginning to slur. I was sitting across from him so I got up and sat on the sofa next to him. I began rubbing his neckline and slipped his tie off as he sipped his drink.

"Can I get you something to eat or another drink?" I said, as he leaned over and planted a sloppy kiss on my forehead.

He was quickly becoming drunk. It was obvious he wasn't used to real alcohol. He slurred. "I'll take another drink."

"Just a minute, let me put my wine down, first." I looked up and kissed him on the lips.

"Your lips are cool. They're very soft but I feel a chill on them."

"Just keep kissing me and they'll warm up. Put your hands on my breast to warm them up, too, while you are at it."

He smiled. "No woman has ever let me touch her breasts before."

I grinned. "I'm not your normal woman." I began unbuttoning his shirt and with each open button, I could feel his heart pick up speed and his color redden.

"What are you doing?" He gasped.

"You said you wanted dessert, so . . . I'm unbuttoning your shirt. Next I'm going to unbutton and unzip your pants. You're not a virgin are you? I mean is this the first time you've ever been with a woman?"

"No . . . no! But I've never had a woman undress me. Even the Italian girls I go out with, don't undress me and they definitely don't let me touch them."

"Remember, first I'm not a girl and I'm not your typical woman. Just lay back and enjoy it. I really like you. That's the reason why we're about to have sex. I don't do this with every man, so don't think I'm a professional woman. I take this very seriously and I enjoy sex."

I removed his shirt and helped him take off his tee shirt. I began to rub his nipples and he sounded like he was hiccupping, the way he was gasping for breath. "Are you okay? Do you have the hiccups or are you short of breath?"

"No woman has ever rubbed my nipples the way you are. I can feel myself growing from the excitement."

I lifted my head and whispered into his ear. "Control yourself. I have more to do and I'm not going to just rub your nipples." I kissed his throat and I could feel his blood vessels thumping with his excitement. It took all my strength not to bite him. Something in the back of my mind was nagging at me not to bite him, yet. Instead I just sucked the side of his neck. This was not going to be like making love to Sally. I felt Johnny had so much he needed to learn about sex before I could even put him on the same level as Sally. I really wanted to bind him sexually to me. He was such a beautiful specimen of a man. I released the band that was holding his ponytail in place and ran my fingers through his hair. He had his eyes closed to take in the moment.

I moved my hands down from his hair to cross his powerful shoulders, down his chest to his stomach, then thighs. He had fine black hair on his chest and thighs. I could see the power in his organ. I took his hands from my breast and ran them down my stomach to my thighs. I heard myself groan as I sipped the air.

"Are you okay?" He asked.

A smile had lit up my entire face. "I'm just enjoying the moment, too." I sat on his lap and he entered me with a large moan. I clasped my legs around his hips and said. "Can you hang on? Don't come yet." I could feel heat radiating from his large organ. I could barely control myself. I began to make small circles with my hips on his lap.

"I can't last." He whispered. "I feel like I'm going to explode."

"Let's come together." I wrapped my arms around his chest and he wrapped his arms around me.

"Nicci!" He softly cried out.

"Johnny!" I whispered into his shoulder. It was incredible. I buried my face in his shoulder and laid there while the heat from his body washed over me. We sat there holding each other for what seemed like hours but it was really only ten minutes.

We separated. I was sorry to let go. I knew he couldn't spend the night. I had to send Johnny on his way. It was nearly 5 a.m. I wanted more but there wasn't enough time. The sun would be coming up soon. He smelled delicious, though. We quickly dressed. "I'll see you tomorrow, Johnny. I've got to call it a night." I kissed him, dressed him, patted him on his fanny and shut the door.

****

Wow! What a way to end the evening. I wonder how she does that. She can get any man to perform sexually for her. I mean, I realize she can enthrall them but she doesn't use that on every man. I wonder if men had more testosterone in those days. I wish I could share her lovemaking activities with my friends. Just maybe there is a guy like that out there for me. I don't want to be a vampire but I would love to be as sexy as one.

I wonder why Nicci couldn't enthrall him. Obviously, he's not a vampire. I wonder if he is really human or something supernatural. I'm almost tempted to skip ahead to see what he really is. But, I'll wait until she finds out.

It looks like the next section is going to introduce a new club with a whole new set of friends. Well, I'm out for the summer so maybe I can get away with having a sleepover with her diaries.

1922-1926/The Jazz Age

The Club Deluxe (The Cotton Club)

Chapter 9

The Club Deluxe opened in 1920 and was our local competition. It was small. Just your typical speakeasy owned by an ex-boxer named Jack Johnson. They weren't doing as well as the Savoy, due to lack of cash flow and talent. We drew better talent and had a larger influx of cash due to our alcohol supply.

****

It was 1922. I was spending a lot of time rotating between Johnny and Sally. So far I had been lucky. Neither one knew about the other. Plus, I had been able to refrain from drinking Johnny's blood. I wasn't ready to make that commitment yet. Life was good. My club was doing well and I had two men in my life.

Johnny invited me to the movies. I hadn't been to a movie since Jack left. I couldn't wait to see this movie. It was supposed to be about a great vampire. All the vamps at the club were talking and laughing about it. I heard Hollywood made us look ridiculous. No vampire I had ever known looked like Max Shreck. He played the vampire in "Nosferatu". I don't know any vampires with pointed ears or raggedy teeth. Even my gypsy friends from Romania don't look that bad. It took all my strength not to burst out laughing. Instead, I gripped Johnny's arm and pretended to be scared.

"Nicci, you're gripping me too tight. Are you that scared? It's only a movie. I'm never going to take you to another scary movie, if you are that scared."

"Johnny, I've never seen such a horrible looking creature. (That was true but Nosferatu looked ridiculous.) He's a vampire and sleeps in a coffin. His bite could turn you into the living dead. Have you ever seen or heard of a vampire? Is that why you're afraid of being trapped in a box?"

"That's no funny. Nicci, there is no such thing as a vampire. That was made up in Hollywood. People don't die then come back to life. They don't sleep in coffins and go around drinking people's blood. Besides, I'm afraid of being trapped in an elevator not being stuck in a coffin."

I smiled at him, all the while thinking, if only he knew the truth. He'd be so shocked. He's never asked any questions about why we sell so many 'Bloody Marys'. He'd probably faint if he knew half the Savoy's guests were vampires.

"I know you had to sneak out of the Savoy, to come to the movies with me, so after the show why don't we sneak back into the Savoy and do a little dancing ourselves?"

I agreed and added. "After I close the club, why don't we go back to my place. I'd love a late night dessert. Do you have to drop off receipts tonight?"

"You know, Nicci, we always go back to your place after I drop off receipts. We've been seeing each other for a couple of years, now, and I have never invited you to my apartment. It's not as nice as your hotel suite but I call it home. I have a real apartment, not some room in a boarding house. Come back to my place and spend the night."

"I'd love to spend the night, but I have to leave by 5 a.m. I have something important that I had to get done tomorrow during the day. (I couldn't take the chance of bursting into flames in the morning just because he didn't have a coffin for me to sleep in. How could I even tell him I needed a coffin to sleep in. I don't really think he would have believed I was a vampire, especially after just seeing "Nosferatu".)

We went back to his apartment, which was in Brooklyn. His apartment turned out to be no bigger than a box. For that matter, it was just a large box with Chinese screens separating the rooms. It was about 600 sq ft. He thought this was huge. I would have hated to see what he thought was small. I had been in bedrooms, in Italy, that were larger than his apartment.

I said. "How quaint! Do you spend much time here?" It was divided into three sections; a tiny kitchen with a sink and stove, no table, the bedroom held a twin bed built into a closet, with a chair that had to be moved so that one could get into the bed and a living room with a loveseat and a collapsible tray for eating with two chairs. One was on each side of the collapsible tray. He said it was called a dinner tray. Johnny called them rooms. I felt if I turned too quickly, I would trip over him. Obviously, he thought it was beautiful because he was beaming as he showed me around. There was no way we were going to make love on that tiny bed! What was he thinking!

Offering me a seat on the loveseat, he said. "Nicci, sit down. Make yourself at home. I know I could use some decorating tips, but it is home. I thought we could have a drink and talk some business, while you're here and then make love."

As I sat down I said. "What did you want to talk about so bad that we can't make love first?"

Johnny cleared his throat a couple of times and began to stutter. "It's . . . it . . . it's . . . about."

"Johnny, take a deep breath. Go pour me a drink and try again. I promise I won't bite you. Just spit it out. Your stuttering is driving me crazy."

Again he cleared throat. He spoke, as he poured me a jar of some red liquid. "I'm sorry I done have any wine goblets or real red burgundy, like you. It's about the Club Deluxe. I know the Club Deluxe is your competition and granted it will never be as successful as the Savoy, but we, I mean, Mr. Luciano, needs some help. Mr. Luciano and I would like to see it make more money than it is. He asked me to convince you to help. I mean, if you don't mind?"

I smiled and said mischievously. "How were you going to convince me? Maybe I should hold out. Also is that a canning jar, you just poured me a drink in?"

"Nicci, you're being naughty." I could feel the heat radiating off his face as he blushed. "Yes, it is a canning jar. I'm sorry that I don't have any fine glasses to drink from No one ever comes to visit. I don't really care what I drink from, as long as it's clean." He was trying to

fit on the loveseat, too. He gave up and sat on the arm of the sofa. "I
was only going to beg you to help, if simply asking wasn't enough."

I smiled and said. "Maybe I should hold out. I would love to see
you beg." I could feel Johnny's temperature rise and little beads of
sweat were forming on his forehead.

"Nicci, now you're really being naughty. This is serious."

"I'm honored that you think I can help improve business. I'm
loaded with ideas, if you're really interested. There are a lot of
changes that need to be done. I have a few ideas that I've been toying
with. I was hoping I would get a chance to help with a new club from
the ground up."

Johnny was looking at his shoes. "I'm sorry to say, even though
we need your help, no one can know you are involved. How would it
look if people knew Lucky Luciano had to get help from a woman to
improve his club and business?"

"That's okay, Johnny. I should be offended but I'm used to the
American way. Even here, a woman can't let a man know she could
possibly be his equal. I still want to help even if no one knows it's me
helping. First, you need to try and improve the quality of the alcohol
you serve. I know Mr. Luciano has connections, so you shouldn't be
serving that bathtub gin. Are you trying to blind your customers?
Then, you need to clean the club up some; paint, new tables, a stage
for a band, add a floor show and improve the music. For heaven sakes,
it's the Twenties. And really! I know you can find better looking
dancers and get rid of Jack Johnson. You need a classier owner/
manager."

"Wow! That's a whole lot of ideas you have been toying around
with. We'll have to close down for a while to make all those
improvements. But, I guess if we want to make money, we have to
make changes. I have to ask Mr. Luciano his opinion first. If he says
okay then we'll close the club and improve it."

With that thought, I stood and smoothed out my dress. "Give it
some thought Johnny. Those are just some ideas to improve business.
It's getting late so I'm afraid we won't be able to have sex. I have to
get home." I didn't really want to make love in that dump, he called
an apartment. Thank God, he started talking business. It made for a
great excuse to get out of there. I'm going to have to find him a better
place to live in, if he thinks we're going to be making love at his place.

Chapter 10

It took nearly a year for all the changes to get put in to effect for the Club Deluxe. Jack Johnson had gotten arrested, which made it easier to have him replaced. Lucky Luciano brought Owney Madden in. He was a popular boxer at the time. Thank goodness, Owney decided to rename the club. It was now the Cotton Club. I heard they had a hard time finding dancers, since the best worked for me. I couldn't wait to see the new floor show. All everyone's talked about, for the last week, was the reopening of the Cotton Club. I decided rather than compete, I would close for the night and check it out myself. Johnny had kept everything a secret so that I would be surprised when it reopened.

It was a Saturday night and I was losing a lot of business, but it was worth it to find out what kind of competition I would have from the Cotton Club. Plus, I had promised Johnny, I would be there opening night.

Johnny and I arrived at the club in my new black Model T Ford, driven by Samuel. He was so handsome in his new chauffeur uniform. Everyone was here. I even saw a few vampires in line. I knew for a fact, that Owney wasn't going to be serving 'Bloody Marys'. Lucky had tried to lure Sally away, with money. Sally was my lover and I knew he wouldn't leave me. Therefore, there would be no vampire chef to prepare food for the vampires. I wasn't worried, though. Lucky didn't even know there were vampires in the city much less in existence, if I had anything to say about it. This would probably end up being a human only club. I wasn't willing to share my clientele.

I didn't stand in line. I was with Johnny. We were both dressed to the nines. He had a black tuxedo and bowtie on. To compliment him, I was wearing a white silk evening gown with a long split up the front. What would an opening be without my ruby choker from Heinrich? Because I wasn't going to cut my hair into the fashionable bob, that was all the rage, I piled my hair on top and used ruby stick pins, that sparkled all over my hair. We were a breathtakingly beautiful couple. (Naturally, I was gorgeous. *I mean, I am a vampire!*) I could hear people whispering about who were we? I pretended, I was famous and just waved my fingertips at the crowd. What fun!

The line was wrapped around the block. I overheard the bouncer say it was a two hour wait. It was 8 p.m. and the floor show was at 9p.m. and 12 midnight. There were people in line that weren't even going to see the first show.

We went directly in and were seated near the back because all the seats around the dance floor were taken by city dignitaries. I didn't mind. After all, I was only there to observe my competition. There was nothing on the menu that I would want or even eat. I ordered a glass of red wine and would pretend to sip on it all night. I was good for once. I didn't need to go to the ladies room and drain anyone. I had "eaten" while I was getting ready for the night. I really wanted to hear Fletch Henderson and see the new floor show. I didn't want to miss anything, because I had been draining someone in the ladies room. Rumor was that the dancers, including the men, were gorgeous.

At exactly 9 p.m. a solo trumpet sounded and the dancers came out one by one. They were dressed in silver sequins, from the top hat to the short shorts. When all twelve dancers, six men and six women were out, the rest of the big band joined the trumpet. It was amazing. (The Savoy only had a piano player. I was going to have to change that.) They began to tap in unison. Only the men had solos but as couples there was a lot of flipping and sliding. The crowd was on its feet, at the end of the show, with a lot of shouting and clapping. After the dancers left the stage, the band continued to play during dinner.

The dance floor was packed. Everyone was doing some sort of tango, foxtrot or the Charleston. Owney Madden was grinning and making the rounds. He finally made it to our table and introduced himself. He seemed like a very nice man. He was definitely not my type. He was too short and a mobster. Johnny was enough mobster for me.

Chapter 11

Immediately, I noticed a difference between the Cotton Club and the Savoy. They had a hat check girl and cigarette girls. This was a new idea. I had to get some. I was racking up a grocery list of things to add to the club.

One particular woman seemed to come to our table every fifteen minutes or so. The cigarettes, she was selling, appeared to be individually laid out on her tray and none were missing. The third time she came by, I paid closer attention to her. This time I realized that she wasn't really paying attention to me or trying to sell me anything. Her entire, rather large smile was focused on Johnny and he was grinning back.

"Can I get you a cigarette, sir?"

"No, sweetheart. I just got one from you, the last time you came by. I don't really smoke quite that fast. For that matter, I don't really smoke." He began laughing and if it was possible, his grin got even bigger.

She laughed. It was then that I noticed, she hadn't blushed. It was so noisy in the club, I couldn't tell if she had a heartbeat. I just assumed, Owney would only hire humans.

"I'm sorry sir. I didn't realize I was coming by that often. Can I get you a drink? A cigar? My boss is going to wonder what's going on, if you don't buy something. How about a cigarette for the lady? I have gorgeous cigarette holders. This white pearl one would look great with her gown."

"What's your name?" He was leaning across the table as he spoke.

It was obvious that she was flirting, as she batted her eyelashes at Johnny. "My name is Anita."

"Do you just sell cigarettes?" I could feel myself smoking with jealousy. I was trying to draw her attention away from Johnny. He looked like he could drown in her glazed expression her eyes were holding.

"That was uncalled for!" Johnny hissed under his breath.

"Wh-Wha-What?" She stuttered. "I sell cigarettes at night and I'm a housekeeper during the day. So far, I make good tips and meet great people in the evening. I'm enjoying being a cigarette girl. I was hoping to get a chance to be a Cotton girl dancer. I think I'm a pretty good dancer."

I knew she was lying, what did she really want? I smiled at that remark. Every girl hopes to become a dancer. I wonder if she knew I was from the Savoy. I didn't like the way she was looking at Johnny. "I'm the hostess at the Savoy and if you're really interested in becoming a dancer, I could possibly arrange an audition at the Savoy." That got her attention immediately.

She turned towards me and began pumping my hand. "Do you really think so? You don't even know me but I would so grateful! When?"

Johnny mouthed the words. "What are you doing? What are you up to?"

Ignoring him, I simply said. "Can you get away tomorrow at 7 p.m.? It should only take a few minutes and that is just before we open. All the dancers will be there and they can decide whether they like you. We just got a new male dancer and it might be fun to add a new female."

It was then I finally noticed her heart hadn't picked up over the excitement of a possible audition. Suddenly, it dawned on me that she wasn't human even if she did say she worked during the day. Not only wasn't she human but she appeared to be a Negro. There must be a coven somewhere around her. Surely, she wouldn't be alone. I'm sure by now she realizes I'm a vampire, too. I was going to have to get her alone to find out about her coven.

Johnny had a big grin plastered on his face. "Can I come early and watch the audition?

"That's up to Anita. You have to ask her, if she feels comfortable with you watching!"

"It's okay, but I don't even know your names."

"I'm Dominique Santa Maria and this is Johnny. My friends call me Nicci. As I said, I'm the hostess at the Savoy and Johnny works for me. I'll see you tomorrow. Do you know where the Savoy is? It's not too far from here."

Anita laughed. "Sure! Everyone knows where the Savoy is. I'll see you tomorrow!" With a little flip of her butt she turned and walked away.

I began to gather my things and took one last swallow from my drink. "Let's go! I've had enough!"

As I retrieved my ticket, from my purse, for my little wrap, I heard Johnny say. "What are you thinking, Nicci? I know you are up to something. You don't need any new dancers."

I grinned and said. "It's not always about the dancing. I saw the way she was looking at you. Besides, I need a new friend. She might be helpful in keeping tabs on the Cotton Club. She is not for you to play with. I want her to continue being a cigarette girl at the Cotton Club. I'll have the girls at the Savoy improve her skills until she becomes a dancer at the Cotton Club. Since it is my competition, she can keep me up to date on the Cotton Club's improvements and I can *run* it out of business or until the Savoy becomes *the dance club* of Harlem."

"You devil!" With that, we left for the evening.

Anita and Robert; as told by Sally

Chapter 12

Johnny had fallen for Anita. He didn't know whether it was love or lust but he had what they called the "hots" for her. Yet, his primary focus remained on Nicci. He was going to be what he considered a typical man; he was going to have both.

****

I had to have Sally investigate her past and her lovers since I knew she was a vampire. I didn't completely trust her. Why didn't she come to the Savoy, first? Almost every vampire in this town knew that was the place to be. Johnny knew nothing about vampires. After much digging it turned out Anita belonged to a coven in Brooklyn, near Johnny. It was full of artists from New Orleans.

It turned out Louisiana was full of vampires. Unbeknownst to me New Orleans was the center for American vampires. There was a lot of musical talent and dancers in New Orleans. The coven had moved as a group from New Orleans to Harlem.

****

Anita had lived in the French Quarter, where all the young beautiful Creole women lived. She stayed in a women's boarding house with a Creole madam. Anita, herself, wasn't a "working woman". She was a housekeeper during the day. She cleaned up after the "girls". Primarily, stripping beds and putting fresh sheets on daily and running perfumed bath water. The Madam ran a very *clean house*. Anita desperately wanted her life to change. She dreamed of being a dancer someday.

In 1901, as a single 23 year old woman, she had a love for music and dancing. On her daily shopping routine, in the evening, after the housework was done, she would notice a group of young musicians. They always seem to travel as a group to various newly opened dance clubs. She had noticed, each person seemed to have some sort of different musical aptitude. There looked to be about twelve in the group. All of them could sing, dance or play some instrument. She had followed them one night and noticed two or three could play the trumpet or the trombone. Two played the saxophone. It looked like they could all play the piano. Some were tap dancers and singers. It was amazing! She'd never seen so much talent in one group of people. Anita didn't think they were actors. They seemed to be just friends. She wanted to be part of that group. She could only sing a tiny bit but she could tap and do acrobats. She was sure she could learn to sing better or even play an instrument, with a little help.

The other thing that stood out, significantly, was that they were all beautiful. I noticed they were all various shades of brown; from high yellow (almost white) to dark brown, even almost blue black. Each person looked like they had sculpted features. People tended to stare at their breathtaking beauty. No one was shorter than 5' 7", well muscled and beautiful hair. The men were all over 6 feet. Anita had only seen such beauty in an art book. To make them extra special, they seemed to be very friendly people.

****

The brothel, she lived at, was at 235 Basin St. in the red light district of New Orleans. Everyone called it Mahogany Hall. There was even a saloon next door. While Anita was cleaning the rooms the women would sit at the windows peering out the curtains, with a red light, behind them. You could hear the women calling men as they walked by.

Every morning, she rose at six, to make breakfast for the house. Laundry was next and there were tons to do, not just sheets. Petticoats, slips, camisoles, nighties had to be hand washed, dried and ironed.

All the beautiful gowns had to be spot cleaned. Sometimes the girls changed their clothes five times a day. Every time they were with another man, they had to put on fresh clothing. They had to maintain the reputation of being a *clean house and clean working girls.*

After laundry, all the rooms had to be cleaned. There were six bedrooms that had to be stripped and have fresh linen put on the beds. Sheets were changed at a minimum of twice a day. In the summer, due to the humidity and sweaty men, they had to be changed more frequently. Anita hated the work but she really cared about the women. Plus, she needed the money to pay for her dance lessons.

Anita loved the evenings, when they served wine, champagne and those wonderful beignets. The women wore evening gowns covered in sequins or lace. It was on one of those evenings that she caught a glimpse of Robert with his friends. It wasn't a special evening but Miss Lulu had just hired two new "girls" and wanted to show them off. She had never noticed Robert before, as part of the "musical" group. She could hardly wait to meet them and him.

First, she decided to introduce herself to them. She needed them to consider her as a friend so that she could be part of their group. Naturally, they welcomed her as if they had been friends all their lives, (That should have been a warning sign, but she so desperately wanted to feel like she was part of their group.) Next, they invited her to some of their group practices. She was surprised but pleased they had asked her to come to some rehearsals. (She had noticed something else strange but brushed it off. They never seemed to do anything during the day.) She wanted to go to lunch with them on her day off or be seen, during the day, as part of this spectacular group.

The more she thought about their strange behavior, the more she realized the few times she had seen them at a restaurant, that no one ever ate.(In her need to be their friend, she let that go, too.) After being with them for about a month, she finally asked Robert, who appeared to be the oldest member of the group, "We rarely go out to eat dinner but when we do, it's usually an exclusive restaurant but I noticed no one eats except me. You just slide the food around on your plate. Is there something wrong with the food that I should be aware of?"

Robert laughed. "No! We've just usually eaten before we go out. As you can see we don't eat much and it's more for appearance sake. We like to be seen around town."

"It makes me feel like a pig because I eat so much. After cleaning all day, at the house, I'm starved, though. Don't you hate paying for food you don't eat?"

"You're not a pig. You're a beautiful woman and we love to watch you eat."He laughed again. "You make the food look so good. We give the food away, so we're not wasting money. By the way, I've heard you say you can dance. Why don't we go back to Nadine's house and everyone can dance?"

She thought it was strange that he said they gave the food away. She'd never seen anyone get food. It was obvious he didn't want to talk about it, though. Again she let something odd go by without really questioning the oddness of it.

This was the first time she realized that she only knew Robert's name. She didn't know anyone else's name, either. "Robert, I just realized I don't know anyone's name. Who is Nadine?"

Just like that, he went around the group spouting off names. "My name is Robert Manchester, as you know. This is: Nadine, Jodi, Rudi, Wanda, Gloria, Emma, Alan, Mark, Renee, Timothy and Steven. Don't worry if you don't remember all the names. You'll learn them over time. We all have special talents that will help you remember us. We'd like to extend a proper invitation to join our group, if you are interested?"

"I'd love to join your group but I only know how to dance. I can't play any instruments or sing very well."

For some odd reason Robert laughed and grinned. "Don't worry. We can teach anybody anything we want to, when we put our collective minds to it. We'd love to teach you some new and extra skills."

Again, Anita thought that was a strange answer. She just didn't know she had consented to being a vampire and would learn those new skills after she had been turned.

Chapter 13

Six months went by and the relationship seemed to be blossoming. Robert worked with her every evening, she had free. Even when she was exhausted, he was able to find energy in her to help improve her dancing. Working only in the evening was beginning to gnaw at the back of her mind. Why didn't they rehearse during the day when she was free? She didn't have the courage to ask him, yet. Anita was happy with the direction her relationship was going and didn't want to rock the boat, so to speak. Her skills were growing and so was her love. It was 1902.

The Spring in New Orleans was beautiful. Flowers were starting to bloom on the trees. Tulips were blossoming everywhere. When Anita walked down Bourbon St. during the day she could hear music lightly drifting out of multiple clubs where musicians were practicing for the evening crowds. On almost every street corner men were harmonizing, tapping and sliding.

Today was the day she was going to tell Robert how much she loved him. Little did she know that Robert had a big surprise for her, too. He was going to tell her he was a vampire. They agreed to meet at 8 p.m. at La Rue de Poisson.

He had brought his own bottle of 'red wine'. She grown accustomed to him bringing his own bottle. He ordered a bottle of champagne for her. After consulting the menu, he ordered her favorite, shrimp gumbo. He ordered two bowls. When it arrived you could see the steam coming from the bowls. It was full of shrimp, crayfish, potatoes and okra. She devoured her gumbo and he played with the little crayfish. Yet, he drank almost all of the 'red wine'.

Anita had finished her gumbo and the champagne. She felt warm and a little drunk. "That 'red wine' looks delicious, too. Instead of ordering some more champagne can I share your wine? I'd love to taste it."

He had mixed the wine with his blood, the various types of blood from the coven and real wine. He knew this was the perfect time to turn her. The wine and champagne would make her tipsy. "If you've finished your gumbo, let's go to my private apartment. I have a special supply of this very brand of wine. We can drink in the privacy of my home. I also have something very special that I want to share with you."

Even though Anita worked at a brothel, she was still a virgin. No man had ever moved her enough to have sex with. She was trying to save herself for marriage. She was a *very* good Catholic girl. She was a little nervous about his invitation. She did love him and wanted him to know how much. She had never been truly alone with Robert, in his apartment. The combination of the champagne and wine was making her brave.

"I feel really good. That's the best wine I've ever had. Mixed with the champagne, I feel like I'm floating on air. I'd love to go back to your apartment."

He lived two blocks away from the restaurant. The weather was beautiful so they walked instead of riding the streetcar. They held hands like two young lovers as they strolled to his home. It was a full moon and a cool breeze was blowing. Robert didn't feel the temperature drop but Anita snuggled closer. When they go to the apartment, she mentioned how chilly she was.

"I need something to drink. I'm cold. There seems to be a chill in the air. I've lost the warmth from the wine and champagne." She hadn't touched him before so she never realized his body wasn't as warm as her.

"Don't worry Anita. I'll warm you up. Have a seat in the living room and I'll bring you a glass of 'wine'."

Anita was trying to take in her surroundings. She had never been in a man's apartment before. They had always gone to Nadine's place. His apartment was very similar, in size, to Nadine's. She did notice a large fireplace in the center of the room. It looked like it had never been used, though. Large over-stuffed sofas were on either side of the fireplace. A very comfy looking over-stuffed chair sat in a corner. On the nearly, bare white wall, above the chair, hung a Voodoo mask. Being from New Orleans, she had seen Voodoo masks before, just not as large as the one Robert had. She wasn't sure what the little statues on the fireplace mantle represented. This should have been another clue, that Robert was different.

"What's that on your wall, Robert?" She asked. "I've never seen anything like it before."

"It's a Voodoo mask. I'm a hougan, a Voodoo priest. I immigrated from Haiti about two years ago and brought my religion with me."

Anita was a devout Christian but had heard of Voodoo. Everyone in New Orleans knew about Voodoo. She was starting to get nervous. She had heard about zombies, Voodoo dolls and curses. She'd heard nothing good ever comes from Voodoo.

He laughed. "I can tell by the look on your face that you're nervous. Don't worry, I don't practice black magic. I do know some curses but I'm interested in the good I can do. I love doing love potions for the local brothels. People are forever coming to me because they are in love with someone who doesn't quite love them."

Anita began grinning. "Are you going to give me a love potion? Have you been using a love potion on me? I really do like you and I hope it's real and not because of a love potion."

"No, I let nature take its course with you. Why don't you come and sit next to me? I hear the sofa calling your name. Its saying 'Anita, come be with Robert on my comfy cushions.'"

"Now isn't that something. I never heard of a talking sofa."

Robert handed her another large goblet of 'wine'. Without thinking, Anita gulped it down. She held out her goblet for a refill. She was feeling good, as she cuddled closer to Robert. It was then she noticed Robert felt cold. With all the wine in her, she had finally gotten her courage up to make a comment.

"Robert, you need to drink some of this 'wine' before I drink it all. You feel awfully chilly. Are you sick? I hope not! Let me warm you up."

"I'm not sick. I am a little chilly. Let me show you how to warm me up." He took her hand and placed it over his crotch. "Just gently rub here."

She started giggling. "Are you sure this will warm you up?" With her free hand she began playing with his left earlobe. She had no experience with sex but had seen the women at the brothel perform with their clients.

He smiled as he said. "I feel myself warming up already. You are moving into dangerous territory."

She had never felt like this before. It felt good. She thought she heard a sigh escaped from her lips, as he wrapped both arms around her. He inched his hands up to hold her head and began kissing her face. Before she knew it, he had placed his lips upon hers and slipped his tongue between them. She felt a shiver run down her spine.

"Mmmm. "She moaned and found herself slowly unzipping his pants. She had a simple button down smock on. She was glad she hadn't worn her corset today. She had a silk camisole on with matching petticoats underneath it. It was one of the working girl's throwaways. Anita broke away to slip her dress off.

He helped her stand to remove it. She just stood in front of him, dressed only in her camisole and petticoats. "Even though I work at a brothel, I don't have a lot of experience with this. Please be gentle."

His face lit up. "I'll be gentle with you. Just do as I say and we'll both enjoy this."

Walking closer to her, he reached out and slid the shoulder strap off. As he did this he leaned in kissing her neck. With her eyes closed, she felt as if she was drifting away on a cloud. She felt a slight pinch on her shoulder and a warm sucking sensation. She couldn't quite explain how wonderful it felt. She felt something warm trickling down her back.

"I'm starting to feel weak. Am I supposed to feel like this? What's happening? Was there something in the wine? I'm a little scared. I feel something wet on my shoulder. Am I okay?"

"Shh! Don't be scared. I'd never hurt you. I didn't put anything in the 'wine'. This is nature taking its course. Just enjoy the moment.

I'm going to bite my wrist and I want you to suck the little bite marks. You'll be surprised at how good it taste and how wonderful you feel. I'll explain what is happening later. This is a different way to achieve an orgasm."

She was really scared. What did she know about achieving orgasms? She was a virgin and proper women didn't talk about what went on in the bedroom. She trusted him. After all, she had known him for six months. Anita began sucking his wrist. He was right. It was delicious. Could his blood actually taste that good? Was she just dreaming? She felt a surge of energy. She wanted more. Just as she felt herself sucking harder on his wrist, he gently pulled it away.

"That's enough for now. You can have more later. I want to teach you other ways to have an orgasm."

She didn't want to let go. Yet, she trusted him. He was the teacher. Now that she was no longer in her dress, he removed her petticoats. She found herself standing in the middle of the room, nude. She opened her eyes to see him smiling and quickly removing his garments. She couldn't believe she was watching his member grow as she stood there.

Robert gently pushed her to the chair under the Voodoo mask. Before she could even ask what was going to happen, she felt a slight twinge of pain as he entered her. As if in response to the sensation, her legs wrapped around his back. Suddenly, her movements were in perfect harmony to his. He slowly pumped his hips. Anita felt the tension increasing in her legs and suddenly they screamed in unison. She felt him fall to her chest and her legs fell to the floor. They both sat there, smiling. He took her hand and walked her to the sofa in the corner.

After a few minutes, he spoke. "Now is as good as ever. I have something I have to tell you. I think you need to know not only who I am, but what I am." He whispered. *"I'm a vampire."*

Anita pushed herself up to a more comfortable position and started laughing. "There is no such thing. Isn't being a Voodoo priest crazy enough? Why would you say something like that and ruin the mood?"

"I'm not joking. This was very hard for me to tell you. Haven't you noticed I never go out during the day? Also you were just drinking my blood. The wine also has blood in it. Everyone in the group contributed blood to make that wine." On that note, the mood was definitely ruined. They broke apart completely, sitting next to each other. "The people that I live with are all vampires. We live in a coven."

"Why are you telling me this?"

"Because, I love you! I'm turning you into a vampire, as we speak. I believed you love me and would want to share this with me. You starting drinking my blood and I drank yours. The blood exchange takes three days. On the fourth, you're a vampire. I decided to change you, after talking to my coven, first because you are a wonderful dancer, then because you are beautiful and finally because I love you. As long as I have been alive, I have never loved anyone like I do you. You'd make a great addition to our coven."

She began shaking her head. "No! No! This is not possible. What makes you think I'd want to be a vampire? This isn't real. I have a whole life ahead of me and I want to live it; I want to dance, see New York, and have children. Can I do that as a vampire?" Tears began streaming down her face.

"Don't cry Anita." Robert tried kissing some of her tears away.

"Stop! What have you done to me? Can we stop it?" She whispered.

"No, I am sorry. I thought because you loved me and let me take your virginity that you would want to do anything I asked."

"But not become a vampire. I wanted children. You didn't ask me. You've never even told me that you love me! I wanted to grow old with my lover. I've heard stories that vampires never change. Their bodies are frozen in time."

"I didn't know if you wanted to become a vampire but I felt if you loved me as much as I thought you did, you would want to share my life." He wiped her face with his shirt that he thrown on the floor. "Being a vampire is a good thing. You are essentially immortal. You become even more beautiful, forever. All your skills either improve or become heightened. You'll love being part of my coven. Plus, sex with a vampire is incredible! Since you're angry with me, I know we're not going to make love right now, so I might as well explain what is going to happen."

He looked down at the floor, as he began his explanation.

Chapter 14

"Don't be scared. First, we exchange blood for three days. It's not as bad as it sounds. You can do that anyway you like. You can drink it from a bottle or straight from my body. You've already drank from my wrist. Even the 'wine' you had with dinner was my blood mixed with the coven's blood. On the fourth day, you sort of die and when you wake you are officially a vampire. Someone from the coven will pick up your body from the Brothel and bring it to my apartment. That night when you wake, you'll be a complete vampire. You won't have fangs yet, though. They take about thirty days to grow in. While we're waiting for them to grow in, I'll teach you the basics of being a vampire.

When you first wake, you'll be starved. You may not know what you're hungry for but it'll be blood. We don't need food to survive but we do need blood. The first month you won't be able to bite anyone so either I'll bring you blood or we'll hunt together. Most important, though, is no contact with your friends or the past. As far as they're concerned you are dead. They saw you die and won't understand how you could possibly be walking around."

"This is so overwhelming." Anita interrupted. "I don't know if I like the idea of drinking all that blood or dying."

"I'm sure you realize by now that blood taste pretty good. I mean it taste like a good rose`. Each person will taste different, depending on their daily diet. You'll smell them first, but most taste like aged wine. The cleaner the person is the better their blood taste. Some will even taste like aged champagne. We even dip bread in our wine, with cheese. We do try to have some class."

Anita started laughing. "Class! Drinking blood can have class?"

Robert was laughing, too. "We do drink from wine glasses, not just the bottle. Wait until you discover how strong and fast you've become. Those skills will improve with time and training." Robert was getting excited, sharing all this information. The words were tumbling out. "Your most important skill will be enthralling your host. We have the ability to hypnotize our host and implant new memories while we are drinking their blood. While your host is enthralled, you have the freedom to drink their blood. Pick a phrase that you can say in a sexually enticing manner. They need to focus on you completely. We'll practice on some of the coven members."

"How will I explain my condition at the brothel? Obviously, I won't be able to work during the day. if I really die, I won't be able to work at the Brothel, at all."

"Remember, they saw you die. You can no longer be a part of the Brothel. I'm sorry! You'll have to let those friendships go."

Anita began to cry. "How'd this happen to you?"

"Don't cry, Anita. Let me tell you my story. I can tell you the truth now. I'm not really 25. I've been a vampire since the early 1800's. I was a slave in Haiti, where we practiced Voodun. I really am a hougan. I was turned by a French landowner's wife. This woman practiced the black arts of Voodun. She had been toying with the spell to make zombies and stumbled on the creation of vampires. She wanted a long term sexual partner. He needed to be unbreakable so that she could experiment with his body, sexually. I couldn't reproduce, so she never had to worry about bearing children. But it turned out I couldn't tolerate the Haitian sun. Yet, I could do the work of five men. I was invincible to disease and the hardships of slavery. The woman decided to educate me and teach me the finer qualities of French society. There was a revolution in Haiti and she was burned to death. The slaves were freed.

I caught a ship going anywhere and I ended up in New Orleans in 1880. Here, I was a free man and I could openly practice Voodoo. Due to both the lightness of my skin and my knowledge of languages,

I was able to pass myself off as a Creole. Being a vampire made me a beautiful specimen of a man. Women have been known to swoon at my feet."

Anita smiled at that comment. "I guess, I'm one of those women who swoon at your feet. That's a fascinating story but let's stop talking about vampires. We'll work out the details later. I feel a chill in the air. Wouldn't you like to use that beautiful vampire body to warm me up, again?"

"Why Anita, are you suggesting what I think, you are?"

"I mean, I am undressed and you don't have a fire going. You did say something about teaching me new skills"

Robert found himself grinning, as he rose to start a fire. Anita slid behind him.

Anita giggled. "It's not like I can change turning into a vampire, now. I might as well make the best of it. Let me see what kind of heat we can generate." She began rubbing his shoulders and caressing his chest. She slid her hands across his chest to play with his nipples, the fireplace logs burst into flames. She hadn't even noticed the logs before. He turned in her arms and lowered his head to begin nibbling her breasts. She heard herself moan as he nipped her skin. She could feel him drawing blood from her body. She wasn't a virgin anymore and she had nothing to compare this wonderful sensation to. She could feel his member growing as he lay on her stomach. As her eyelids grew heavy, he released a surge of power.

"Oh. My! Mr. Manchester I think I'm going to like being a vampire."

****

Johnny

Chapter 15

I was going to have to put lovemaking to Johnny on hold. I had an audition to plan. I knew Johnny would be there. Why did he care about Anita's audition? He didn't even know if she could really dance. All we really knew about her was that she was from New Orleans.

She was due at the club at 8 p.m., tonight. All the female dancers would be there. I would let the dancers decide if they wanted her. I didn't want anyone to think I was involved in the decision.

Johnny and I sat at one of the tables and Linda and Tracy at another. I could feel Robert's presence in the back of the club. For some reason he was in the shadows. What was he up to? I wondered if Robert knew her. He's from New Orleans, too

Every time Anita did a new routine or twirled, she threw a big grin at Johnny. He looked like he could eat her, like a piece of candy. I felt heat and smoke rising from the shadows. I didn't know if Robert was smoking or what was happening in back.

Martha clapped with excitement. "Let me show you these new tap routines. I want to see how well you catch on to choreography." She did some complex tap move with a shuffle and flip thrown in. Only a vampire would be able to copy that. I knew Martha had just made that up. I know I've never seen that dance combination on the Savoy's stage. Everyone was cheering that she'd been able to repeat it. I felt like Martha was checking out her vampire skills.

Anita was smiling at Johnny, as she spoke to Martha. "How was that? I learn pretty fast but I get better with practice."

I got the feeling she didn't know we knew she was a vampire. We *expected* her to learn fast. I had the feeling a dance war between female vampires was going to begin. Poor Johnny had no clue what was about to happen, he was falling in love.

Tracy did a jazz number. Naturally, Anita repeated it. They knew she was a vampire but I was sure *she* didn't know *they* were vampires. You could hear Johnny's heart thumping loud enough for two people. He was so excited about all this female flesh flashing around him.

Tracy laughed. "You're quite good. Maybe we could work you into the troupe. If you don't dance in our troupe, we would at least, love to work with you. Maybe, we can get you in as a dancer at the Cotton Club."

"Do you really think so? Do you really mean, you'll dance with me? I've been at the Cotton Club as a cigarette girl. I can't even get an audition. I think I'm the right color and I'm definitely tall enough." She was at least 5'9" without heels. (The Cotton Club had a reputation for accepting fair-skinned, extremely tall Negro women.)

"Calm down!" Martha said. "Let's do one thing at a time. Why don't you come to our rehearsals on your days off and we'll work on some routines?"

"Yes! Yes! Thank you." She climbed off the stage and came to my table. She bent and kissed both of my cheeks. "Thank you, Nicci. I can just tell this is going to be a life changer."

Suddenly, she kissed Johnny, too, on his cheeks. I was surprised, well, really shocked. I mouthed. "What was that for?" It looked like I was going to have competition. I don't compete well. *I don't like to share, either.*

I heard a chair crash in the back. I knew it was Robert. What the heck was wrong with him? What was he so angry about?

****

Closing the journal, I realized I needed a bathroom break. I really hated to put the journal down. It's just starting to get juicy. I wonder what Nicci is up to with Anita.

I ran to the bathroom on the next floor down. I had stocked the bathroom with toilet paper, soap and towels. No one ever came through the house so I was pretty safe in the bathroom. I quickly used the toilet, washed my hands, and splashed my face to get some of the dust off it. I towel dried it and headed back to my little hole in the attic.

It was noon and I was hungry. Mom hadn't gone grocery shopping, in a while, so I only had PBJ sandwiches, bologna, Fritos, (I hate Fritos but I need the salt.) and a Coke. I found a slightly dehydrated apple in the fruit crisper with a chocolate candy bar. Chocolate never seems to really expire. Someone must have dropped it when they were putting food away, the last time Mom went grocery shopping. I even found a package of stale crackers.

While I was chewing I thought: what the heck is Nicci thinking? In over 200 years she has never had to compete for a man. Even when it came to Antoine, Martinique's lover she just set her eyes on the prize and took it. Every man that she has wanted has sort of fallen into her arms. She must be losing her touch or Johnny isn't human. I wonder why he's so hot for Anita. She hasn't enthralled him or bit him to make him fall in love with her. From Nicci's notes, it sounds like he's all googly-eyed over Anita.

I noticed Nicci didn't describe Robert. He must be drop dead gorgeous, (No pun intended.) if a French woman turned him when he was a slave. I bet he's tall, coffee cream colored, muscular, with beautiful hair. Obviously, he's in love with Anita. Johnny had better watch out.

It looks like Anita has been a vampire for less than fifty years. She still a baby as far as vampires go. She still has a lot to learn. Obviously she doesn't know the vampire code. One vampire doesn't usually cross another, especially Nicci, if one values their life.

Finally, I finished eating, threw my garbage away and readjusted my pillows. I did a couple of stretches. One can get very cramped sitting in a ball, reading. I flipped back to the next section. It looks like she is going to explain more about Johnny.

Chapter 16

Anita was practicing every other weekend. Johnny seemed to be focused more on Anita than me. I was wondering why all my vampire tricks weren't working on Johnny. Something was wrong. He smelled delicious but something told me not to bite him. I had this strange feeling that Johnny wasn't quite human. I knew he wasn't a vampire but what was he? My vampire tricks should have been working. I needed Sally to ask around and see if anyone else thought there was something strange about him.

Friday, after just rising, I called Sally. "I have this strange feeling that Johnny isn't human. Do you think you could quietly check out his background for me? We need to find out who and what he is. Why isn't he affected by my vampire enthralling words?"

"Sure, Nicci! You know I'm basically a very nosy person. I have some friends I can ask. I f that doesn't work, I have a friend that can do a few little spells that may help us find out what he is. We'll need some of his blood for that, though. But let me ask around before we try that."

The club opened at 10 p.m. Nothing special was planned for the evening. This was the perfect night for Sally to mingle and ask questions about Johnny.

I saw Sally come out of the kitchen and wander to the back of the club. He sat at a table with four other vampires. They were all drinking 'Bloody Marys' and laughing. I could only hear bits and pieces of conversation over the noise of the club. I heard someone say Johnny was from the old country. What the heck was "the old country"? The next time around I heard someone else say "two years and the mob". My fifth time by the table, someone else said. "I noticed his blood smelled funny." That got me to thinking about the smell of his blood. It was like nothing I had ever smelled before. Maybe, that was why I was so nervous about drinking his blood. But I was still no closer to finding out what or who he was.

Between shows I caught Sally before he went, into the kitchen, to check on his staff.

I was so excited. "Well! Sally, what did you find out? I tried to eavesdrop but I could only pick up bits and pieces of different conversations. What is the "old country"?"

"You are just as nosy as me, Nicci. You just couldn't wait until I got all the information. Sean is from the old country. That's what the Irish call Ireland. I've never noticed an Irish accent when Johnny speaks, though. I've never notice any type of accent when Johnny speaks. Sean said he heard Johnny had just arrived about two years ago. He immediately went to work for the mob. He's a pick up man for them. I'm sure you already know, he picks up the receipts for the night, from all the clubs that Lucky Luciano either owns or supplies with alcohol. Sean doesn't know what he is only that he's not a vampire."

"Did anyone recognize the smell of his blood? It's a sweet fragrance I've never smelled before."

"Sean said he'd smelled it before in Ireland. But he said only on fairies. Johnny definitely couldn't be a fairy because; one, they never leave Ireland and two, they are only about two inches tall, plus they are only in fairy tales." Sally was laughing at his own humor. "I guess we'll have to get some blood and cast a spell. Do you think you could get us some blood?"

I found myself laughing, too. "Two inches tall, you say. His sex organ is larger than two inches."

"Nicci, I didn't need to know that. Focus on getting the blood!"

"Sorry, Sally. I just couldn't resist saying that. Getting blood won't be difficult. How am I supposed to transport it?"

Sally laughed, too. "Remember all those times we dripped blood into wine bottles in Italy? You could do the same with Johnny's blood. Just drip some in a flask. The only problem is that you can't enthrall him to get him to cooperate. Just get him drunk, slash his wrist, then drip it in. Make sure you don't taste any. We don't know what we are dealing with and I'd hate to see you get sick. Don't forget to seal the wound so that he doesn't know that you cut him. Don't lick it. Please be careful. Make sure you take enough, in case we make a mistake we'll have enough to do it again."

"You know better than that! I just hope the alcohol won't interfere with the spell. I'll take him home tonight after he makes his final pick up. I'll have Maria deliver the blood and your friend can get right to work. Where should she bring it?"

"Why not bring it to the Savoy and we can cast the spell here in the kitchen. Have Maria be here by noon and put in the cooler. Make sure she understands not to put it near any food or any food near it. We don't want it contaminated or to contaminate any food. I'll be here after sundown with Jules. You're welcome to come and watch." He smiled, knowingly.

"You know I'll be here. I have to know right away. I can't wait until you bring me the results. By the way, how does Jules know any spells?"

Sally looking rather wicked said. "He's a special kind of vampire. He'll tell you when he gets here."

Chapter 17

Just prior to closing, I invited Johnny to come back to my apartment at the Waldorf-Astoria after he finished making his pick up rounds. I offered him a drink and breakfast.

He showed up at 3:30 a.m. That didn't give us much time. He didn't seem to be concerned about the lateness of the hour. I felt as though he thought the lateness of the hour didn't bother me. He thought I could sleep at any hour. I had to be in my coffin before sunrise. The sun would be rising in a few hours. I had to get his blood, wake Maria for the delivery, all before 6 a.m. I had to work fast. I still had to get him drunk.

It was 4:30 and he still wasn't sleepy. I finally realized there was no getting him drunk before the sun came up. I was going to have to use a sleeping draught. I woke Maria. "Can you throw some breakfast together with a sleeping mixture in it?"

Maria was used to Nicci's idiosyncrasies. She didn't even ask questions."Sure."

We had a small cooling box in our room, in the corner. I heard Maria scrounging around in the box. Then cabinet doors were opening and closing. She came out of the kitchen carrying a large platter with small sandwiches and cheese, placed in a decorative pattern and a goblet of orange juice.

"Eat up!" I said as I grabbed a bottle of 'wine' from the bar. "I know you are starving. It's nearly 5 a.m. and you probably haven't had time to eat since you rose this morning."

"Nicci, you're reading my mind! I didn't realize I was so hungry. Are these Italian pastries and cheeses?"

"Yes! They are some of my favorites. Sally, from the Savoy, makes them special for me and Maria. (I had to make sure he didn't get any with blood mixed in. I would have a hard time explaining that.) Try this canola. The ones with the chocolate are my favorites. I can have Maria make some coffee, if you want some?"

I could put the sleeping draught in the coffee or a glass of orange juice and he would never taste it. I had to get it in his blood stream. Even, if he only slept for a few hours. While he sleeps, Samuel can take his car home and he'll never know what happened. I would leave a note with Maria explaining I had to go to an early morning fitting and would see him later. Maria could drop off the blood after they dropped him off.

Maria made the coffee, as he was eating a sandwich. Finally, he went to sleep after two sips of coffee. I slit his wrist with a straight edge razor and dripped some blood into an empty, dark wine bottle. I didn't want the sun to affect it. I used some of my saliva to close the wound. As an afterthought, I brushed his hair to get a few strains, in case we needed hair, too.

I gave Maria a note reminding Sally to wait for me before the starting the spell. I would come as soon as the sun went down.

Chapter 18

Jules and Sally were waiting for me, in the back of the kitchen. I was so excited. I really liked Johnny and couldn't wait to find out what he really was. I hoped whatever it was, was compatible with vampires.

Sally was running around the kitchen gathering spices and herbs for the spell. Jules was standing by the sink in the back of the kitchen. He had a large mixing bowl, on the counter, by the sink. If anything went wrong, he could dump the spell in the sink. He'd be able to quickly wash it down the drain.

Jules had a large metal bowl with some of the herbs already stirred in it. "Sally, bring me the blood from the cooler. Did you get any hair to grind up in it?"

"I think Nicci sent his hairbrush with a few strands still in it. We can use that. I'm glad Nicci thought to gather the hair." Sally winked at me.

I saw the wink, but I was frowning. "Sally, do you really think this is going to work? I've never known any vampire that could do a magical spell."

Jules started laughing. "In the 'old country', vampires do more than just drink blood and live forever. When you've lived as long as I have, you meet people that call themselves; magicians, shaman, high priest, even witches. Not all of it is real, but you would be surprised at what really exists. All we are trying to do is find out what Johnny really is. Obviously, he's not a vampire but he doesn't smell quite human, either. America is different from Europe. Non-humans aren't persecuted here. They are drawn to the Savoy. Creatures and people of all types come here because they can practice almost anything without being harassed or even noticed.

Let's start the spell. Drip some blood over the herbs and after you grind that hair up add it to the bowl."

I was still frowning. "This feels silly! Do you really think this will work?

"Shh! Just add the hair and be quiet."

Just like a magician from one of the Nickelodeons; he lit the bowl, and waved his hands over it. "Ira, ironia, iradiare."

Smoke started rising from the bowl. "Do you read the smoke?"

"Shh, you're interrupting my thought process. Don't be silly! You can't read smoke."

I looked at Sally and he looked at me. He shrugged his shoulders. "Are you sure it's not on fire?" It was obvious he didn't know what was going on. Suddenly, the bowl flew up in the air, exploding. I put my hand over my mouth trying not to laugh.

Jules looked at me and said. "Don't say a word. I'm a little rusty, that's all. Maybe the bowl wasn't clean. We'll just do it again."

He dumped all the ingredients in the sink, washed and wiped the bowl out with a clean towel. Sally got the herbs together again. He dripped the last of the blood into the bowl again. I ground some more hair and added it.

"You better get it right this time, Jules. We are out of blood."

"We'll read the results after the smoke fades." Jules said before I could ask another question. "Just light the blood and I'll say the words."

I quickly lit the blood and moved away from Jules, in case it blew up again. I stood next to Sally by the big metal cooler.

He waved his hands. "Ira, ironia, iradiare."

Green smoke began billowing out of the bowl. The most unusual thing I had ever seen in my life began to occur. Suddenly, the smoke began to form a word on the ceiling. When the smoke dissipated the word 'faerie' was spelled.

"What's a 'faerie'?" I said, looking up at the ceiling.

Jules smiled. "It's a supernatural creature from Ireland. I'm sure you heard of fairies or pixies from children's stories. They really *do* exist."

"We didn't have fairies or faeries in Portugal or Italy that I know of. We had Pinocchio, the puppet, in Italy. My childhood stories, from Portugal, were about the Moors being wizards and them turning children into wolves."

"Well," Jules said. "Faeries are the Irish fairies. The old ones would tell stories about faeries as being magical creatures that could sprinkle magic dust on you. This would allow you to be invisible or become a wee folk. They stole babies like your Moors did. I even heard they could make you fly. I doubt if that's true though. Why would you want to fly? They also can't lie. If they sprinkle dust on you, you can't lie either. What's important in all this is that he doesn't know that we know he is a faerie. Oh, by the way, they are immortal, too, like vampires.

The story goes that faeries live forever, so every 200 years, they can go on sabbatical and become whatever creature they want to be. Usually, they become humans because they want the opportunity to try out human love. They have at least twenty-five years. But they don't get to stay human. They must return to their faerie self. They look completely human, even with a heartbeat. Faerie blood smells like candy, but if you try to drink it, it will drive you mad. It's a definite poison to vampires. You can't even sip it. Even though, I know it smells so wonderful, you can barely control yourself to keep from drinking it. You have to be strong. There is no cure for the madness. Also, there is no way to turn him into a vampire, so don't even try.

Remember, he can't know, you know what he is!"

I felt bloody tears streaming down my face, from the laughter. "Are you teasing me? Blood can't drive a vampire crazy. It makes us stronger. That sounds like some cruel joke. Are you sure someone didn't make that up about faerie blood being poisonous, just to keep us from draining them?"

"Nicci, I don't know how true it is, but I'm not willing to try it. Remember there is no cure. There are more than enough different types of blood to drink without drinking faerie blood. Make sure none of the girls drink it either."

Suddenly, I heard one of the large kitchen doors swing open. Someone called out. "Is anyone in here?"

I didn't recognize the voice of who had just come in. I just shouted. "Sally and I are in the back of the kitchen, going over inventory, for the next weeks order."

I started grabbing things off the drain board and dumping them in the garbage. I wiped the tears from my cheeks, with a kitchen towel. Jules was dumping the spell remnants in the sink. He quickly turned the faucet on, to wash it down the drain. Thank goodness the word on the ceiling had faded. I heard footsteps coming further into the kitchen.

Sally grabbed Jules by the arm and shoved him out the back door. He quickly pecked him on both cheeks. I heard him whisper. "Thank you. We'll talk later." The door slammed behind him.

Sally said under his breath. "We now know what Johnny is. We'll have to be more careful around him. I don't think he knows we are vampires. If you are too weak, and I know you Nicci, to keep from really making love to him, you'll have to keep your fangs hidden."

"That's going to be really hard. You know how I like to nibble when I make love."

"No sparks either! He knows humans don't cause sparks When they have sex I know that."

I couldn't stop laughing. "Now Sally, its sound as if you're jealous. *Are you jealous?*"

"Hmm"

Vampire Hunters
Mikael Dragomir/Petyr Apostal

Chapter 19

Lately, two strange looking men had started coming to the club. They were definitely European. I could tell by the out dated suits they had on. One looked to be about in his late thirties and the other was in his twenties. I don't know if they were brothers but they were always huddled together at a table in the back of the club. I noticed, they tended to stick to the shadows of the room. I never saw a woman with them. I thought it was odd. They did enjoy the female dancers, though. They seemed to be studying the women especially me.

I had Martha, a human, sit and talk with them first. I needed to know if they were human. Although Martha wasn't a vampire, she was in tune with our bodies to know if someone had a heartbeat. I could tell by the way the older looked at her, he liked her. After a brief conversation, she found out they were Mikael Dragomir and Petyr Apostal. Finally, I worked up my courage to go and sit at their table. I had to find out what they were up to. Extending my hand I said. "Good evening, gentlemen. My name is Dominique Santa Maria. My friends call me Nicci. You may call me Nicci. I've noticed you coming to the club a lot, recently. I pride myself on knowing almost all my guests. I would love to know more about you, if you don't think I'm being too forward."

I noticed right away that Mikael loved to talk. He said they were from Romania. It was a very small village near the Carpathian Mountains. They had lived in a Seminary run by the Brothers of St

Gerome. Both of them supposedly had decided they didn't want to be Brothers and left the order. Because they had decided they didn't want to join the order, they had been thrown out of the Seminary. Since they had no family in Romania, they decided to come to America.

Something in their story didn't ring true. I told them of my life at the Convent of St Theresa's in Italy. "Why did you leave the Seminary? Isn't that a calling from God? Why didn't you at least accept the education the Seminary had to offer?"

Mikael did most of the talking. "Yes, it is a calling from God but we didn't get that calling. The Brothers had raised us since we were children. We wanted to see the world and women before we made that final commitment to God."

"Are you telling me you've neither one of you have ever been with a woman?"

Petyr looked at Mikael. "Is that how all American women talk? What kind of question is that to ask, from a woman?"

"First, I'm not American. Second, I was curious. Have either of you ever been with a woman?"

Mikael was blushing. I could feel the temperature rise in his entire body. "If you must know, yes. Now, let's change the subject."

"Why are you really here? I don't believe it's because you didn't get some calling from God."

Petyr lowered his voice. "Can you keep a secret?"

Mikael looked at Petyr. "Are you sure you should be saying something? I mean, we just met her."

"We have to trust someone. Since she knows all her guest, I bet she could help us find out who the local vampires are. Hopefully she believes in vampires."

"Gentlemen, I do know my guests. I have never heard anyone speak of vampires. What are they?' (I just couldn't believe they were dumb enough to ask me about vampires. Obviously they didn't know any real vampires.)

Mikael cleared his throat. "Surely, you've heard of vampires. You *are* from Italy. Don't you remember when the Church had that big execution and had those two vampires turned to ashes in the sunlight? We were there."

I almost choked. "No. Maybe I was already here in New York when that happened. I would remember something like that." (Thank God, they didn't know those two vampires were my best friends. I was devastated from that loss and it ruined my relationship with Antoine.)

Petyr said. "Mikael, she doesn't really look old enough to remember that. We were both kids when that happened. The Brothers from the Seminary took us to see it. They thought it would be a good lesson to learn on how to destroy vampires, if we were to be future vampire killers."

Thank goodness vampires don't blush. "Is that what you are? Vampire killers? How exciting. Have you killed any vampires?"

"No. Here in America, we don't call ourselves vampire killers. We are vampire hunters, but you can't tell anyone. We were sent here because after the execution, all the vampires in Europe started disappearing. It's as if they went underground, so to speak. Or into hiding. We had been following one particular vampire during the war but we lost his trail. I think his name was Heinrich something or other. He kept changing his last name and we lost his trail. We were ordered to come to New York. The Order heard they're a lot of extremely rich and beautiful young people in this city. We're to find out if they are vampires."

"Good luck. What does a vampire look like? I'll keep my eyes open, in case I see one."

"They are very difficult to spot, though. They tend to be very beautiful people, much like yourself. They don't have a heartbeat, or eat. They drink blood. The important thing is that they never come out during the day. They don't like sunlight. Also they sleep in coffins."

I started giggling. "I almost said that could be my entire dance troupe. They dance all night so they sleep a lot during the day. They are all very beautiful, too. But I think I can truly speak for the group when I say they don't have any coffins lying around here, as far as I know of. But I'll keep my eyes open."

Martha had not said a word during this whole conversation. She just rolled her eyes at me and snickered. "Me too. I'll keep my eyes open. If I see the undead walking around I'll let you know."

Chapter 20

The Cotton Club was growing in popularity. The dance troupe had made quite a name for itself. They couldn't compete with the Savoy but I wasn't going to take any chances on losing any of my clientele. I had to keep tabs on it.

Anita finally moved up from cigarette girl, at the Cotton Club, to dancer. She was even featured on one Saturday and Sunday night a month with a fellow dancer named Levi. Levi was human. He had no idea that Anita was a vampire. She had been secretly seeing Johnny on Wednesday nights after he dropped off his final receipts. She didn't know I knew but I could smell her on his skin when he came to pick up the receipts on Thursday nights. He was now coming twice a week. I couldn't do anything about it because I couldn't enthrall him. I couldn't drink his blood or bind him to me. I needed a love potion!

Two nights prior to New Year's Eve, Johnny and Anita snuck and made love for the first time. It was obvious they were lusting for each other. At least, it was obvious to me. She still didn't know he was a faerie.

****

It was New Year's Eve, 1926. Naturally, we had a big gala for the coming of the New Year. Even the vampire killers were there.

WuYi and Su Chi were passing champagne around to get ready for the midnight toast. Lucky Luciano and I had decided to join forces for one night and have a big dance and show at the Savoy instead of splitting the customers for one night.

Because of the joining of both clubs, Anita was at the Savoy tonight. Everyone knew that I still wanted Johnny. They thought Anita was in love with Robert. I knew that people assumed when you kissed at midnight that it meant nothing. I knew differently.

I warned Johnny. "When you kiss tonight, only kiss."

He laughed. "What's that supposed to mean? What else would I do besides kiss? The only person that I may even consider going home with, to bed, is you. Nicci, don't be so jealous. Just take in the exceptional beauty of the night and look forward to going home with me." As he said this he was looking directly at Anita not me.

I grabbed his face and kissed him on the lips. We toasted. "I have to make the rounds and greet my guests, but I'll be back before the last show." I could feel my blood beginning to boil from anger. I had to get away from him for a while. With such a large crowd the smell of blood and the thumping of their hearts was intoxicating and adding to my inability to control my emotions. I saw Anita with Robert and my anger went down a couple of notches. I felt a little reassured.

At 10 p.m. the dance troupe performed with Cab Calloway. Of course, he had to sing 'Minnie the Moocher'. Normally, Cab Calloway only performs at the Cotton Club but he was doing a favor for Lucky. He knew tonight was special because I had quite a few couples that were planning to get engaged tonight. Lucky hoped I was going to marry Johnny.

"You know, Nicci, if you marry Johnny, we can join the clubs into one large club. It will just be on two different properties. We can pool the profits and everyone involved will make money. Let me toast with you."

Suddenly, Sally was at my elbow. "Did I tell you how exceptionally beautiful you look in that red and white gown? I see you even have your ruby choker on. But, who can help but notice Anita in that orange gown. It looks like the feathers are floating down from heaven when she walks. She looks almost inhuman, ethereal, even. Johnny also has a radiant glow about him as if he is one of God's angels. I wonder what is causing that glow. Maybe it's love or is it my imagination"

****

After the show Anita came to sit with us. She was radiant from the sweat of dancing and enjoying herself. Somehow her body was cover with this sheen from head to toe. Vampires don't sweat so I wonder what it really was. As Johnny pulled the chair out for her to sit, he scratched his wrist on the back of the wooden chair. Suddenly, blood began to trickle from the tiny wound. The candy fragrance of fresh blood began to fill the room.

I could hear other vampires saying. "Do you smell that?"

"What is that fabulous odor?"

"Is Nicci cooking something special for the New Year?"

"Where is it coming from?"

It was then that I noticed the vampire hunters looking around the room to see what everyone was talking about. Not being vampires, themselves, they couldn't figure out what people were talking about. They didn't smell anything.

I immediately knew it was Johnny's faerie blood. I had to fix the problem. I saw the blood dripping down his wrist. Even with my vampire speed and reflexes, before I could grab a napkin, Anita had grabbed his wrist and licked the blood. (*I couldn't believe she had gotten there before me.*)

Anita said. "I'm sorry you scratched your wrist when you pulled the chair out. I hope it didn't hurt too much? It looks like a tiny scratch. And look since I licked it, you can barely tell what happened."

Johnny laughed. "I don't even see a scratch. I didn't even feel it. You're amazing." He leaned over and kissed her on the cheek, as she seated herself.

Anita began playing with the roses and pretended to stick herself with a thorn so that she would bleed. (*I knew she was faking. I personally oversaw the de-thorning of all the roses.*) She said. "Look I stabbed myself and I'm bleeding. Can you stop it?" Before he could answer she had put her bloody finger in his mouth. He didn't even have a chance to grab a napkin. I saw his eyes light up as he began drinking her blood.

I heard myself almost shouting. "Anita, stop that! If your finger is cut we'll get a band-aid. You don't stick your sweaty fingers in his mouth. You haven't even washed your hands after dancing." She couldn't have ingested any more than a few drops of Johnny's blood. I had no idea what he took from her.

I turned to talk to Sally and she started sucking his fingers. Suddenly, she looked up and saw me watching her. I felt Robert's presence lurking in the back of the club. I was worried that a fight might break out over Anita. When she saw me staring at her, she dropped Johnny's hand, but it was too late. She had swallowed more than a few drops now.

I stood and announced to the table. "I must get the balloons ready with Sally. Sally, can you come to the kitchen and help me with the balloons? When are the balloons supposed to drop?"

He was sitting at the table transfixed by what had just occurred. He knew Anita didn't know Johnny was a faerie. "Nicci . . . ? Nicci . . . ? Let's go to the kitchen and work on those balloons."

In the kitchen Sally said, frowning. "Oh my gosh, Nicci. What are we going to do? They just exchanged blood. I have no idea how long it takes before she goes mad. Did you see Anita tried to create a sexual blood bond right before our very eyes? It's a good thing it takes a couple days with more blood exchanged. We have to stop it and try to break the bond."

"Sally, you're not thinking. Johnny is not a normal human. There is no bond to break. We have to worry about her sanity. Did you forget faerie blood drives a vampire mad?"

Chapter 21

Suddenly, I heard a chair crash. People were screaming. What the heck was happening in the club? I came out of the kitchen and started running towards my table. Anita had kicked over some chairs and thrown bottles at the guests. She was sitting on a table in front of Johnny, with her dress hiked up over her knees.

She was preaching. "Did you know as a vampire, I think humans make a very good meal? I bet most of you didn't even know I was a vampire. Yes, I am a vampire and I drink blood."

Robert had come from the back and was trying to get her to stop talking. Johnny didn't understand what was happening. His expression said it all. Fear was written on it.

She was babbling. "The world was theirs first. It now belongs to us. In the vampire hierarchy the educated humans can work for us and we'll drain the rest. If the vamps won't work for me I'll let them burn in the sun."

Johnny said. "What's wrong with her? Why is she talking like that?"

Sally whispered to me. "I guess we were wrong about the length of time before the madness kicks in."

"You think!"

Anita was struggling to free herself from Robert's viselike grip he had on her arms. "The world should belong to the paranormal. I'll be the queen and Johnny you can be my King. Robert you are fired!"

****

People in the club are either frightened or laughing. They're not sure if it's an act or if Anita has gone mad. Sally and I know she is going mad. Johnny has no idea that his blood caused her madness. Robert knew Johnny was a faerie because he had overheard Sally and me talking about keeping the girls away from him. Robert didn't think Anita cared for Johnny that much. He thought they were just business friends. He'd heard stories about the madness caused by faerie blood but had never seen a vampire go mad before. He was frightened because he loved Anita.

Robert began pointing his finger at Johnny's chest, with his free hand. "What did you do to her? You weren't supposed to be sharing blood. Obviously, you're not a human! What are you?"

Suddenly, Anita grabbed a waiter passing by the table.

"I'm just a mobster. What the <u>hell</u> is she?"

As Johnny was screaming at Robert, Anita had gotten free. She ripped the waiter's throat out and drank his blood. I'd never seen anything like that before and I've seen a lot of evil things over the years. You could hear gasps throughout the club.

Anita seemed to be calmer after drinking the waiter's blood. She had wiped her mouth with the back of her white glove. Her orange feathered gown was streaked with blood. She looked down at her gown and began screaming. "What happened? Who did this? Is someone dead? Am I bleeding? I don't feel any pain!" As she calmed down she patted herself and her clothing. "I'm okay!" She frantically looks from Johnny to Robert.

Johnny tried to talk through his shock. "Anita, you just ripped out that waiter's throat. You looked like you were drinking his blood. You were ranting about being a vampire and vamps should rule the world."

"I would never do or say anything that horrible!"

Johnny grabbed her and held her close to his chest. For the moment she was completely lucid. "I couldn't have done that!" Anita broke down in his arms crying. She began to accuse Robert. "How could you do such savagery? Why? What did he do?"

Robert was beginning to get angry. "Why would you think I would do something so horrible?"

Bloody tears were streaming down her face. Because Johnny still didn't believe she was a vampire, he thought her face must be cut or blood had splashed on it. He began to pat her face slowly and realized the tears were real blood coming from her eyes and not a cut.

He shoved Anita away. "What are you? You're crying tears of blood! You can't be human. You're crying tears of blood. All that talk about vampires ruling the world, you meant it. You're a vampire." He let go of her and began crying into his hands. He fell to the floor and curled up into a fetal position. "Help me! Don't kill me. The only thing I did was love Anita."

Robert had just discovered he couldn't enthrall Johnny. He didn't know what to do. He couldn't have Johnny telling people what he just heard and saw. He was debating whether he should just kill Johnny. He could then focus all his energy on fixing Anita or would he solve the problem by killing them both?

Everyone in the club was watching. No one said a word. Finally, after hearing the racket, Sally came out of the kitchen holding a bottle of blood. He had gone back into the kitchen looking for bottled blood when she started ranting. He thought maybe if she drank some fresh blood from a bottle, it would calm her down. He was too late. Only Sally, Jules, Maria, and Nicci knew that Johnny was a faerie and that his blood would drive you insane. I quickly filled Sally in on what had just transpired. I tried to explain that after he returned to the kitchen to get the bottled blood, she had another brief moment of insanity when she ripped out a waiter's throat and Johnny saw it. She seemed to be sane for the moment. The problem was Johnny had seen her drink the blood. She also had cried bloody tears. How were we to fix Johnny's memory if he couldn't be enthralled?

Sally whispered to me. "I knew this problem was going to arise, the way they were goo-goo eyed over each other. Robert can fix Anita's memory for now and we'll explain to her later what happened. Hopefully she won't go crazy again. We have to worry about Johnny's memory. We need to give Johnny a Mickey to knock him out. Let's give him a shot of good bourbon. We'll tell him it's to calm his nerves. I'll add a Black Shade petal. It will cause him to black out and sleep for at least twenty-four hours. We can explain he passed out at the club and has slept for a day and half. He had been running a fever. He seemed to be having nightmares. We'll only let him see

Anita if she is lucid. I don't know how to take care of faerie blood madness so I'm making this up as we go along. I have to ask Jules is there anything else we can do? We can't let the vampire community know that Johnny is a faerie. Like I said before, we also can't let Johnny know we know he is a faerie.

I said. "What a mess! We should have at least told the troupe he was a faerie."

****

Mikael and Petyr were sitting in the corner during all the commotion. No one even noticed they were there.

Mikael whispered to Petyr."Did you see that? I had no clue they were vampires in this club. Look at all of them! When that man cut his wrist abut twenty people turned their heads. Then that dancer, I think her name is Anita, began sucking his arm. Vampires can be so disgusting. Did you see him sucking her dirty fingers? Do you think they were exchanging blood?"

Petyr laughed. "Anything is possible. But in public! I think her blood lust got the better of her. Do you think that owner woman, Nicci, is a vampire? We can't kill them all unless we burn down the club."

"I don't think burning down the club is practical because they would just move on to another club. They could just move to the Cotton Club. I wonder what happened to that woman. I've never seen a vampire drink blood in public."

"What's wrong with that man? Obviously, he's not a vampire. Did you see that woman just rip that waiter's throat out? She even drank his blood. He looked like he was going into shock. I hope someone helps him. We can't help him. We don't want anyone to know we are vampire hunters. I think we should follow Anita and find out what is going on. Somehow we have to listen in and get Anita alone. I don't know if we've stumbled upon a coven but we obviously need to get rid of Anita.

Chapter 22

The club was closed immediately 'for repairs'. Robert took Anita with him. Johnny drank WuYi's drink and passed out before it was finished. Samuel drove Johnny home, with the explanation that he had gotten sick. I rode with Samuel. I told him I was going to play nurse. He helped me carry him to bed. I stayed with him while he slept. I had to be there when he woke. He had to think it was just a wild nightmare.

We finally got him settled. I knew he was going to wake with a terrible headache and thirst. We had to find out how much longer he was going to be human. The smell of his blood was just too tempting for vampires. It was just like candy. I might be forced to have Johnny and Anita killed, especially if we couldn't cure Anita.

****

Sally, Anita, Robert, and Tracy went to Robert's apartment, while Anita was lucid. Sally explained to everyone what had happened to Anita during the blood exchange.

Anita began to cry again."Why didn't someone tell me! I wouldn't have been so quick to drink his blood."

Robert had a tremendous amount of pain etched across his face. "Anita, I thought you loved me? Why would I even think you would try and drink his blood? I just found out his was a faerie, too. But,

I've always known faerie blood will drive you mad, although, I've never met one. The smell is highly intoxicating. You're not through with the madness yet. I don't know how much you drank, but you'll definitely go mad again. I don't know if there is a cure. We may have to wait until it circulates through your whole body unless we can find someone who does Blood- letting. How much did you drink?"

Anita whispered to herself, while she gave it great thought. "It couldn't have been too much. He only scratched his wrist and I sucked the cut. That can't be too much, can it?"

Tracy moaned into her hands. "You silly girl. Sally, how could you and Nicci have kept this a secret? It's such a dangerous secret. You should have at least told the dancers."

Sally wasn't sure if a great load had been lifted off his shoulders or if he just added to the weight. "That's why we kept it a secret. If the information had gotten out . . . . Do you know how many vampires could have used his blood as a weapon? We thought we were safe if only a few people knew. Who would have thought Anita would be sucking on Johnny when she had Robert?"

"I know I was wrong. Robert, I'm sorry! Now I have to fix this. When will I go mad again? Sally, please help me!" She began crying again.

Sally frowned. "Don't cry Anita. You realize this is all new to us? We'll just have to wait and see." He didn't want to tell her he knew every time she was near a human host, she would go into a blood frenzy. It didn't matter how much or how little she had ingested.

Sally and Robert went into the kitchen to talk in vampire whispers. They couldn't afford to have Anita overhear them. "There is no cure, Robert. Not unless you know a faerie doctor or witch. I know, from whispers, you're a Voodoo high priest. Can you use any of your magic to cure it?"

Robert turned on Sally, exploding with anger. "Why would you keep this a secret? Hougans only practice white magic. A cure would probably involve black magic. How did you find out about my Voodoo practices?"

"That's not important now. Do you have a cure, or not?"

"I've never seen an infected vampire before. Until I can come up with a cure we have to keep her isolated. We may have to kill her if she gets out of hand. Sally. I love her, though. I heard the vampire hunters were in town. We can't let them find out about her. It would be too dangerous. No telling what they would do. In the meantime I'll work on a cure."

"For now, we have to keep her away from humans if we want her to stay sane. Try to keep her appeased with bottled blood and I'll look for a cure, too."

****

Keeping to the shadows, no one knew Mikael and Petyr had followed Robert, with Anita, home. They were curious to find out what was going on. Mikael and Petyr were really excited. Had they stumbled on a coven? They had just arrived in America. Could they be that lucky? They felt it was a sign from God, supporting their mission.

They knew Anita was a vampire by the way she had torn that waiter's throat out and drank his blood. They weren't sure if Nicci or Robert were vampires. It didn't really matter. It seemed as if they were in league with the vampires. They could easily get rid of Anita and put fear into the vampire community. Eventually, they would come out and gather, if not just to talk about the vampire killers but their safety, too. They always did when one of their own was killed.

Mikael could see Sally and Robert talking through the kitchen window. He whispered. "Petyr, while they are in the kitchen talking, Anita is alone except for a woman she seems to be talking to. It looks like the dancer called Tracy. Do you have a weapon?"

"I always carry my long blade!"

"That will be perfect. Anita is probably still crying to that woman while the men are in the kitchen. Go knock on the door and depending on whom answers, will determine what to do next. Ask for Anita if that woman comes to the door of if Anita answers quickly stab her.

Before she has time to react or anyone else can get to the door, decapitate her. As soon as her head comes off, get out of the doorway. *Do not stand* there to admire your work or success. Remember, the men, possibly two male vampires are in the kitchen. The other woman will be too busy screaming to attack you. Just get away and meet me at the Cotton Club tomorrow. They'll be looking for us at the Savoy. We'll have to stay away from the Savoy for a while.

The Depression Years
1929-1939

Chapter 23

I don't know whether to cry or just be angry. I can't believe poor Anita not only went mad from drinking Johnny's blood, but she literally lost her head over it. I'm glad Nicci was able to control her lust enough, not to drink his blood. Who'da thought fairy or faerie blood would drive a vampire mad. I always thought they were invincible. I was just beginning to love the sex Nicci was having with Johnny. I never expected Anita to be involved with a Voodoo priest, either. That could have really gotten ugly for Johnny.

Obviously, this is information they kept out of the history books. I wonder if Robert is going to try and get revenge for the beheading of Anita. Do vampires go to their coffins instead of mattresses like the mob, when they are at war? How do Petyr and Mikael think they can keep the vampires from knowing they beheaded Anita? I mean, they were Vampire Killers. They didn't keep it a secret.

It is starting to get dark but I hate to stop now. A quick stretch and maybe I can get at least another hour in before it gets too dark and my mother begins to wonder where I am.

****

No one spoke after the loss of Anita. Everyone was pointing fingers at each other as to whose fault it was that she got beheaded. We did celebrate her brief life as a vampire at a private memorial, but then all went quiet. The entire vampire community was nervous. From 1926 to 1929, vampires kept disappearing. We heard stories of vampires burning in the sun, beheadings and staking. I knew it was Petyr and Mikael but I couldn't prove it or even catch them. No one seemed to care we had Vampire Killers in our midst. The community kept saying it was just some sort of mob war.

Time passed and for a while the vampire deaths seem to decrease, but then The Depression hit us. Many vampires had their money in banks and the stock market. When it crashed, they were suddenly poor. As if that wasn't bad enough, bodies were reappearing without heads. The Harlem Community newspaper had a story every week. No one called them vampires but we knew who they were. We had to figure out a way to stop them. The local police didn't care that vampires were dying. They weren't going to arrest Mikael and Petyr, even if we had proof.

After the 1930's New Year's Eve party, the thirteen major covens of New York came to the Savoy to discuss the problem. They needed to stop the killings. We knew the Vampire Killers were doing it but we hadn't been able to prove it. This was America. We couldn't convict them without proof. We also had to discuss the impact the Depression was having on our food supply and cash flow. If the people were starving, the amount of blood we could get was decreasing.

Instead of partying for the New Year, we argued all night. Of course, they wanted to set up a committee to research the feasibility of just killing the Vampire Killers. (Who were they kidding!) They wanted to weigh our options on just killing them without anyone knowing or turning them into the law.

I stopped that idea. "All we need to do is hunt them down and kill them. But if you insist on wanting to talk to them, maybe we could reach an agreement and return them to Romania. We don't want to make them martyrs in the vampire hunter/killer community. That will just bring more of them. We have to see how many vampires they feel they need to kill.

Maybe they have reached their 'quota'. Are we all in agreement, though, we definitely have to kill them? Just carefully! We don't want a war."

Sally laughed. "Nicci, you are being unrealistic. Do you really think once we reveal ourselves as vampires, they will say they have reached their quota of killing us? Eventually, we may have to go to war, now that they know who we are here. We just need to kill them and be done with it. We can make their deaths look like they were a result some great financial loss from the Depression. Let's take a vote. We have a board of thirteen members representing all the major covens in New York. I think we should take a vote. Does everyone agree?"

Everyone said yes, in unison, except Jules and me.

I frowned and shook my head. "I think you are making a mistake."

I could sense Sally's frustration with me. He said. "We are vampires. We are the strongest of the paranormal races. We should be in control, not hunted down like animals. No one has to know we killed them."

"I agree, Sally. But, if we are going to kill them we need a plan. We can't just walk up to them and murder them. We need to find out where they are hiding out, first. I think we should interrogate them to make sure they are alone. It would be a waste to kill them only to find out later that they were part of a team. They are human so they won't be difficult to kill."

Jules spoke up. "I agree with Nicci. We can't just rush into this. We are smarter than that. We need to plan. We have to know how many of them there are. We can't have a bloody war on our hands. We don't want Romania sending replacements. Also, you're not thinking with your brains. How are they finding out who's a vampire? Haven't you notice that only vampires are being murdered? How do they know who we are? No one has spoken about Anita, yet ever since her breakdown at the Savoy we've lost at least one vampire a month. Where are they getting their information from?"

The looks went around the room. Everyone had the same question on their face. "He's right. How do they know who is a vampire and who isn't?"

Sally spoke first. "You're right Jules. We never stopped to think. How *do* they know who's a vampire and who isn't? Someone must be feeding them information."

I could hear the grumbling in the room. Everyone was giving each other and accusing look, while saying. "It wasn't me."

I stood, this time, to speak. "Let's not sit here and accuse each other. We need to find out who the informant is and kill him too. I suggest we set up a trap to catch them. We need to start a rumor that there is to be a large vampire gathering to draw them out. We can either follow them to see if they meet their informant or just capture them. Once they're our prisoners we can figure out what to do with them.

Okay, today is January 1st, 1930 and the Depression is in full swing. There are a lot of starving people out there and face it, you cannot drink blood from a starving host. Some of you have very little food to share with your coven members or have no food at all. We know the local food stores have very limited, expensive supplies. After giving this much thought, I am going to turn the Savoy into a food bank during the day and early evenings. The Savoy will still be a club at night and we'll serve good meals just like before. The Vampire Killers will know vampires are running it because I'll hire Negroes to stock it during the day and vampires will distribute the food at night. I will mix in a few normal people so that the only way you'll know who a vampire is, is if someone has singled them out. The two vampire killers are bound to show up for free food. By March, we should know who is giving Mikael and Petyr, the Vampire Killers, information. We'll have to rotate the staff and make sure a human is always working with a vampire. The food bank has to look as real as possible.

I figure by March, we should know who the contact is for Mikael and Petyr. They will have let their guard down because the vampires will appear to be out in the open. We already know they are vampire killers because they haven't kept it a secret. The first time I met them they told me they were Vampire Killers. They'll come to the food bank to investigate.

We'll offer food to everyone. If they can pay, we'll take whatever they can pay. If they can't afford to, we'll still give them food. We want people to think we're good Samaritans. I want the Vampire Killers to think twice about killing us. This will also provide us with a healthy food supply. Remember, though, no killing unless absolutely necessary. We can't have dead bodies lying around the food bank. People will become too frightened to come."

Everyone was in agreement. The meeting was adjourned.

Chapter 24

Flyers were posted and handed out everywhere. The Savoy was to become a Food Bank, during the day. Food would be given to everyone, not just those with money. It was to be open Monday—Thursday. Friday and Saturdays the Savoy would have dinner and shows as usual. We would still cater to the rich on the weekends. Business was closed on Sunday's for church. (We had to maintain a good image.)

Shantyville had been set up in Central Park. It was about six blocks away. Samuel and his friends from the Waldorf-Astoria distributed food to the families living in the park. Sally made full meat soups to feed the working men in Shantyville. I would make rounds in the evening, getting to know some of the men and their families stranded in New York City with no food or jobs. They were taking the Depression the hardest. People were getting to know me and were growing comfortable talking about what was happening on the streets.

Johnny didn't come around too often in the beginning. I think he was too scared. I didn't really care how he felt at the moment. My primary responsibility was to the vampire community and to find out how Petyr and Mikael knew what vampires to kill. I had to find out and get rid of all of them.

Samuel didn't know the Vampire Killers by sight. One night he told me that he had noticed two strange men, dressed as migrant workers. "They are in line every Thursday night. They wore the same grey coat and denim jacket. I noticed they seem to have a two day beard growth and dirty hands. The dirty hands are what made me notice them. All the other men in line always made sure that if their clothes weren't clean at least their hands were. They claimed their hands were dirty from selling newspapers. They claimed they sold them a penny a piece and some of the ink came off on their fingertips." Samuel said. I heard one call the other Mikael. Mikael had two coats on under the grey coat and gloves with the fingertips cut off. He said it was to make it easier to handle the newspapers and keep the bitter chill of the New York winter out."

I asked Samuel. "What about the other man with him. Did you hear his name?"

"I didn't catch a name. The other man had managed to find a hat. You could tell it wasn't his. His earlobes were exposed and red from the cold. He had the denim jacket on with a raggedy red sweater underneath. Neither of them had boots or galoshes on to protect their feet from the snow or slush. They'd be here tonight because it's the night we get donations of extra fried chicken from Tillie's Chicken on 133rd."

Every night, the line to the food bank was wrapped around the building. Since word had gotten out that on Thursday's, Tillie's Chicken donated left over chicken, the line extended past the corner. No one ever asked where did all the food come from? They seemed to be just grateful that they were able to get some. Usually, only men stood in line. They took the opportunity to discuss if there was any work to be found. On a rare occasion, we got a woman with her family.

A pattern was beginning to develop with the two young men. They'd get food on Thursday night and then show up at the club clean shaven, on Fridays. WuYi pointed them out to me after they showed up three Fridays in a row. I decided to say something to them after WuYi got them seated and handed them menus.

"I noticed, you gentlemen ordered one of the most expensive items on the menu. Samuel, my chauffeur, noticed that you seemed to be in line at the food bank every week, though. How is it that you can afford such an expensive meal?" I began to examine their clothes a little closer. Even though, it was dark in the Savoy, I could tell they were wearing black tuxedos and cashmere coats. "You look awfully familiar. Have you been here before? (I knew who they were but I didn't want them to know I remembered them.)"

I was surprised when the older one said. "No, it's our first time here. I'm sure your chauffeur is mistaken about us being in the food bank line. Why would we stand in a free food line if we can afford to eat here? We've heard a lot about how good the entertainment and food was. We noticed, even though, New York City is in the midst of the Depression, the Savoy is still partying. How is that?"

I wasn't sure how to answer that. "Do either of you two gentlemen have a cigarette?"

Petyr opened his tuxedo, flashing a gold cigarette case, and offered me one.

Taking the cigarette, I placed it to my lips. Before I could say anything, Petyr had whipped out a gold lighter with a ruby in the center. As I bent to light my cigarette, I batted my eyes and flashed a big grin for his sake. I made sure we made eye contact before I took my first puff. I knew he was hooked.

I laughed. "We're not just partying. I'm sure you noticed our signs for the Food Bank, Monday to Thursday. We can't feed all of Harlem and New York City, but we try. (I felt they were going lie about knowledge of the Food Bank since they lied about coming to the club.)

Petyr smiled at me. He was beaming. "We've never seen your food bank, we're new in town and wanted a night out on the town. We've heard so much about the Savoy."

Mikael added. "Everyone is struggling! It's good to see that you can still get a good meal and a drink in New York. And entertainment!"

I laughed and said under my breath to myself. "They're unbelievable. How could they think we wouldn't recognize them? I don't know any stupid vampires!" I felt my anger growing. Out loud I said. "Well enjoy your meal." I walked away with a secret smile on my face.

I went into the kitchen to talk to Sally. He looked like he was baking bread. "We've got them. I just can't believe they don't think we know who they are. They are dumber than I thought. It's a wonder they've lasted as long as they have. It just goes to show someone is helping them. We've got to have someone follow them and find out where they live. They must have money tucked away somewhere if they can go to the Food Bank once a week and then show up at the Savoy on Fridays. They ordered about $20.00 worth of food. No one has money like that to throw around. The Food Bank must be the point of contact. Someone is paying them to kill vampires. They must be getting names from this person. We have to find out who is supplying the information and dispose of them."

Sally was dusting his hands together. I could see flour in his hair and on his cheeks. He looked like a movie vampire with a white face. "For once I agree with you, Nicci. I think someone is paying them to kill vampires, too. Johnny has been laying low every since Anita was beheaded. He would be perfect to follow them. Or we could get Martha to act like she is falling in love with Petyr or Nicci you could make a play for Mikael *or* Petyr. You haven't had a human lover for almost five years. After the fiasco with Johnny and the faerie blood, Mikael would be perfect for you. Although, I did see the way Petyr was looking at you when he lit your cigarette. You didn't think I was watching but I was."

"Sally, you know I'm content with you as my lover but maybe it's time to play with a human again. I've been good for a long time. I haven't turned anyone in years. Do you think I should turn someone to kill Mikael and Petyr or just kill Mikael and Petyr myself?"

"Don't get ahead of yourself, Nicci. First, we have to find out who's paying them before we kill them.

Chapter 25

Petyr and Mikael sat and ate until the Savoy closed. Without close inspection, they appeared to be two gentlemen just eating and enjoying a floor show. I knew they were really trying to find out if there were any vampires at the Savoy. I decided after the final dance number to have Martha sit with Mikael. I had plans for Petyr. He was the younger of the two and probably would be easier to manipulate. Next, I called Johnny from the kitchen phone. I didn't want to be overheard by the staff. He arrived just before closing.

Johnny was still depressed over the loss of Anita. The Mickey and the shock of Anita ripping out that waiter's throat caused him to block out the fact that she was a vampire. He had yet to come to grips with the loss or understanding of why she was beheaded. We didn't even have to worry about implanting new memories.

"I came as quick as I could. Nicci, what's going on? You know I don't work for you or Lucky anymore' Whatever you people are, I've had enough of the ugliness that seems to surround you. I came because I wanted to say it to your face. Please leave me alone!"

"Johnny, I know you're still hurting, but we all miss Anita. Maybe I can help you ease some of that pain."

"What are you talking about? The only way some of this pain will fade is if I can get some revenge."

"I think I can help with that. I finally found the men responsible for her murder."

You could feel the heat radiating from his face. "Are you sure? This is not some trick to just get me to work for you again, is it?"

"Johnny, I'm not that mean. I can't quite prove it, so I need you to follow them to help me gather the proof and question them."

"What makes you think it's them? What will following them do?"

"Johnny, I don't know if you've been reading the newspaper lately but ever since Anita died there have been a large number of beheadings happening in New York City and Harlem. It has to be their work. I heard them bragging about how they had beheaded this woman they thought was a vampire. You and I both know, there is no such thing as a vampire. That shows you they are mad! We must stop them, but I need help. Your help!"

"Why would they think my beautiful Anita was a vampire? She was so innocent and pure. I loved her. She never hurt anyone."

(*They say love is blind and he really is blind. I don't know how she kept it hidden that she drank blood. Well, whatever! I can make this work to my advantage.*)

"Oh, Johnny, I know you loved her. Can you help me?"

"For Anita's memory, sure! Just point me to them."

"I want you to follow those two men in the back. Martha is sitting with them. They just finished eating. They both have black cashmere, knee length coats. They both have blond hair and are wearing black bowlers."

"Who are they? Why would they kill her? Why chop off her head? What's going on?" I could see the tears streaming down his face and dripping into his hands, as he pretended he wasn't crying.

I put my arm around his shoulder. I gently kissed him on the cheek. "Johnny, just do what I ask. We'll solve this problem together. Just follow them and find out where they live." As I finished speaking I rested my head on his shoulder. I hadn't been that close to Johnny in over a year. I had forgotten how wonderful his candy scented blood smelled I could feel it pulsating through his body with the excitement of possibly finding Anita's murderers. I wanted to drink his blood so badly. Just a taste. Suddenly the thought of Anita screaming and ripping out a waiter's throat to drink blood flashed by. I restrained myself. I thought. "*How much longer is he going to be human?*"

Johnny spoke, waking me from my reminiscing. "Nicci, you're not going to kill them are you? As much as I want to kill them myself, we have to let the law do it, right?"

(*Who's he kidding!)* "Of course! Now, hurry before they get out of the club." I realized I couldn't completely trust Johnny to not have the police or the mob interfere in their capture. I knew I had to find out who was giving them names and *then* kill them before Johnny could have them arrested.

Chapter 26

Mikael and Petyr wiped their mouths with the white linen napkins and pushed their plates away. I saw Mikael pull a $5.00 bill out of his wallet and leave it on the table as a tip for WuYi. If he split that with SuChi, they could have food for a week. Even though, they both had good jobs, money and food was hard to come by. WuYi and SuChi had lost their homes to the bank and were sharing a small apartment, near the Savoy, in Harlem.

Mikael helped Petyr slide into his coat and Petyr helped Mikael. It was strange to watch. They both put their hats on and headed for the door. Johnny waited until they went out the door to fall in step behind them. A taxi had been sitting out front, hoping for a fare, and they both got in.

Johnny ran out and jumped in the cab with them. "I hope you don't mind sharing your taxi? I'll pay my share. It's cold out and I don't want to have to wait for another cab."

Mikael was shocked at Johnny's abruptness. He said. "Well, uh! You're already in, you might as well ride with us. We're going to Brooklyn. Where can we drop you?"

"Isn't that funny, I live in Brooklyn, too. I live near the Greenwood Cemetery of 25th Street. Are you near there?"

"We're new to the country but I think that's near us. We're at 43rd Street near the 18th Police Precinct Station House."

Petyr just looked at Mikael and shrugged his shoulders and added. "Sure. You're right it is cold tonight. By the way, my name is Petyr Apostal and this is my close friend, Mikael Dragomir. We didn't see you at the club. Where were you sitting?"

"I'm Johnny Vittini." He reached over and shook their extended hands. "I was behind you. I noticed you getting up to leave so I thought maybe I could catch a taxicab with you. I hope I wasn't too presumptuous?"

Mikael still didn't trust him. He hadn't noticed anyone sitting behind them in the club. He kept his comments to himself, for now. He would discuss it later when they got home. Mikael knew Petyr could be overly trusting when he met new people.

Petyr smiled. "No. No, not at all. We love to meet New Yorkers. Do you go to the Savoy often? You don't look like you are suffering from the effects of the Depression. We've heard stories about men throwing themselves out windows and off buildings because of the Depression. How are you surviving?"

Johnny thought awhile before he answered. "I help with the food bank, Monday through Thursday. So I always have food. During the day I go to law school. On Friday's and Saturday's I also help Nicci with small jobs at the Savoy. She is helping me go to law school. I try to work for her as much as possible." Quickly, before they could ask him anymore personal questions he might have had to lie about, he turned the conversation to another subject. (Faeries were not able to lie. But they can manipulate the truth.) "I must say, you both are very well dressed, too. If I didn't know better I'd think you were bankers. You're both wearing cashmere coats. How are you doing that?"

Mikael answered before Petyr had a chance to say anything. "Well, um, we are specialist. We're a type of contractor that gets paid per job. We're quite busy right now."

Petyr started laughing. He choked out the word. "Contractors!"

Johnny said. "I see you're laughing. It must pay well. If you ever need a lawyer, look me up. "With that last comment, they pulled up to his apartment. His still didn't know their actual apartment number but he was closer. He knew they lived near him and it was in Brooklyn. He would find them at the food bank the next night they came in. At least, they exchanged phone numbers when he got out.

The Seduction of Petyr

Chapter 27

On Sundays all the clubs were closed. Most people went to church, praying for the Depression to end. The food bank also took advantage of the closure to restock for the coming week. Both Johnny and Samuel worked during daylight hours to get ready. Neither one of them questioned why the bank was only opened at night. Food was scarce so no one asked questions.

I had decided to seduce Petyr partially because I felt Mikael was interested in Martha and because he appeared more naïve than Mikael. I also couldn't afford to have a rivalry between the men. Petyr was extremely handsome, so why not woo him?

****

I was wondering how long it would take Nicci to replace Johnny. It looked like from her history she didn't, as my mother would say, allow much grass to grow under her feet. I think that meant she'd barely end one relationship before she would start another. Even though, Sally was still floating around he didn't seem to rock her boat anymore, so to speak. I mean she must still have had sex with him but she hadn't talked about fireworks or sparks in a while. They had been lover since Italy. I wonder why she never showed affection to Robert.

She knew he was a vampire and handsome, yet she didn't go after him. I wonder if she knew about his voodoo roots. He didn't know she was a mulatto so that couldn't have been an issue. He accepted her as a white woman of wealth. I guess times hadn't changed enough yet for a Creole to date a 'White' woman. It didn't really matter because she was having fun seducing Petyr. Seduction seems to be an art form with Nicci.

I think I've read at least 40-50 more pages and my butt is beginning to hurt. The sun has started to go down. I have to get home before my mother can think of anymore crazy questions about where I could be spending my days. If it's not about shopping, she wants to know if I'm actively hunting for a boyfriend. Please! I get enough excitement just reading Nicci's diaries.

I wish I could take one home so that I could read in the comfort of my room. I'm just not ready to bring it home and have to explain what it is and where I got it. I only have one more journal to finish.

I put Book II back in the hole with the other two and replaced the floorboards. I picked up all my garbage and wished I could bring a small fan up here. There was no power in the house and the attic was getting warmer. Summers in Massachusetts can be hot and humid especially trapped in a non-ventilated attic. I desperately needed a fan. I would have to freeze a couple of bottles of water and put a frozen blue cube in my lunch bag. Maybe I can find a battery operated fan? I needed more snacks too. Reading exciting books with sex in them is hard work. The more exciting the book gets, the hungrier I get.

✳✳✳✳✳✳✳✳✳✳✳✳✳✳✳✳✳✳✳✳✳✳✳✳

My alarm went off at 5 a.m. It was still dark out. Who'da thought I'd wake up this early and not have a job to go to? I slammed my snooze button on the clock radio. I told myself. "Just 10 more minutes."

Alarm clocks never cheat. It gave me exactly ten minutes. "Beep-buzz, beep-buzz."

I whispered rather loudly. "I'm getting up. I'm getting up!" I finally dragged myself to the side of the bed and sat. "Why am I doing this? School is over. There is no reason to get up at 5 a.m. Those books aren't going anywhere." I reminded myself.

I, still, got up and jumped in the shower. I dressed and packed my lunch, snacks, and an extra blueberry muffin for a late breakfast, while my oatmeal was cooking in the microwave. I made a large pot of coffee, to put in a thermos, to take with me. I was prepared for a long session.

I thought. "Today is the day Nicci is going to start the seduction of Petyr. No man can resist Nicci and I don't want any hunger pangs causing an interruption. I wonder if she'll kill him or turn him. Either way she's going to enjoy herself."

I was packed and headed back to the house. By the time I had finished packing and headed to the house, the sun was staring to rise. It was still creepy reading her diaries in the dark so I liked having the sun rise. I fluffed my pillows, got comfy, grabbed Book II and settled in for the seduction of Petyr.

Chapter 28

Usually, Mikael and Petyr went to the food bank on Thursdays, but they were afraid they had been spotted. They changed their plans to Wednesday nights. They assumed (wrongly) that the Wednesday night staff would be different from the Thursday crew. They were almost right. Everyone but Johnny and Samuel were different. Samuel was in the back filling boxes with food so he hadn't noticed them. Johnny was at the food counter taking names and information from men looking for work and not just food.

This first Wednesday, Mikael and Petyr joined the work line with what they thought was a new disguise. They didn't want to be recognized. They both had a two day growth of stubble on their faces. Both had dirty hands and faces. They had put soot in their hair so you couldn't tell what color it was. Still Johnny recognized them.

"Mikael, Petyr is that you? What are you doing here? Last week when I saw you, you looked like you were doing well and had plenty of money. What happened? Why are you so dirty? Do you need a place to clean up?"

All the men in line and those within hearing distance turned to see who Johnny was talking to.

Petyr was looking at the ground. "You're wrong, sir. This is our first time coming here. You must think we're someone else."

Because it was the usual Wednesday night crowd, no one recognized them. You could hear the men grumbling about whom *could they* possibly be? A man standing near Mikael said."Don't be ashamed, sir. We're all hungry and we'd rather no one knew who we were, too. But Miss Nicci is nice enough to give us free food without asking questions."

You could hear other men around them agreeing. "He's right. We're all hungry. There's no shame in being hungry. You do what your family needs. We can't let our families starve. There's no shame in the food bank." You could hear grunts of agreement throughout the long line.

Mikael was staring at Petyr. "We aren't ashamed that we can't find work. Yet, I still think this man must be mistaken. This is our first time here."

Johnny didn't want to argue so he let it go. He knew he was right. Samuel came from the back to see what was going on. Johnny whispered. "That's Mikael and Petyr. They don't want to be recognized. We need to find out what they are up to. I need to follow them when the food bank closes or after they get their food box. May I use Nicci's car? They won't recognize it because they have to take a taxicab to get back to Brooklyn. If that doesn't work can you just ask the taxi driver where he took them?"

When they got to the beginning of the line Johnny apologized. "You're right, I'm sorry. I really thought you were someone I knew."

"It's okay. With all this dirt on our faces we could be easily confused with someone else. We have familiar faces."

I watched the whole conversation from behind the bread pantry. I thought the whole conversation was strange. They were definitely up to something. She had to get Petyr away from Mikael if she wanted to seduce Petyr and find out what they were up to. I knew dinner at the Savoy, with wine and dancing, could make any man talk.

Chapter 29

Friday night rolled around and sure enough, Petyr and Mikael were at the club. There were only a handful of customers that night. Not only was it an exceptionally cold night but people just didn't have extra spending money. The troupe did their usual dance number at 8 p.m. and I made the usual rounds of all the tables. As I got to their table I pulled out a chair.

"May I join you, gentlemen?" I was dressed to kill tonight. I had on an emerald green evening gown with emeralds in my hair. "Aren't you Petyr Apostal and Mikael Dragomir? You must be doing well to come here for dinner as often as you do? Are you finding a lot of vampires to kill?" Petyr began blushing, as I smiled and batted my eyelashes. I looked directly into Petyr's eyes as I spoke. "Can I get you gentlemen anything? We do serve some alcohol. It's still Prohibition, so I can't offer you much."

The men were at the Savoy, clean and in their cashmere coats as if they'd never been dirty. Mikael laughed. "I can't say we're killing lots of vampires but we are paid well for whatever work we do." Smiling, he added. "We'll just have two whiskeys, for now."

I motioned for WuYi to come to the table and get two whiskeys for the men. Sally had made some good old fashioned pasta with a red sauce. He called it spaghetti. Everyone in Italy ate spaghetti in some form or another. After WuYi had gotten their drinks and menus in their hands, I sauntered back over.

"I recommend the spaghetti, gentlemen. It's very filling and can even warm the soul they say. Sally even made bread this morning. It rested all day and was cooked about an hour ago. This means, you can have fresh bread with your spaghetti."

They looked at each other and Mikael spoke. "We've never had spaghetti before. For that matter, we've never heard of spaghetti. What is it?"

I laughed. "It's long skinny noodles, a type of pasta. Sally pours a red tomato sauce with or without meat over the noodles. We also make loaves of bread every day. When they are first removed from the oven, the bread is soft and butter or olive oil is delicious with it. What we don't sell on Saturday nights, we sell or giveaway, as stale bread, on Monday, at the food bank. We make fresh bread on Tuesdays and Wednesdays, for the food bank. People seem to love it. You don't have to be Italian to enjoy fresh bread."

"We'll try it. It sounds delicious."

"I'll show you how to tuck a napkin in your collar. The spaghetti sauce tends to splash. Would you like to add some wine? That's still sort of legal."

They both smiled and I winked at Petyr.

"That's alright. We are pretty much tea totalers and we've already had a shot of whiskey. One shot of whiskey should warm us, for the whole week. Which I might add was quite good, for Prohibition. We'll take a tall glass of milk, if you have that to offer. We don't get milk very often."

I laughed. "No, I'm sorry. We don't get many requests for milk. I do have ice cream for dessert. That's about the closest I can get to milk. I can get you a glass of water, though. WuYi can you get two orders of spaghetti and fresh bread. I'll take a Bloody Mary."

I pulled up a chair and sat next to Petyr. I could feel his blood picking up speed as he blushed. WuYi placed two servings of spaghetti and a basket of fresh in front of the men. Petyr's hand was shaking as he brought the fork with the spaghetti, to his lips. Because he didn't know how to roll spaghetti on a fork, he slurped it. Even though I had emerald gloves on, I brushed the back of his hand and grabbed a napkin to wipe spaghetti sauce from the corner of his lips. "You're getting messy. I know I'm not you mother but I thought I could help."

Petyr blushed. "Not even my mother wipes the corners of my mouth."

I leaned over and licked the corners of his mouth. "Is that better?" I got up and walked back to the bar, smiling. I could feel his eyes following me.

I could hear Mikael questioning Petyr. "What was that about?"

"I don't know but I liked it. I can't wait to find out what it was about. No one has ever licked my face before."

I could hear his heart rate pick up, all the way from the bar.

****

I stood at the bar and watched them. They didn't know with the use of my vampire hearing, I could hear their conversation. The crowd was small tonight and the dance show was over.

I realized it was going to be easy to seduce Petyr. The trick was going to be getting him away from Mikael. Somehow I need to plan a double date with Martha. She was human and wouldn't make any vampire mistakes.

I went backstage to talk to Martha. "I need a big favor." She was trying to change clothes to get ready for the next show.

Martha was shimmying into a pair of silver stockings. I don't often look at women's legs but she was 5' 9" and had a pair of long, beautiful, coffee-colored legs. No wonder the men loved to watch her dance. "What do you need, Nicci? As long as it's not too crazy, I'd love to help you. Does it include a free meal? You know, even though I have a good job, times are tough. I've been taking leftovers from the kitchen, to share with the families in my apartment building. I have enough money to take care of myself, but I saw a couple of old men selling rotten apples for a nickel. I heard them say they had gotten them from the International Apples Shippers' Association. They were trying to pass them off as fresh apples."

"Martha, I didn't know things were that bad. I don't have all my money in American banks so this Depression hasn't affected me as severely. I still have the Savoy and we are managing to break even. People love to be entertained and will always find a way to drink. I want us to go on a sort of double date to the Cotton Club. Cab Calloway is playing and I heard he has a new Negro singer named

Ella Fitzgerald. It should be fun. I need you to go with Mikael. Will anyone question a Negro woman with a white man? I'm still learning all that stuff about races."

"No one will question it, if I dress like a show girl. They'll just attribute it to my being in the theater. We are considered a different class of people, especially in the evening. Anyhow, people will be looking at how beautiful you are, not me. Make sure you wear your rubies and an evening gown. They see people in rags all day long. It will be a treat for them to see your rubies and one of your fabulous gowns. Make sure you wear a mink coat because it's March, meaning it's extremely cold in New York. Have you heard about this thing called the "Harlem Renaissance"? All these famous Negroes are allowed to come to the Cotton Club. Lucky Luciano will do anything for notoriety and to get his name in the society pages. Maybe Langston Hughes will be there. He's a very popular Negro writer. It's funny how Lucky will bend the rules for the rich but not the poor."

"Martha, life is always hard for the poor. It was hard in Italy for the poor and we didn't even have this thing called the great Depression. Enough politics! I want you meet me next Friday at the Cotton Club with Mikael and Petyr. Petyr will be my date."

"What are you up to, Nicci? Why would you date that man?"

"Don't worry, Martha. I like him and I want to separate him from Mikael. It looks like they are always together."

"Sure Nicci, for a real hot meal, I'd be glad to."

We made plans to date the following Friday, when they made their usual visit to the Savoy, for dinner.

Chapter 30

Wednesday came again. Sure enough, the two of them were back at the food bank. Again, they had a two day growth of scruff on their faces and raggedy suits on with salt stains on the pant legs and scuffed shoes, still no boots or galoshes on in the snow. I was hidden in the pantry. I couldn't figure out what they were up to. Another vampire had been beheaded the previous night. I knew they had gotten paid. I could hear Samuel talking to them.

Samuel said. "I see you're back again for more food."

Mikael looked at Samuel and remarked. "We've *never* been here before. What are you talking about? I don't know you."

I could hear Samuel's deep baritone voice, laughing. "I just saw you last Wednesday. There is no shame in coming to the food bank. We all have to eat. I even saw you standing around at the blood bank. Many men have to give blood to get money to buy food. Hunger doesn't recognize pride. As I said there is no shame in coming to the food bank."

Petyr looked at Mikael and said. "Not us! We've never sold blood. We don't even know where the blood bank is." You could hear the anger building in Petyr's voice. "We're just trying to get food. Why do you care what we are doing?" (They had been to all the blood banks, looking for vampires. Mikael had been convince that some vampires would go there looking for fresh blood. They had tried two weeks in row with no luck.)

"Calm down, sir. I don't care. I'm just curious as to why you keep denying who you are. I'm no one special. I'm not investigating you. I was wondering if I could use one of my connections to get you and your brother a job."

I was tempted to come from behind the pantry and intervene. Instead I whispered to Johnny. "I need you to follow them again. They are definitely up to no good. This time don't jump into a cab with them, again. If they get into a cab, keep walking and catch the next cab. I don't want them to know you are following them."

I pushed Johnny back behind the cash register and slipped through the open doorway, back into the club.

Petyr and Mikael left with a box of food. They looked like they had enough food to feed a family of five not just the two of them. They eased out of the front of the line and Samuel picked up the conversation with the next man in line.

Johnny slipped on an old overcoat, made of cotton, and slid out the door behind them. He just nodded to Samuel, to let him know he was leaving. They grabbed a cab and he grabbed the next. He followed them for about five blocks before they came to an old rusty playground. Petyr sat in a tattered swing and Mikael sat on a park bench that had one slat missing. He put the box under his feet for protection from the slush. Johnny stood behind an old, bare oak tree. Since it was already dark he didn't have to hide in the shadows. Streetlights had been turned off to conserve electricity. They were only on from 7 p.m. to 8 p.m. to allow people to get home from work safely.

Fifteen minutes had passed and a well dressed man just kind of appeared behind the park bench. Johnny had been watching. He thought was carefully. He didn't see anyone walk up but there the man was. He appeared to be dressed in all black—from his bowler to his cashmere coat. From where Johnny was standing he could see that there were no stains or tatters on his slacks. Due to the darkness, he couldn't tell his race. He kept his face in the shadows. He even had black gloves on. Johnny saw him pass a large bulky envelope to Mikael. He appeared to be having a brief conversation with Mikael. Petyr remained on the swing the entire time. Again, the man appeared to just disappear. Upon his departure, Petyr ran over to Mikael. Only then did Mikael even look at the envelope. It looked like he pulled a large bundle of bills out. Johnny couldn't tell what denomination they were, but it looked like a lot of money. He could hardly wait to get back and tell Nicci. Suddenly, he stepped on a twig and it snapped. He couldn't believe he was making so much noise.

Mikael looked up in his direction. He whispered to Petyr and slid the envelope into his coat. He picked up the box and they left the park. Johnny wasn't sure where they headed but he knew it wasn't Brooklyn. He couldn't figure out where they were going. They were walking and it was too far to walk to Brooklyn.

As they left the park, they headed down Lennox Avenue towards a rundown tenement near the Cotton Club. It was just off 133rd Street. Johnny didn't follow them in. He could see lights flickering in the windows upstairs. It looked like candle light not electric. He didn't see any people but when Mikael and Petyr came out they were both clean shaven and had clean clothes on. They were no longer tattered. Mikael had a cream colored cashmere coat on and Petyr's was black. It was nearly 2 a.m. *Where were they going?* Naturally, a cab appeared and they were gone.

Johnny went closer to the tenement to see if there were any names on the mailboxes. There were six boxes but he didn't know if only six families lived in the building. Dragomir, Apostal, Smith, Jones, Brown and Wiesenberg were taped across the mailboxes. What a combination. Nicci wouldn't even believe they were real. Johnny figured since he couldn't follow the taxicab he'd knock on a door.

A young girl in dirty, shabby night clothes answered the door. She was rubbing her eyes. "Yes!" She yawned.

"I'm sorry I knocked on your door, so late. Did a man with a foreign accent, just leave you food?"

"Momma! There's a strange man at the front door asking questions!" She yelled.

Johnny was glad it was dark out so they couldn't see how embarrassed he was. "Again, I'm sorry. Can I talk to your mother or father? I don't mean to intrude. My name is Sam Johnson. (He gave a fake name. He didn't want anyone knowing he had been there.) I work at the Savoy Food Bank and I was checking on the neighborhood needs."

A frail woman with pink rollers in her hair and a dirty yellow scarf holding them in place, pushed the girl aside. "What can I do for you, sir? Do you not realize its' 2 a.m. in the morning? We are trying to sleep."

"Ma'am, I'm so sorry. I was trying to find out if a man with a foreign accent just dropped a box of food off. He's a close friend of mine and I've been trying to catch up with him all evening. I lost sight of him when he entered this building."

The frail girl interrupted. "That's not what he said, Momma!"

"No! And if he had, I wouldn't tell you anyhow. Go away! Can't you see we are poor here? Do I look like I just ate?" Her laugh had a grating sound to it. "Unless you are here to offer my husband a job, I suggest you go away." She slammed the door in Johnny's face.

He thought that was strange. Usually, he thought, people were friendlier since we all had hunger in common. Maybe it was just because the hour was so late. He headed back to the Savoy to tell Nicci what had happened. By the time he got back, both, the club and the food bank, were locked up tight.

Chapter 31

Johnny didn't talk to Nicci until Friday. He told her everything he had seen, even how badly the woman had treated him at the tenement apartment. He hadn't seen the man in black's face because of the shadows. When he really thought about it, he didn't have much information to give her. They still had no idea who Petyr and Mikael were working for. They didn't have a clue as to what they were doing with the food boxes. Johnny would follow them again next Wednesday.

Tonight was my turn to seduce Petyr. I knew they'd be here before the 8p.m. show. Both Martha and I were taking the men out. Expectations were high for the outcome of the evening. Tonight I had on one of my favorite ruby-colored gowns, with the huge dip in the cleavage. Naturally, I had a ruby choker on, with my hair swept up into curls on the top of my head. I had never cut my hair into a bob like the "Roaring Twenties" called for. I enjoyed sticking ruby hairpins in my hair. Due to my height, I had ruby ballet slippers on. I didn't want to tower over Petyr.

Both Petyr and Mikael had black tuxedos on. They appeared to be new ones, not like the usually shabby or frayed ones most of the men wore. Even their shoes had a spit shine.

I pulled up a chair next to Petyr. "How are you boys?"

I again leaned on Petyr's shoulder, making sure he could see down the front of my dress. I felt Petyr's heart pick up its' speed and him trying to steal glances down the front of my dress. I knew tonight was the perfect night to take Petyr home and interrogate him. I had to find out what they were up to. I knew he had to tell me of his own free will. If I enthralled him it would be the truth but he wouldn't have any memory of it. I needed him to know he knew me and to trust me if I was going to have sex with him. The sex needed to be unforgettable. I needed him to be willing to tell every time the two of them were planning to kill and to eventually expose who was giving them information.

Martha had just finished dancing her first set. She pulled up a chair next to Mikael. I could feel his heartbeat racing, too. He had shown interest in her when they first met. I wanted to use that interest to redirect his friendship with Petyr. I wanted Mikael to completely focus on Martha and Petyr to be able to think without checking with Mikael first. Martha was still in her feathers and body suit from the show. She had left the majority of the feathers backstage so they could eat without feathers floating down into their food. I did notice, though, Martha kept brushing a few feathers under Mikael's nose or brushing his cheek with a feather. Every time she brushed his cheek I heard him take a sip of breath. I desperately wanted to laugh. I knew what she was up to even though she apologized every time she did it.

Martha was grinning. "What are you gentlemen eating? I'm starved! Dancing always leaves me hungry. With money being tight I have to pack a dinner instead of being able to buy it here. Don't get me wrong, sometimes Nicci lets us eat here for free but it depends on the size of the crowd. I can smell fresh bread baking. I would love some of that bread and a bowl of minestrone soup." She began rubbing the feathers across Mikael's forehead and cheek.

"It's so cold outside! I bet some bread and soup would really would keep me warm in this skimpy little outfit." She pretended to shiver.

Mikael took his jacket off and wrapped it around Martha's shoulders. "Are you cold? You look like you are shivering. Keep this around you until I can get you some food. Soup and bread sound good. I'd love to get you that bowl of soup. We can't have you be cold. It might affect your dancing." WuYi suddenly appeared at his elbow. "Can I have a large bowl of soup and some of that fresh bread for the lady? Petyr and I would like some too. We had a hard day today. We'd like a bottle of the house's finest champagne."

No one asked me if I'd like some. They were too focused on Martha's chest, legs and feathers. WuYi bowed and left to get the champagne.

"How's your private contracting business doing? Are people really hiring you, with money so tight?" I had heard another head had turned up on Friday. That was just a day after they met with the man in black. There was no body to be found. I knew the head belonged to Henry Hayes. He'd been a very quiet vampire for nearly three hundred years. I knew he was from England, but he usually kept to himself. I only had contact with him when he needed blood. He had no enemies that I knew of.

"We seemed to be in high demand." Petyr smiled mischievously at Mikael.

"It must really pay well if you can pay to eat like this." Martha laughed and I smiled.

WuYi had returned with the drinks. "WuYi can you bring my usual? I ate earlier. I'll just sit and watch you three eat."

Between stolen glances, Petyr said. "I'm sorry. I just realized Mikael didn't ask if you wanted anything to eat. Now that I think about it, Nicci, I've never seen you eat. All you do is drink 'Bloody Marys'."

Mikael showed his teeth in a wicked sneer. "I'd swear you weren't human."

"Mikael, how can you say that? I'm very human. Don't you feel you're body heat rise when I sit next to you? Petyr always blushes when I rub up against his arm."

Martha piped in. "I thought you were just being naughty, Nicci and trying to be ladylike by not eating in front of the gentlemen."

I gave a knowing smile.

****

WuYi brought all the food and drinks out, serving the women first, then the men.

I put my glass to my lips and batted my eyelashes at Petyr. I frowned at Mikael. I knew he was going to be trouble and dangerous. I was going to have to watch my step or end up headless myself.

Chapter 32

Martha asked Mikael out after her last show. Mikael's whole face lit up. "Should we bring Petyr, too? He can be a lot of fun."

"No, I think he has plans with Nicci. I don't think they involve us. "She began laughing. "You know she lives at the Waldorf-Astoria. They can go there and have a night cap and breakfast. You don't have to work tomorrow, do you?"

"No, but how will they get there? It's too cold to wait for a taxicab."

"Nicci," Martha grinned, when she said this. "Has a private chauffeur, Samuel. He also works at the food bank. She even has a lady's maid, Maria that will take care of all their personal needs at the hotel."

Mikael heard me say. "WuYi, can you ask Sally to lock up for me? I have a date tonight. Please have Samuel meet me out front in fifteen minutes."

****

Sure enough Samuel was sitting out front in a black Model T Ford, holding one door open. I had gotten my coat on with the assistance of Petyr and we were out the front door. I had gotten in first and Samuel went around to the other door and opened it for Petyr.

"Were to, ma'am?"

"Home, Samuel. I have a guest this evening. This is Mr. Petyr Apostal. Is that a Romanian name? I've been really curious but felt it might be too intrusive to ask you that. You know I'm Italian. Presently, I live at the Waldorf-Astoria on the twelfth floor. We will take the elevator up. Have you ever ridden an elevator? It's quite fun." It was too dark to see Petyr's expression at that question, even with my vampire sight. He didn't say anything so I just assumed he was okay with it.

As we arrived at the Waldorf-Astoria, we were greeted by the usual late night Negro doorman. "Good evening, Miss Santa Maria. I see you have a guest. Would you like anything special sent to the room? We have your standing breakfast order; croissants, butter, strawberry and two jars of raspberry jelly, some cheeses and a pot of coffee." (One jar of raspberry jelly came from a special café because it had blood in it so that I can eat with my guests if need be.)

"Thank you, Jonah, for noticing my guest. I think that should be plenty unless Mr. Apostal would like to add something."

Petyr thought long and hard. "We just ate a large late dinner. I don't think you need to add anything. That seems to be plenty. Do you have guests so often, this late in the evening, that you have a standing order for breakfast?"

I didn't answer. Jonah and I shared a knowing smile.

Caleb opened the elevator door with a rattle. I noticed it wasn't Jimmy, the usual elevator operator. Jimmy and I usually got a good laugh at the first time elevator riders. I wasn't sure he was in on the joke."Mr. Apostal, may I take your coat? It gets a little warm in the elevator. Seeing as we are going to the twelfth floor you may get hot."

Petyr slid his coat off and handed it to Caleb. After they both got into the elevator, Caleb rattled the gated security door close first. Next he closed the heavy metal doors with a crank he manually turned. With a jerk, we quickly rose to the twelfth floor. I was used to the ride so the jerking didn't bother my stomach. Also, I slept in a coffin so being in a tight box didn't bother me. As soon as the first door banged shut, Petyr began sweating, turning green, pale, and then green, all in that order.

Caleb started laughing. "Rarely does anyone vomit. I have seen a few late night dinners come up, though. Did you leave your stomach on the first floor? You seemed to be changing colors."

Petyr shook his head no. But he did grab the bucket he had noticed sitting in the corner. He didn't even ask what it was used for. He just retched into it. He continued to have dry heaves until we reached my floor.

I could sense Caleb was trying to hold back more laughter. "I think you'll be hungry again once your stomach settles down. I have some milk of magnesia I save for just for occasions just like this." (I was planning to add a small amount of aphrodisiac to the milk of magnesia to increase his enjoyment of the night. I couldn't risk enthralling him due to the possibility of Mikael finding out. Mikael would quickly figure out I was a vampire then I would end up headless.)

I heard Caleb whisper under his breath, to himself. "Silly white people." I laughed. that was every operators' comment when we got off the lift.

(*I hadn't been able to relax at my suite for nearly a month. It seemed like I had been using my suite as just a holding space for my coffin and a place to sleep. Trying to keep the food bank and the Savoy running were more time consuming than I realized. Plus, I was trying to compete with the Cotton Club. So far, Owney Madison was winning. He was doing a great job with the Cotton Club. We both seemed to have continued having a positive customer flow. Even between the Depression and Prohibition we were both making money. Yet he seemed to have a better stream of talent; Cab Calloway, Duke Ellington. Just looking at my coffin reminded me to focus on the task at hand. I could worry about talent and Owney after I solved this problem of vampires getting beheaded. The local community didn't know that only vampires were being beheaded. They thought anyone with money was at risk. We, vampires, knew the truth. Sally and I had to put an end to this if I wanted business to improve. Even the best talent in the world wouldn't help business if all my customers had no heads. I really missed lounging in my suite, entertaining and drinking bottled blood.*)

Petyr entered my suite complaining of an upset stomach. He was glad to be free of the elevator. After removing his tuxedo jacket, I offered him the milk of magnesia. I laid his overcoat on the desk chair.

He drank the milk of magnesia, I had laced with the aphrodisiac before handing it to him. "This milk of magnesia has a sweet taste to it. Do you think it will really settle my stomach? I've never had this type before. It usually tastes chalky."

"It should. I have to keep it on hand for all my guests after they get off the lift. It's my own special blend. It seems almost everyone has an upset stomach and I like to be prepared."

"Let's change the subject while my stomach settles. You smell awfully good. Women in Romania usually smell like farm animals after working all day on the farms, except when they just wash their hair. I love the smell of freshly washed hair."

I laughed."I hope I don't smell like farm animals/I've never been on a farm. I grew up in the city. Women in the cities tend to use perfumes sprinkled on their pulse points instead of talc that men use. I think Roman women bathe more than Romanian women. We love a good bubble bath. I'm not saying Romanians are dirty people but Romans will use any excuse to take a bubble bath and a Romanian woman has to work the farm, cook and clean all day before she can take a bath. I think I'm making a mess of this conversation. Why don't I just be quiet."

Petyr murmured something and began snuggling against the side of my neck. The aphrodisiac was taking affect and I could smell his blood. I was fighting control over my fangs. He smelt like good old-fashioned European blood-a touch of garlic and oregano. I was trying not to be an overly aggressive woman but I couldn't stop from sliding my hands into his shirt. As I ran one hand across his shoulders, unbuttoning his shirt with the other hand, I slid his shirt off and let it fall to the floor. He looked down at it, briefly, and looked up at me, smiling. I moved my hands again only to find a tee shirt underneath.

"Damn, he has so many clothes on!"I said under my breath. Out loud I said. "I know it's cold but all these clothes makes lovemaking that much harder." Trying to keep my thoughts to myself I whispered."I don't want the aphrodisiac to wear off. I have to use my vampire speed to get all these things off before he knows what hit him."

Suddenly, he was sitting on the side of the settee without a shirt. His suspenders were hanging at his sides. I wasted no time getting his pants off. Within five minutes he was sitting in the nude and I had changed.

He was staring at me. "What happened? Where are my clothes? I don't mean to be stupid but are you standing there in just a camisole and a petticoat? I've never been on a date with a woman by myself. Is it supposed to move this fast? I mean, are we supposed to be undressed already? I mean, does this mean we are going to have sex? Oh Nicci! I don't know what I mean. Do all women do this on the first date?"

I was laughing so hard I thought I was going to choke. "Are you telling me you're a virgin?"

He stuttered. "W-w-well, yes. I'm always with Mikael; training, studying or even on a date. Women are not usually part of the curriculum. *And I definitely never had a female teacher!* I was taught by the Brothers of St. Gerome."

I continued to giggle. "I was taught by the nuns at St. Theresa's in Italy. I haven't known a lot of men in my life, either. (*What a lie!*) I don't think I'm much of a teacher on sexual behavior but if you let me, I can teach some of the basics. (*Who knows what that entails?*) Let me assure you, though, being a virgin is nothing to be embarrassed about or even frightened of. You *will* have to keep this from Mikael, though. It must be our little secret. I know he cares for Martha. I'm not quite sure how he feels about me. I don't think he would approve of me taking your virginity."

"Don't worry, I won't tell a soul. I'm twenty-five years old and still a virgin. Trust me, I would be too embarrassed to tell anyone I lost my virginity with you. I mean that's not a bad thing. I would love to brag about you. I think, no one would believe that at twenty-five I just lost my virginity."

"You can't Petyr. Not yet anyhow. It has to be our secret for now. There will be many things you won't be able to tell Mikael. For now, let's start with this one. Come here!"

This time he was laughing. "You're not a vampire are you? You're not going to enthrall me then drink my blood?"

"Of course not. We're would you get such a silly idea. Do I look like a vampire? If I wanted to drink your blood would I go to all the trouble of undressing you then plan to make love to you? (*Naturally, I was going to drink his blood. I just hadn't figured out where I could bite him and neither he nor Mikael would find the punctures. I needed a sex bond with him if I wanted to figure out how they were getting the names of local vampires to kill. I couldn't depend on his love for me to be enough to get him to tell me everything.)* I don't even know what vampires look like. Are there female vampires? *(It just flashed through my thoughts. The best place to bite him would be near the scrotum. If it itched he'd think his underwear was rubbing. Mikael would never touch him there.)"*

"We were taught there are female vampires. I've never seen one, though. You know, I am a trained vampire killer." He covered his mouth, laughing. "I don't think I was supposed to say that. Please don't tell Mikael I told you."

"Don't worry, but what is a vampire killer?"

"We privately contract out with the Catholic Church or communities that think they have a vampire problem. Usually we behead them as a warning to other vampires to leave town. If we just kill them they turn to dust or ashes and the vamps don't get the message."

"How horrible!" I covered my mouth and raised my eyebrows as if in shock. "Do people really hire you to kill them. I heard they were monsters and ate your babies."

Petyr started laughing. "I think that's an old wives tale. I've never heard of a vampire eating a baby. Why would they? They only drink blood! Right now, though, we have been hire by a very wealthy man. I don't know who it is, but, Mikael gets paid almost $5000 a head. That's a lot of money, especially during this Depression. Please don't tell Mikael. He says I have such a big mouth that I can't keep a secret."

"I won't."*(I didn't realize I had gotten so lucky. I had just planned to bind Petyr sexually and get him to talk. Who knew Petyr would be such a talker all by himself. It couldn't have worked out any better.)* I leaned over and his nibbled his shoulder and rubbed both his nipples. "I'm sure we can find something else to talk about besides vampires."

I could feel his body temperature rising and him gasping for air. I was afraid he was going to pass out. I stopped playing with his nipples so he could catch his breath. When his breathing slowed to normal I suck each nipple, flicking my tongue across the tip. I heard him moaning. It was obvious he knew nothing about sex. He just laid there, not even attempting to touch me. Each time I moved his hand to my breast, it slid off. It was like he was in some sort of trance. His body was reacting though. I could see and feel his manhood grow. As I stroked it, I bit him near the base and sucked. I sat on it and he passed out. That was a first for me. No man had ever passed out upon entering me. I wanted to quickly take advantage of his being unconscious. While he was out, I slashed my wrist and dripped blood into his open mouth. Gently massaging his throat allowed him to swallow enough to bind him without turning him. I had learned my lesson about turning someone without their permission. I only needed a good sexual bond, for now. He had to *need* me and follow all my commands, including giving me information about Mikael's doings.

I shook him and sprinkled water on his face. He was out cold. His eyes were still rolled up in the back of his head. Oh my gosh! I called Maria to come help. I was praying I hadn't killed him with too much of the aphrodisiac! I could hear his heart beating rapidly. Well, at least he's alive. Finally, Maria suggested we try a shot of whiskey to see if that would bring him around. He sputtered some of the whiskey at us but I think he swallowed some. Yet, he just laid there and moaned. At least, he wasn't dead!

Maria was beginning to get worried. "Nicci, you didn't try to kill him did you? He still has a little bit of color so obviously you didn't drain him completely. His chest is still moving. I think he's still breathing. What in the world did you do to him?"

I was grinning. "I just made love to a Catholic, virgin boy. He's twenty-five, but has never had sex. He passed out before we could even finish. I'll tell him it was fantastic, though. He'll never know the difference."

"Nicci, you're so bad. I put some vodka in the orange juice. If you can get him to drink it. It should definitely perk him up."

As I put the juice to his lips I got him to gulp some. As he came round, he began sputtering. "What happened? What in the bejesus am I drinking? Did I die and go to heaven? Are you real or an angel?"

"Don't be silly, Petyr. Of course, I'm not an angel. First, you're fine. You're just drinking orange juice because you passed out. I still can't believe you passed out while we were having sex. You *really don't* know anything about sex! Hasn't a woman ever touched you other than your mother or a sister?"

"No, my mother died when I was little and Mikael is the only family I have. He definitely never touched me. The Brothers at St, Gerome don't teach a class about sex."

I laughed. "You should have warned me! I didn't expect you to pass out. Well, now that you are quite satiated on sex, you should be hungry for food. It's getting late and you did vomit all your dinner up, in the elevator. I always have cheese, crackers, possibly some left over croissants and wine if you want something light. You can even spend the night. It's 3:30 in the morning and I have a 12 noon appointment. I have to get some beauty sleep if I want to look good. If you don't want to stay the night, eat and Maria will have either Samuel or a taxicab take you home. Good Night! Maria will help you get cleaned up and dressed."

"Good night, Nicci." He reached up, from his seat on the sofa and kissed me on the forehead.

I smiled, heading towards the back bedroom. I turned and wiggled my fingers in a wave, Next, I blew him a kiss. *He was hooked.*

Chapter 33

Mikael saw Petyr leave with Nicci. He was nervous about Petyr leaving with her. He knew she was worldly and Petyr was a virgin. He still wasn't sure if she was a vampire or not. He hated to admit it but he was going to have to wait and see.

Petyr was a 25 year old man. He was no longer the little boy that had been entrusted to him. He had to let him grow up at some point. He'd always been his pretend brother but he wasn't sure he had taught him enough about the world and women. The Brothers had taught them about religion. He had taught him about fighting skills No one had taught them how to be with a woman. He wasn't a virgin so he wasn't worried. Although, he had never been with a colored woman and he'd heard rumors about how exciting they could be in bed.

Martha was a very tall, possibly 5'8", elegant, mahogany colored woman. The Cotton Club had all fair colored women as dancers and she was little too dark for them. He had never seen a more beautiful human woman next to Nicci. He was sure Martha was human. He could see her heart thumping after her shows. He loved watching her dance. He couldn't wait for the final show to be over. He also loved to watch her eat. She loved food.

He finally had someone to share all that money with that he was making, other than the families in the tenement. He wanted to do something special for someone. Mikael had no clue where to take her. He definitely couldn't take her back to that sad tenement he and

Petyr were temporarily living in. He had to find a nice hotel or motel. Maybe Martha had a place to go to. It would have to be place where it was okay to bring a white man to.

The show ended and Martha, dripping with sweat, came out to talk with Mikael. "I need to change and put some warmer clothes on if we are going out. What did you have in mind? The club closes at 2 a.m. We don't have to stay here. Did you have somewhere in mind we could go? I don't have to be back until 6 p.m. Monday, for rehearsal."

"I'm new to the area. I don't know where a white man can take a colored woman without problems. It is 1931 and there are still some racists. Not everyone is as accepting as I am."

"Don't worry! We can go to Tracy's house. She is staying at Harry's tonight. They have a standing date. When we have minestrone soup and bread at the club, they take a pot home for a late dinner. We'll have the place all to ourselves. We can talk and get to know each other (*Earlier, Nicci told me she had no intentions of just talking to Petyr and she gave me a jab in the ribs meaning I better do more than just talk. She needed to find out who was paying Mikael.*) Let's go. It's within walking distance."

Martha watched Mikael slip his cashmere coat on. She couldn't believe he was wearing cashmere when people were starving, due to the Depression. "Is that real cashmere?"

"Yes. It's nothing special but it's warm."

Mikael helped Martha slip into a thread-bare black wool coat with a fake fur collar. He thought maybe once he got to know her better she might accept a new warm fur coat from him. He really cared for her. Once she had her coat on, he helped her gather her soiled costumes. They had to be cleaned for the following night of shows. He slid into his galoshes and asked."Don't you have boots or warmer shoes? Your feet will get soaked in the snow."

"No, but its okay. I can't afford boots. My money has to go to food and rent. Heat is more important than boots. My parents lost their jobs when the stock market fell. I have to send extra money home. My parents moved back to Waukegan. That's in Illinois, not far from Chicago. They lost everything. At least, I still make money, but I lost my savings, too. The bank I had it in went out of business, without giving me my savings."

"I'm sorry. I've never trusted banks. Petyr and I have never kept large sums of money in the bank."

"You must be doing well if you can come here and eat. I've heard strange stories, though, about you and Petyr going to the food bank every week, picking up a box of food. You look like you have so much money. Do you really need to get a box of food from the food bank? Also, why do you deny it's you? You shouldn't be ashamed if you're picking up food for some family in the neighborhood. You should be proud."

As they walked out the front door, Mikael spoke, looking at the floor. "That's not us. Petyr and I never go to the food banks."

He couldn't tell her the truth. He and Petyr just used the Savoy food bank as a contact point to get their next assignment or to the let their contact know the job was completed. It was simply a cover even if they took food home to the people in their building.

****

They walked to Tracy's apartment about two blocks away. It was on top of the Radium Club. It was a small speakeasy that served illegal alcohol and had small gambling tables. Martha made plans for him to spend the rest of the night. It was already early Sunday morning. When they rose they would go to Sunday mass at St. Joseph's around the corner, and then go to lunch. They could possibly meet Petyr and Nicci there. Martha called the Waldorf-Astoria, knowing Nicci could get a message from the front desk. It would tell them to meet for mass at St. Joseph's or lunch at Tillie's Chicken Shack. This would prove to Mikael that Nicci had to be human. She wouldn't go to mass at a Catholic Church and then lunch if she was the spawn of the devil. *(Martha knew Nicci would make up some excuse as to why she would be running late. She'd probably use her standard; she was helping set up mass at another church and would have to clean the sacristy when mass was over. It would be near 6 p.m. before she was finished with the last mass.)* Mikael thought Nicci can't be a vampire if she is going to church. The church would destroy her if the sunlight didn't. When they did the Stations of the Cross and holy water was sprinkled, she would burn. He felt safe with Martha but meeting with Nicci and Petyr would calm his nerves. He'd killed so many vampires lately. He couldn't tell who was real and who wasn't.

****

After she explained her plan to Mikael, he was in total agreement. She still wanted to make love to Mikael. The thrill of finding out that Nicci wasn't a vampire had increased his libido. All that talking and walking had him sweating and blushing in his big coat. He looked at all the snow on the ground and decided he would rather sweat than freeze. It felt like they had walked forever down Lennox Ave. but it had really only been two blocks.

"This is it. Her apartment is on the second floor. As I told you before, Tracy has her room and I have mine. Tracy isn't here so we have the whole place to ourselves. Let's go up. We can finish talking upstairs where it is warm. Before we go too far—what did you do in Romania that keeps you so busy here? Should I be worried?"

"I worked for the Church in Romania. I taught self-defense. We were a small village with very few jobs except farming. One of the Brothers from the Seminary saw how well I could handle myself in a fight. They decided to hire me as a teacher for the young men in the Seminary. I also taught etiquette. ("Ha-Ha") Don't laugh! It's very important for a man to not only kill but know how to behave like a gentleman."

Martha kept sniggling. "How many gentlemen did you teach?"

"It was considered a great honor to be in one of my classes. I had ten students a year. Not everyone always graduated. Some dropped out because it was too hard and some died in warring games. I take my craft seriously so some of the battles were very realistic. I also, had to teach them how to handle themselves if they were confronted by a vampire. (Ha-Ha) You're laughing again. Killing a vampire is very dangerous work. We had to clean our village of vampires and the neighboring villages, too."

"You don't really believe in vampires do you? I've never seen a vampire before. I did see that vampire movie 'Nosferatu'. He drank blood. What man or woman would want to show him their neck much less drink blood from it? Did your vampires look like Nosferatu?" She giggled.

"You're right. I've never seen a vampire look like Nosferatu. Just because they don't look like him doesn't mean they don't exist. Most vampire look like us. I mean normal people. It's just that they are immortal and they drink blood. I thought Nicci was a vampire."

"You're kidding, right. How could she be a vampire? She eats and drinks alcohol. She even goes to church." This sent Martha into near hysterics. She was laughing so hard.

"I know. I know. I was wrong. But she is exceptionally beautiful and I never see her eat."

"That's only because she is so busy trying to run the club alone. Ever since Jack died, the previous owner and her partner, she's been trying to run the club on her own. She just doesn't have time to sit and eat. Believe me she eats." (Martha hoped she had done enough to get him to stop thinking Nicci was a vampire.)

"But just because you've never seen a vampire doesn't mean they don't exist. They drink blood, rip out throats and I heard they even eat babies."

With that statement Martha doubled over in laughter. "Eat babies! Really! Eat babies! No one eats babies. Those are just stories to scare children. I don't believe any of that stuff. Are you sure you didn't just have brutal men in your village pretending to be vampires to scare the villagers?" (Martha knew not only was Nicci a vampire but so was Tracy and Harry. They had *never eaten* a baby!) Where would you get stories like that?"

"We use stories like that to keep the hunters on their toes."

"Humph!" She snorted. "Let's call it a night before your stories get any crazier. Plus, we have to get some sleep if we want to go to Mass in the morning. I have one last thing I want to show you, though, before you drop off to sleep."

"What's that?"

"Let me show you." Martha took his hand and slid his heavy coat off . . . "Now that you are warmed up and through telling crazy stories we can get this date started."

"Those stories aren't crazy. What do you mean get this date started?"

"As I said, let me show you." Martha led him to the overstuffed sofa and pushed him onto it. Before he could say anything she began unbuttoning his shirt. Next, she unzipped his pants. He sat there in shock, unsure what he was supposed to do.

"Are you undressing me?" Mikael had never been undressed by a woman before. Usually, when he had sex, they undressed themselves and just climbed into a bed. He thought maybe this was the wildness he had heard about.

Martha smiled, showing almost all her beautiful white teeth."Yes and I'm gonna do more than undress you. Just let me slide your shirt and pants off." Before he could answer, she had them off and was trying to get his long johns off. Because of the cold, he had a complete set of long johns on.

"I can't get these long johns off. Are they glued to you or what? They feel like they are stuck to you. Where did you get these things, anyway?"

Mikael was laughing, now. "I brought these from Romania. The winters there are very cold. Don't all men wear these under their clothes?"

"To be honest, I haven't slept with a lot of men. But I don't ever remember taking these off any of them. I mean, how do you pee?"

He chuckled. "There's a flap in the front that opens. But for what you have in mind, I think I should take the whole thing off."

Martha just smiled and helped him get out of them. Finally, he was undressed and she could remove her clothes. She only took her outer clothes off. She left her pink camisole and petticoats on.

Mikael's eyes opened wide and blinked slowly like a night owl. He had never seen anything as beautiful as Martha's body. She approached him slowly and sat in his lap. He could feel his power growing but she didn't climb on him.

"I'm ready. Climb on me and let's do this."

"That's not how you have sex. Let me show you a few things. There's no hurry. No one is going to interrupt us. Just sit here and enjoy." She began kissing his shoulder slowly. Next she began licking his right nipple. She heard a moan. "Doesn't that feel wonderful?"

"Oh, oo-h! My God, what was that?"

"Let me show you a few more things. Just lay back and enjoy." As she spoke she rubbed the left nipple between her forefinger and thumb. The moan grew louder and more guttural. Martha felt a smile growing on her lips. She didn't even pause or skip a beat as she slid down his abdomen. She did little tongue flicks like an anteater hunting for food. Mikael could hardly hold still.

Martha noticed the linea nigra line down his abdomen was blond instead of the usual black she had seen so often. Just the coloring seemed to excite her more. She felt her nipples grow hard and her pocket get wet. As she reached the end of the blond hair, her tongue touches his member. It bounced with rigidity and excitement. With one last flick of her tongue, she mounted him. They groaned in unison.

"I feel like I'm going to explode. I've never felt this way with a woman before. WHAT HAVE YOU DONE TO ME!" He was screaming.

Martha thought thank God they were alone. "You're about to have a orgasm, as they say. In other words you're going to come. Enjo-o-oy." She collapsed on his chest and he wrapped his arms around her back.

"That was wonderful. I've never felt anything that wonderful before. I'm even exhausted and I think you did all the work." He said laughingly.

She found herself laughing, too. "I bet you sleep like a baby. So let's go to sleep if you want to make mass in the morning.

He was already snoring, sitting up on the couch. She dismounted and covered him. As she gently slid him into a lying position he moaned, again. He had a small smile on his face this time.

Chapter 34

They overslept, missing early morning mass. They arose at 11a.m.and planned to walk to lunch at Tillie's. By the time they finished kissing and trying to shower it was already 12:30. It would take at least fifteen minutes to walk through the snow to get to Tillie's. Mikael felt energized after that sexual experience, he had with Martha. He could hardly wait to share it with Petyr. He was wondering if Petyr had lost his virginity to Nicci. Petyr didn't know that Mikael knew he was a virgin still.

****

Petyr showed up at Tillie's just as they were seated. Sunday was usually very busy at Tillie's especially after church. Everyone in the neighborhood tried to get a fried chicken dinner from Tillie's Chicken Shack. Each dinner consisted of fried chicken (1/2 of a whole chicken), mashed potatoes or candied yams,(your choice) macaroni and cheese, green beans and a side of hot water corn bread. No one made corn bread like Tillie's. It was worth a week's pay to be able to eat there on Sundays.

Martha spoke first after Mikael got her seated. "Where's Nicci? Didn't you spend the night with her?"

"Yes, but she was gone before I woke. She had given Maria a note to give me, explaining why she couldn't make it. It said she had a prior commitment but would meet us at St. Joseph's for the Stations

Of The Cross at 6 p.m. (Because it was still winter the sun set early and she could make it to church.) The note said something about she had agreed to serve lunch at the Salvation Army."

Martha was nodding her head. "I had forgotten that she did that almost every Sunday. I thought she might skip it today. She is such a dedicated and giving person." Martha felt like she was going to gag on all the sugar she was pouring out to make Nicci look good.

(I *knew if I hurried, after the sun went down, I could make it to Mass without risking any danger to my skin from the sun.)*

Neither Petyr nor Mikael thought anything further about my missing Mass. Mikael was convinced I couldn't be a vampire. He had never seen nor heard of a vampire going to church or stepping on hallowed ground. He thought we were the spawn of the devil. Although, we were children of the dead, undead so to speak, I think we were the spawn of the devil when we did evil things. Like my old lover, Franco.

****

After speaking with Martha, I confirmed the men were from Romania and trained vampire killers. I decided to put a new plan into action. This wouldn't be about love but control. Since Petyr was still a virgin, he would be easy to control. I'd be his first and he'd be completely mine.

After Mass I would take him back to my apartment and we would really make love. This time we would exchange blood during sex. Eventually, I was going to have to turn him but I wasn't sure how I would explain his being a vampire to Mikael. For now, though, we would just exchange blood. I wonder if I just share blood with him once a week will this strengthen the bond without turning him. I couldn't afford to cause any problems with the vampire killers, yet. I didn't want to get myself beheaded. Also I didn't want any sanctions against me for turning someone again, without their permission. I had to figure out how they were getting their information about who was a vampire. Hopefully, Mikael will be committed to Martha and I'll have Petyr. We had to drive a wedge between the two of them.

Chapter 35

Johnny would have to follow them tonight, again. They hadn't killed anyone in the past two weeks. Johnny had followed them every night to no avail. I think no one had been killed because they were involved with Martha and I. Johnny *has* to find out who hired them. Neither one of us has been able to get the information from them.

It was Thursday and as usual, they were in line at the food bank. Johnny was three men behind them. He was trying to watch both of them. He saw Robert come up to them and slip a note in Mikael's pocket. Mikael nodded in recognition.

Johnny thought. "That can't be. He's a vampire! He wouldn't hire vampire killers. But I know I just saw him slip a note into Mikael's coat pocket and Mikael nodded."

Robert didn't notice Johnny in the line. Johnny had to find out what was on that slip of paper.

As the line moved up, both Mikael and Petyr received a box of food. Johnny got out of line and bumped Petyr. He immediately dropped his box. Mikael put his box down to help Petyr. As he squatted, helping Petyr, Johnny slipped the note from his pocket, read it and returned it to his pocket. The note simply said; Walter Polsky, 223 N. Santa Fe St., Brooklyn. That meant nothing to him but he was sure it would mean something to Nicci. He wasn't sure Mr. Polsky was a vampire, yet, it didn't really seem important if he was.

The question was, why was Robert giving names to Mikael? He did remember that Nicci had told him that the two men were using the food bank as a cover to get information. Was this the information they needed?

Johnny rushed around to the back of the Savoy, to the storeroom, to talk to Samuel. "Samuel, where is Nicci? I didn't see her in the food bank. It's imperative that I talk to her right away."

"I think she is in the kitchen getting ready for tomorrow's opening."

The storeroom led to the kitchen. "Nicci!" Johnny called out. "Are you in the kitchen? We need to talk."

I called out. "I'm here, putting things in the refrigerator. Sally is trying a new recipe tomorrow. We had to order extra vegetables. I thought I would help out. Is the food bank in trouble? Are they fighting in the line? Should I shut it down?"

Johnny answered, sticking his head in the kitchen. "It has nothing to do with the food bank. You won't believe it! I saw Petyr and Mikael standing in line to get food boxes. They didn't recognize me. Suddenly, Robert walked up to Mikael and slipped a note into his pocket. I got the note and read it. It said; Walter Polsky, 223 N. Santa Fe Rd., Brooklyn. Does that mean anything to you?"

I ran out of the kitchen so that we could talk a little more privately. "Yes! He's a vampire. He doesn't come to the club very often anymore. He used to come every Saturday night to watch the show and pick up a host. Why would Robert give his name to vampire killers? You don't really think Robert is supplying the names? He's a vampire! He wouldn't sell out his own. Maybe it was for something else. Let's just wait until Saturday night when they come to club for dinner."

"I would think Robert wouldn't have anything to do with them after Anita died. You're right, let's wait 'til Saturday and see what happens."

Saturday night when I got to the club there was a newspaper clipping waiting for me. WuYi handed it to me to read:

ANOTHER MURDER IN BROOKLYN

Walter Polsky, age unknown, found

beheaded in his apartment. It has been

determined it was murder. This is the 8th

beheading. There are no

suspects at this time. If you have information

Please call: 216-555-4820

Brooklyn Police Department

I could feel the tears starting to gather. I was truly angry. "Oh no! Robert wouldn't sell us out! Why!"

WuYi was frightened. "What is it, ma'am. Did the paper say something you didn't want to read? Can I help? I do not read English so I don't know what the paper said. I did not mean to upset you ma'am."

"It's not your fault, WuYi. I will handle this. Please let me know when Mr. Apostal and his associate, Mr. Dragomir, have arrived."

WuYi nodded and returned to setting up the tables for the night. I turned my rage to Martha. She had come in early to check some of her costumes. "I have to find out what's going on. I have to take Petyr home tonight and seduce him. I think the time has come to stop all these killings. Something has to be done with Robert, too, if he's the one that's supplying the names. If I have to, I'll turn Petyr, and kill Robert, if that's what it takes. We'll have to do something about Mikael, too. I have to be careful, though. I can't have Romania sending replacements." At that moment, the front door opened and Johnny walked in.

"I warned you! I can't believe Robert sold you out. I thought he truly loved Anita. He knew she was a vampire. Do you think it was some kind of revenge? We didn't plan to have Anita killed. What's his motive? What could he be thinking? I'm not a vampire and she *did* love me."

"Johnny. I'm not sure. You didn't know Anita would go mad or that the vampire killers would follow them home and behead her. You didn't even know she was a vampire. Sally and I were the only ones who knew you were a faerie. Not even you knew what would happen if she drank your blood. Why would he want to work with the men who killed Anita? I have to step up my new plans with Petyr. *I have to find out what's going on."*

****

As usual, Petyr and Mikael came for their Saturday night dinner. WuYi told me of their arrival. I sent him to take their dinner order and make sure they were comfortable. Tonight we were having a type of beef burgundy with egg noodle pasta. This was a relatively inexpensive meal to prepare and allowed us the opportunity to buy wine or blood to add to the dish. Sally was able to make two pots-one with burgundy wine and one with blood. It was one of my favorite dishes.

Naturally, I was 'dressed to kill'. I had a gold lame` gown on. The collar came to my chin, Victorian style, but was split between both my legs and between my bust. The back was cut open into a diamond shape. The gown was so long that it swirled around me when I walked. It dragged across the floor. As I progressed, across the dance floor, the rays of light bounced off the gold giving me the appearance of a sparkling star. I headed straight to their table.

Petyr and Mikael were there early, having arrived just after opening. I pasted my best smile on my face while I promptly pulled out a chair and sat next to Petyr. "Good evening, gentlemen! You're early. You must be hungry. The beef burgundy is delicious. We use real burgundy wine to flavor it. The egg noodle pasta is hand made by Sally."

"Good evening, Nicci." Mikael said without even noticing how beautiful I looked tonight. He was looking around for Martha, I presumed.

"It's great to be here tonight, Nicci. If I must say so, myself, you are breathtakingly beautiful tonight. If the beef burgundy taste anything like you look, it will be delicious." Petyr laughed and stared at my bust with his dreamy eyes.

"Are you comparing me to food or do I look good enough to eat?" I felt very wicked with that comment to Petyr. I blocked Mikael from the conversation and kept Petyr focused on me. I don't think Mikael even noticed. He was focused on getting a glimpse of Martha.

I decided tonight was going to be the first blood exchange. It wouldn't turn him but he would be bound to me. Before the night was over I hoped to have really made love to him. I wasn't going to fake it tonight. "Enjoy your dinner, boys."

Before Mikael had a chance to start a conversation with me, I rose. As I rose I whispered into Petyr's ear. "Before the night is over, we'll make love again." I kissed him on the forehead and started to leave. I could hear his heart rate pick up and his body was giving off heat as he blushed.

I heard Mikael say, as I stepped away. "What did she whisper in your ear? Why are you blushing like that? What is she up to? You know, I still don't completely trust her. She may not look or act like a vampire, but she is definitely up to something. I don't want you to be alone with her anymore."

"Mikael, please don't order me around like a child. And please don't ask so many questions about Nicci. I am no longer that little boy from Romania. *If I want to see Nicci, I will!. I'm* a grown man now. I *am no longer a virgin.*"

Mikael began sputtering. "Did I hear you just say you were no longer a virgin? When? How? Who did you make love to?"

Petyr was laughing. "Aren't those rather personal questions? Should a man really tell who his lover is?"

"You're stalling. Who is it. I mean who was she?"

Petyr was grinning from ear to ear. "If you have to ask that question and don't know who I made love to, then you're not the man I thought you were. As far as when and how, is none of your business. A man should never reveal what he and his lover do."

"Where did you learn that? You don't know enough women to have a lover. *Have you been with Nicci?"* Mikael was squinting as if was trying to see me clearly for the first time.

(Petyr didn't know he was still a virgin. He wasn't aware of the fact that he hadn't really had sex, yet. I didn't have the heart to tell him that he passed out when he got undressed.)

He began blushing again, when Mikael began talking about Nicci and he thought about that night. He could honestly say he hadn't had sex with Nicci. In his mind they made love. It was incredible lovemaking. He could barely eat for thinking about lying naked with Nicci. He could feel his manhood growing under the tablecloth. He pretended to drop his napkin as he leaned over to readjust his pants for comfort, from the bulge. He carefully placed his napkin over his lap. His smile was growing larger, too. He almost began to laugh. He so desperately wanted to tell Mikael about his first experience with lovemaking.

"Petyr, what are you grinning about? I know you say you haven't slept with Nicci, but you seem to blush and smile a lot, when I talk about her."

"Mikael, you're imagining things. Although, I do dream about sleeping with Nicci, I haven't yet. Let's just finish eating. I have an appointment with Nicci tonight after the Savoy closes. We are planning a special Christmas party. She needs my input. Although, she runs the Food Bank, she feels that I have a closer connection to families struggling from the Depression. We don't want to overdo the Christmas party. With people struggling to meet their everyday needs it wouldn't be fair to have too big of a Christmas party."

"Petyr, what do you know about people struggling in the Depression? You are sitting at the Savoy eating and you wear a cashmere coat. She's not supposed to know we stand in that food bank line every week. Even if we give the food away, we still aren't struggling. Are you sure she couldn't use both of us? I mean, I can gather more information about who she really is."

"Not yet. And she doesn't know it's us, standing in the food bank line. We are in the early stages of planning, anyway. I also want you to stop thinking she's a vampire. I know what she really is. I mean she's too beautiful to be a vampire." Petyr felt himself beginning to blush again. He knew he had no intentions of planning a Christmas party tonight with Nicci."Let's just eat, Mikael. I'll think about asking Nicci whether you can help us."

Petyr knew he didn't want Mikael there. He was having all sorts of fantasies about undressing Nicci and lying in her arms naked. He couldn't quite remember what lovemaking felt like but his member seemed to have an excellent memory of it.

Mikael tried to focus on his food but he noticed that Petyr seemed to be getting redder and redder. What was he thinking about? Now, he recognized the signs. Maybe Petyr *was* really no longer a virgin. He prayed Nicci wasn't the one who stole it. If she turned out to really be a vampire, he'd have to kill her. That would destroy Petyr.

Chapter 36

Dinner was over. WuYi brought two containers, full of beef burgundy, for them to take home. Petyr had to get rid of Mikael. "Mikael, why don't you take the food home and share it with our neighbors? I'm sure they're hungry. I'm going to stay and watch the final show. I'll probably help Nicci clean up. I'm going to escort her home at the end of the evening. I will see you tomorrow."

"Petyr, do you think that's a good idea? I mean escorting Nicci home. Do you think it's safe?"

"Mikael, you worry too much. It's only proper that a gentleman walks a woman home that late at night. Naturally, I may stay for a nightcap. Just one drink."

"I think she's your lover and you don't want me to know it. *Please* be careful! I'd hate to see you become a vampire and I'd have to kill you." He laughed, then added. "But of course, Nicci's not a vampire so I shouldn't have to worry. I'm still a little nervous about this vampire thing. I know she went to Mass but something just doesn't feel right about her. Maybe it's her beauty. I just don't know."

"You worry too much. If I didn't know better, I'd swear you were my mother. Even if she is a vampire, she can't turn me without me knowing it. *I am a vampire killer! I will not be turned!*" He started laughing, too, and felt Mikael was beginning to relax.

****

After closing, Samuel picked both of us up and drove back to the Waldorf-Astoria. We went straight to my suite for drinks. Petyr was much more relaxed this trip in the elevator. I already had a 'special' bottle of red wine made for him. Maria had made mini sandwiches for Petyr to eat while he drank his 'special' wine. I decide I would start the process of turning him. I would ask his permission when his lust was out of control. In the middle of an orgasm, he would agree to anything. I just couldn't allow any more vampires to be killed.

My biggest concern was not that Mikael would figure out what I was doing to Petyr but that Robert would recognize the signs of someone turning; the feelings of being ill, the weakness with the burst of energy in the evening, plus the euphoria after drinking my 'red wine'. I couldn't risk letting any bites being seen after we'd had sex.

That night we made real love. This time, he would not forget. We made love like that expression, 'with reckless abandon'. I made sure he 'walked' me home every evening for the next three nights. He was so in love that he never noticed the weakness. He thought it was from too much sex.

Petyr was turned without Robert and Mikael finding out. It wasn't until the fourth night that he realized I had turned him without really asking him. I assured him I did ask, even if he was lost in the grips of lust. He didn't care. He was in love. As far as he was concerned that meant he could be with Nicci forever. He had one major problem. He was still a vampire hunter.

The more he thought about it, he realized he had more than one problem. He had a whole list of problems:

1. He had to disappear during the day.
2. He didn't have a coffin to sleep in.
3. How was he to get a coffin without Mikael knowing?
4. Where was he going to keep a coffin?

How was he to drink blood and not eat food without Mikael knowing he was drinking blood? The more he thought about it the worse it got. Well, Nicci turned him, let her figure it out.

I sort of figured it out and told him to relax. I would get him a coffin and he could store it at my suite with mine. I would get blood for him until his fangs grew in. Finally, we would tell Mikael he was moving in with me for a while, to help with some business I had to take care of. That would keep Mikael's thoughts elsewhere for a while, until we figured out what to do with Mikael.

Chapter 37

It was Christmas, 1930. Finally we were ready for the big Christmas party. Everyone that came to the Food Bank was invited. I had gotten a large evergreen tree from the lot near Gladys's Clam House. It was beautiful. All the dancers had hung their favorite ornaments on it. The price of admission was to bring one favorite ornament from your home. Naturally, nothing matched on the tree. This made it all the more beautiful. Sally had cooked five 20-lb turkeys, one pig was roasting on a spit out back in the snow. It created quite a look. I had never seen anyone barbeque in the snow before. We had all the southern home cooked fixins. All the local restaurants had supplied food, especially Tillie's hot water cornbread.

Everyone that attended had their best, clean clothes on. Everyone was determined to eat a good meal and take home any leftovers that might be available. We didn't have a gift exchange but Samuel handed out five dollar bills to everyone that attended. I thought the five dollars would go a lot further than a gift. It cost me $1000, but with all the money the community had given me in support of my club I could spare it. That night everyone slept with a full belly.

****

With Christmas planning and party behind us, I was looking forward to the New Year. It was now 1931. Petyr had been lucky so far. Mikael had yet to figure out Petyr's secret. He didn't seem to question anything. He truly believed Petyr and I had moved in together. Well, we had in a sense.

Petyr got a call from Mikael to meet him at the docks in Brooklyn. They were to meet a Romanian ship. Mikael had received a telegram the night before, simply saying a friend was coming. It was signed by the Brothers of St. Gerome.

Mikael knew that 'a friend' was code for assistant. He didn't think they need any help. He felt that he and Petyr had done quite a good job killing vampires. Although, they had stopped for a while, out of respect for the holiday season. Who were they sending?

The ship arrived at midnight. Due to the lateness of the hour, Petyr was able to meet Mikael. After what seemed like hours a tall, young blond man disembarked. He handed Mikael a letter: *Mikael and Petyr,*

> *You are no longer to try and kill one vampire at a time.*
> *We need to see more dramatic results. We have received*
> *word from out spies in New York that the Savoy is the*
> *home of a large coven of vampires. We want the whole*
> *place destroyed. You are aware that the Catholic Church is*
> *not supportive of you working with a Voodoo priest. We*
> *are sending Boris Yemnov to assist with these killings.*
> *He is carrying explosives to help with this destruction.*
> *The Council*
> *Brothers of St. Gerome*

Mikael read the letter out loud to Petyr after first reading it to himself. The men shook hands and exchanged kisses, in the traditional sense, first one cheek then the other.

Boris smiled and spoke in their native tongue. "I'm so glad to finally meet the two of you. It was a long journey from Romania. I passed the time by daydreaming about how the three of us would behead many vampires."

"It's so nice to speak Romanian again. Petyr and I have gotten lazy. We rarely speak in our native language anymore. What village are you from? Have you been in training long? I have many questions to ask you about our homeland and your training."

Petyr didn't say a word. He was just glad they had met the boat at night. He didn't want Boris asking questions about his coloring. He was lucky his thirty days hadn't passed otherwise he'd have to worry about his fangs popping out when he smelled fresh blood. He was having a hard enough time controlling himself around Mikael. Now Boris was here with smells of Romania mixed in his blood. He knew if he'd had fangs he'd be drinking Boris's blood without thinking. He hadn't smelled calf foot soup since he left home. Boris said his mother had canned a few jars that he brought with him. Even Mikael was talking about the smell of the soup. Suddenly, both men were homesick for their motherland.

Chapter 38

Boris couldn't stop talking about the small town he came from. He said because it had at least 100,000 people in it, it was too large to be a village anymore. It was near the Carpathian Mountains in Romania, just outside of Transylvania. It was called Brasov. All the young men, in the town, were trained to be vampire hunters. He was ranked number one in the killing of vampires. Even though he was only 21, he'd been killing vampires since he was 15 years old. The council voted he should come to the United States and help them. He believed he knew the latest techniques in killing vampires. Petyr and Mikael stuck to the tried and true techniques to kill—just behead them. Still, they were interested in hearing about his new techniques.

Boris could hardly contain himself. He'd been planning, during the entire journey, what he was going to tell Petyr and Mikael about how they had started using explosives in Brasov to kill vampires. They'd never heard of explosives being used for anything other than clearing land.

Boris explained that one of the Brothers had used some dynamite to clear some stones away, near an old church. Well, it turned out a coven of vampires were stowing there coffins in the crypt of the church. When the Brother blew the stones up, the explosion was so massive that part of the church and the entire crypt went up too. All the vampires hidden there were killed. It turns out vampires can't grow back every body part. If the head and extremities are separated from the torso, there is no chance the vampire can recover.

"I can't wait for you to show us how to work this dynamite, Boris." Mikael said. You could see the excitement written all over his face.

Petyr quickly changed the subject, before Boris could explain any further. "Tell me, was it hard to leave your home?"

Boris blinked his eyes rapidly to keep tears from falling. "I remember getting on the ship to America and the entire town turned out. They were singing "Desteapta`-te romane, (Awaken thee Romaniani) the National Anthem." You could see tears of pride roll down his face.

Mikael spoke with tears rolling down his face. "Boris, your town must be really proud that the council chose you, at such a young age, to come to New York City? We will keep you busy. I see you even brought dynamite, with blasting caps, with you. I think I can figure out a way to connect a timer to them so they won't go off until we want them to. We'll take you to the Savoy. It seems to entertain a lot of vampires. I even think the hostess, Dominique Santa Maria, is a vampire, too. Everyone calls her Nicci. I'm sure Petyr will disagree with me because he's in love with her.

Petyr started laughing. "You're just jealous that I let Nicci take my virginity. He didn't get to introduce me to many of his friends."

"Is that true, Petyr? You are no longer a virgin? Does this Nicci have any friends that might be interested in taking my virginity or educate me in the ways of sex?"

"Boris, relax! You just got here. You're only 21. You have plenty of time to lose your virginity or learn about sex. I will say though, Nicci is quite proficient when it comes to teaching sex. But first, we need to get you a place to stay and work on planning this explosion. I have to meet Nicci at 2 a.m. to help close up the club, so you can stay with Mikael tonight. I'll ask Nicci if she knows where you can rent a room for a small amount of money. Americans are still suffering from the effects of this Depression and any amount of money is considered helpful."

Mikael and Boris began plotting how to use the explosives. No one seemed to notice that Petyr was unnaturally pale or that he was sticking to the shadows. Even his natural good looks had seemed to improved. They were both so caught up in the idea of now having dynamite to work with that they just brushed Petyr off.

****

Petyr met me just as I slipped the key into the lock of the Savoy. "Hi Petyr! Where have you been? I was starting to worry that things didn't go well when you went to meet that ship. Are you coming back to my room or are you going to that new apartment I found you in Harlem?"

"We have to talk, Nicci! The Brothers of St. Gerome sent a new vampire hunter. He arrived tonight from Romania. He brought explosives, dynamite with blasting caps. Mikael figures he can make a timer and destroy both you and the club with as many vampires as possible. He hopes to kill you, too. I don't think *even you* can recover from that. I'm scared! He still doesn't know I'm a vampire, myself. He's dead set on destroying you. I don't know if he really believes you're a vampire or just jealous of our relationship. No matter what I say he still wants to argue you are a vampire."

"Well, I am. Petyr, you worry too much. Even if he blows up the club, it won't kill me. I'm pretty tough to kill. We'll just make sure the club is empty before the explosives go off. You're going to be involved in the planning, right?. You can let me know where the explosives are and what time they are set to go off. I'll make sure I get out before they go off. We can always rebuild the club."

"I love you, Nicci! I'll make sure I'm involved in the planning. How do I explain not being around until the evening? That could cause problems. If they realize I'm a vampire, myself, they'll just behead me and complete their plans without me."

"We'll continue like we have been. I'll create a project that supposedly you'll have to work during the day. Petyr, you can help at the food bank. Mikael already knows about the food bank, so we just have to tell him that's what you're doing, You can say I asked you to start making deliveries during the day. I'll make a list of things I want you to do. Just show Mikael and Boris the list and tell him you should be done by 6 or 7 p.m. Saturday nights, you'll just spend the night with me and not be available until the evening. Petyr, Petyr, I'll say it one more time, Petyr, you must remember to drink, at the minimum, one bottle of blood before you meet them. This will keep you from being so pale and your thirst for Boris's blood will be controllable. It will still be tempting, but when your fangs grow in they won't drop down when you're near him."

Petyr laughed. "Don't worry, Nicci. I think I can remember to drink when I get up. Most of the time, I'll be sleeping with you or near you. You always keep a supply of blood around. I also haven't figured out where to put a coffin. I'm afraid if I try to keep a coffin where I live or near Mikael and now Boris, I'll get caught."

I agreed. "You're right. Living with vampire killers is putting oneself in unnecessary danger. My apartment at the Waldorf-Astoria is the safest. Maybe you can use Jack's old coffin at his home. Sally is staying there but . . . ."

"You never told me Sally was a vampire, too. Who else is a vampire that I don't know about?" Petyr interrupted, with a flash of anger and jealousy.

"Don't worry, Petyr. I let you know who is a vampire on a need to know basis. And right now you don't need to know. It's not open for discussion so just worry about your coffin."

"Nicci, I don't think that's fair. Now that I'm part of the community, I should at least know who is in it with me."

"I'll think about. After all, you *do* live with a vampire hunter/ killer. This way if you don't know, you can claim innocence. Now, as I was saying, Sally is staying at Jack's old house and I'm sure he bought himself a new coffin. That leaves Jack's old coffin. I'll speak with Sally. Eventually we can have a new coffin made for you. And before you ask, yes, I do know a few morticians. They supply my bottled blood and extra coffins if necessary."

"I was wondering how you managed to have bottled blood. I didn't think you could buy it in a store."

"You're silly Petyr." I was smiling as I said." I've got a great idea on how to hide your being a vampire; let's get married!" I started laughing. "I know we haven't known each other very long, but we're both immortal and we're not going anywhere. That's the perfect excuse to have vampires gather. You can steer Boris and Mikael into planting the dynamite that night. You just have to make sure I know what time the explosion is set to go off."

"Nicci, are you sure you want to marry me? I mean, I love you and definitely want to be married to you. But, do you really love me? When do you want to get married? Do you want a fancy ceremony? Should we make a really big deal of this?"

"Petyr, I can see the excitement in your face. Naturally, I want it to be fancy and huge. I mean, you only get married once. I'm glad you don't have a heartbeat anymore or you'd faint." I started laughing. "I think it should be May 30th. It's a Saturday. It gives us two months to get everything together. Do you think that's enough time for the boys to get their dynamite together? I don't think you could keep our relationship a secret much longer than that. First, I'll give you a list of things I want Mikael to think you are doing for me. Then, we'll start working on the wedding.

Here's the list:

> Deliver meals to the needy and home bound.
> Pick up supplies for the food bank and Sally, with Samuel
> Pick up supplies and laundry for the dancers.
> Restock the shelves with Samuel or Johnny.

Johnny and Samuel will cover for you in case Mikael or Boris should ask where you are. Your fangs should be in by the first of May. You'll need to learn how to control them. You can't have them dropping down every time you smell blood."

(Only my new maid, Remi, will know the wedding is a fake. I sent Marie back to Italy. She had aged beyond her desire to be a vampire. People were also beginning to ask questions about Marie aging and I wasn't. Poor Petyr won't even know the wedding is a fake.)

"Take the list and go back to Mikael's. I'm sure Boris and Mikael are going to want to do a dry run with the dynamite. Make sure they set the date as May 30th."

Chapter 39

Petyr could hardly contain himself as he went running to tell Mikael the good news. He spoke as if it was his idea."Mikael I'm getting married! I don't know what came over me. I asked Nicci. I kind of blurted it out, and she agreed!"

"Petyr are you crazy! You lose your virginity to her and now you want to marry her! You haven't had enough experience to be marrying her or any woman for that fact. You're too young. Obviously she is a woman of the world and you're just a country boy." You could see the anger building in Mikael's face. He looked like he was going to explode.

Boris just laughed and offered his congratulations. He began slapping Petyr on the back. "You're one lucky fellow. You came all the way to New York City and fell in love with a rich American. May I be so lucky."

"She's an immigrant, just like us, Boris. She's from Italy." Petyr was wondering why Mikael was so angry.

You could actually feel Mikael's anger growing but he decided to quickly change the subject. "We need to start planning the bombing of the Savoy. Petyr, I think the night of your wedding would be perfect. I bet every vamp in town will be there. I know you don't believe Nicci is a vampire but we know vampires hang out at the club. Because I love you and you're my best friend, I'll let you leave before we trigger the explosion. I'll do a dry run with Boris. Have you got a date picked out for the wedding, yet? Is it going to be a long engagement?"

"No, Nicci wants a Spring wedding. Saturday, May 30th seems to be the perfect day. We won't have the summer heat and we'll still have the beauty of the Spring flowers."

"Petyr, you sound like you are getting romantic already. Boris, do you think we'll be ready to do a dry run by May 1st? There is a lumber yard outside of Harlem. We should be able to set off dynamite there without stirring up too many questions. I've had a chance to look at the blasting caps that Boris brought from Romania. I think I can attach an alarm clock to them and have them go off at a set time."

Petyr began picking at his shirt. He was nervous but since he was "dead", he couldn't sweat. He was so glad it was 3a.m. Plus, Boris and Mikael were both so excited and concerned about his announcement, they weren't aware of his nervousness. Now, he had to tell them he wasn't going to be available during the day because of his new job at Nicci's food bank. Hopefully, they wouldn't ask too many questions and just accept what he said.

"Mikael, I won't be available for the dry run or even until after 6 during the week. I promised Nicci and Samuel I would help out at the food bank. Of course, on Sundays Nicci and I go to church and then have a long lunch. She actually gave me a list of jobs to do."

"I don't believe you!" You could see the doubt that flashed across Mikael's face. Before Mikael could say anything, Boris said. "Can I see that list? Is there anything I can help with? I need to get to know more Americans. That will possibly help improve my English."

Petyr showed Boris the list;

Boris looked at it. "Petyr, I can do any one of these things. Please check with Nicci and see if she would like another volunteer. She won't have to pay me at all. I can ride around with this Samuel or Johnny and get to know New York City."

Mikael was laughing. "Don't you think you should at least meet Nicci first? I think once you meet her, you'll agree with me. She must be a vampire. I'll take you to meet her tomorrow, at the Savoy."

****

Nicci is amazing. I figured she was going to turn Petyr but I never expected her to marry him. Obviously, Petyr doesn't really think Mikael's attitude is serious. Doesn't he realize that Mikael really believes Nicci is a vampire? That should be the perfect clue that he was entering into a dangerous situation. Now, Boris is added to the picture. I wonder why the Brothers of St. Gerome sent Boris. I bet they suspected something was wrong between Petyr and Mikael. Maybe they read between the lines of Mikael's letters home. Now Petyr is marrying a vampire. Who'da thought! This wedding should be quite exciting. It's like watching a soap opera on TV or reading a tabloid magazine. I wonder if Heinrich will show up at the wedding. If I remember my history correctly, WWII should be starting soon and Heinrich always shows up when there is a war in the making.

First, she turns Petyr into a vampire. I realize she's always plotting something. But, I say again, is she crazy! He's not just any man. He's the vampire killer's best friend. To make it even more exciting, they are going to try and blow up the Savoy with dynamite. I don't think plastique explosives had been discovered yet, in the 1930's. I hope none of the dancers get hurt. Really, I hope only Robert, Mikael and this new man, Boris get hurt.

I wish I could have taken Petyr's virginity away. (Not that I'm an expert on virginity taking!) Petyr sounds young and gorgeous. I can just see that shoulder length, blond hair. It's probably blond with streaks of white and red from the sun. Mikael is never really described. But I see him having that tall, dark Romanian look. That's just with my mind's eyes. They both seem to be soft spoken with their choice of words and ways. (Sorry, I seemed to have wandered off.)

I can't wait to see that guest list and the menu. I wonder if Sally is going to make some of those blood dishes he's so famous for?

Nicci doesn't have a father to give her away. I suppose she'll make some excuse about her father being dead in Italy. I wonder if Sally will give her away or possibly Johnny.

Wedding Plans

Chapter 40

Mikael and Boris arrived at the Savoy, the next afternoon just pass 4 p.m., looking for Nicci or Petyr. Naturally, neither was there. Johnny covered for them. "Nicci and Petyr are out picking up the last of the ingredients for tonight's dinner. Nicci announced she was getting married last night. Sally was so excited that the first thing this morning he went looking for a Romanian cookbook. He said something about a dessert called, I think, koutete. I think he said they were white chocolate covered almonds. You pass them to your wedding guests to symbolize the bitterness and sweetness of life. Plus, you know how women are. She had to go get measured for her wedding gown, right away. You'd think the wedding was tomorrow! Once she starts talking to her seamstress, she'll be there for hours."

Boris noticed Samuel standing next to Johnny, although Samuel had not spoken. "Is he a Negro?"

Samuel heard this comment and began laughing. He whispered to Johnny. "I wonder what he thought I was."

"Why are you laughing? That's very rude. I meant no insult. I have just never seen a Negro before. I have only heard wild stories about them. You have normal clothes on and look like a regular person."

Mikael laughed, too. "He is a regular person. You'll soon see there are lots of Negroes in Harlem. Samuel is Nicci's chauffeur. He is also her protector. Let me introduce you properly. Samuel, this is Boris Yemnov. He just arrived from Romania. He's from near my home. I hope you'll accept him as a friend, as you do me?"

"I'm pleased to meet you, Boris,"

"I'm pleased to meet you, Samuel." Samuel reached out to shake his hand but Boris grabbed his face and kissed both cheeks. "This is how we greet our friends."

Both Samuel and Mikael laughed. Samuel smiled. "I've never had a grown man kiss me before. As I said before, though, Nicci and Petyr are not here. You're welcome to stay and help me get the food bank ready for the dinner lines."

****

Petyr had been sleeping with Nicci. They rose together as the sun set. It was close to 7 p.m., as the sun went down.

"Nicci, we have to hurry. I just know Mikael is at the club, with Boris, looking for me. He's trying to prove to Boris that you're a vampire. We'll have to tell him, we were out getting your dress measurements taken by your seamstress and picking out fabrics. We also went to pick out paper for the invitations and whatever else may be needed to have a wedding. We need a guest list."

"Stop worrying, Petyr. Remi will create one. She'll take care of the paper for the invitations, too. We just have to give her a little input."

Just then Remi walked into the room. Having overheard them speaking, she spoke. "I have created a guest list for you to review. I know you want a small wedding and a large reception. You need to pick a maid of honor. What I did was create a small guest list for the wedding and made the reception open to the public:

The Guest List

All the dancers; Martha, Tracy, Linda, Robert, Harry, Ricardo

Lucky Luciano

Cab Calloway (performing 'Minnie the Moocher')

Duke Ellington (Band to come to reception)

Johnny Vittini

Mikael Dragomir

Boris Yemnov

Sally (Salvatore) Regnosco

Mayor of New York-Fiorello La Guardia

* Father Murphy from Holy Cross will perform the service. Sister Mary Margaret will assist with communion and carry the white wedding vestments for Father Murphy.

* (Petyr will have to find one.) A Greek Orthodox priest will help with the Mass

* Nicci will get to walk down the center of the Savoy on white virgin paper. (We'll pick it up before the reception.)

* Flowers-bouquets of red/yellow/purple carnations on the tables with white linen tablecloths.

* Social column journalist from the <u>New York Daily News</u>

Menu

(No one will actually know the difference between the two menus, except the vampires will know when no blood had been added.)

*'Red' wine, White wine, pink champagne,

Humans: Choices of: Turkey, Ham-roasted pig on a spit, iceberg lettuce and ambrosia salad

Or

Vegetable lasagna with white sauce and fresh pasta

Vampires: cheeses blended with blood, pink ambrosia-mixed with blood, creamed whipped with blood and chunks of fruit

Lasagna with red sauce and fresh pasta (Vampires will be able to smell the blood)

Wedding cake: topped with two red bells, alternating layers of red velvet and vanilla. Chocolate whipped cream(blood added) between the layers. (Humans won't taste the blood and because everyone knows that you love rubies they won't question the red coloring on the food.)

****

"My goodness, Remi! I think you've thought of everything. You must have worked on this all day. Now, I just have to get a wedding dress. Do we have time to send invitations or should we just make phone calls? I've never done this before so I don't know what's proper."

"*Nicci, you can't just call people! That's so gauche!* People assume you have class so you must maintain that air. Your wedding definitely has to be a class act." Remi laughed. "We'll send invitations. I've designed them. I just want your okay before I have them printed."

<u>Invitations:</u>

Dominique Santa Maria and Petyr Apostal

are happy to announce their union of souls.

Saturday, May 30, 1931

At

The Savoy on Lennox Ave. and 133rd St.

At 8:00 p.m.

A reception will follow immediately after the wedding.

RSVP

****

"Remi, it's beautiful. You must have worked the entire time we slept. It's amazing—you made a guest list, a menu and an invitation. Are you sure you weren't a vampire in another life? I don't think even I could have completed all that.(The invitation appeared to be on heavy high grade white paper with black scrolls swirling around the print. It was handwritten in olde English calligraphy. She'd used real black ink. Each invitation had a piece of blotter tissue. She had handwritten a small envelope with RSVP on it.) How did you even know Petyr's last name?"

"Nicci, *I do pay attention!* You *did* introduce him the first time he came over. I have a very good memory. If you remember that was one of the reasons you hired me."

****

Petyr was running around the suite, trying to gather up his clothes and get dressed. "Nicci, we've got to get to the club. Mikael and Boris may show up early, looking for us. If they do, they will begin asking questions when they don't see us."

"You're right, Petyr. We should get to the club. Remi, I love your plans. I'll give that menu to Sally. He should be able to make all of those items."

Both Petyr and I gulped down two goblets of cold blood a piece. (We didn't have time to let Remi warm it up.) We quickly dressed and caught a taxicab, sitting in front of the Waldorf-Astoria. I knew Samuel was working at the food bank. We didn't have time to wait for Samuel to come across town to pick us up. I wasn't sure what lies Samuel had been forced to tell all day to cover for us. It was just easier to take a taxicab.

Chapter 41

We had barely arrived at the club and gotten out of the taxicab, when we were swamped by Mikael, Boris and Samuel's questions. Everyone was talking at the same time.

"Where were you?"

"Did you get fitted for your dress?"

"What took the both of you so long?"

"Don't forget, I need to be properly introduced to Nicci."

"Gentlemen, one question at a time, please. Who is this beautiful young man with you, Mikael?" I gave Mikael my best and biggest smile I could muster for the moment.

Both Mikael and Petyr were laughing. Petyr took the conversation over."I'm sorry, Nicci. This is Boris Yemnov. I forgot you two haven't met, yet?"

"My name is Dominique Santa Maria, but my friends call me Nicci." I switched all my charm from Mikael to Boris. I kissed his cheeks in the traditional European fashion. "Where are you from, Boris? Have you known Mikael and Petyr for a long time? Did you grow up together?"

"You sure ask a lot of questions." Boris was blushing beet red, "And it's my pleasure to make your acquaintance, Nicci. To answer your first question; I'm from Romania, like Petyr and Mikael. Only I'm from a small town closer to the Carpathian Mountains than their village. I met Mikael and Petyr for the first time when I got off the ship in New York. But we were all trained by the Brothers of St. Gerome."

I grinned because Boris had no idea that Petyr had already told me about him.

****

Boris,, still wasn't quite as sure as Mikael was, that Nicci was a vampire. Yet, he had orders that had to be followed. He was ordered to destroy the Savoy and everyone in it. If she was killed during the bombing and not a vampire, it would be a horrible loss. *But if she was a vampire* the council would be thrilled.

Today he was going to meet Mikael at an empty lot behind Club Hot-Cha near Seventh Ave. and 134th Street. They were going to try a dry run with the dynamite, Neither of them had used a timer before. They didn't want to blow themselves up. Not only was he hoping that Mikael knew what he was doing, he was praying.

Mikael showed up at noon, just as they had planned. Boris had been sightseeing all morning. This lot behind the Club Hot-Cha, supposedly, was near the Hudson River. He supposed if the bomb started a fire or blew too many things up they could run for the river for protection. The only problem was that Boris couldn't see the Hudson River from Club Hot-Cha. He was a little nervous about the Mikael's safety back up plan.

Being the end of April, the lot had very little garbage in it. The snow had almost completely melted, revealing old broken bottles and cans. Weeds had just started to grow, so the dirty snow looked like a small field of Spring wild flowers. The lot was bordered by the club and an empty building, the hidden river in the center and a new apartment building going up on the left. No one was around at this time of the day. It was still a little too cold to do much construction.

Mikael had brought a wind-up alarm clock to use as the timer. "When the alarm clock rings, the dynamite will explode. We'll wrap the blasting caps around the bells on the clock. When they ring, the vibration of the bells rubbing together will cause a spark and set the dynamite off. We have to time the ringer to see how long it takes before the dynamite explodes. We don't want to be caught in the blast."

Boris looked behind Mikael and asked. "Where's Petyr? Is he out running errands for Nicci? I bet they are still making wedding arraignments."

Mikael laughed. "I'm sure he is. He didn't even answer his phone this morning. He and Nicci are pretty kissy kissy, since they announced their engagement. We'll have to practice without him and just fill him in on the details."

Boris was laughing, too. "I sure hope I meet a woman as beautiful and nice as Nicci." As he spoke he went to the middle of the lot and began stacking dynamite. "How high do you think I should stack the dynamite? First, we don't want to level the block from the explosion and second, we need to hide the dynamite so that no one knows it's there."

"Boris, you're right. Do you think we should place the dynamite in more than one spot? It could create a chain reaction or just place a stack in a central location?"

"I was thinking, Mikael, if we put dynamite in various spots the vamps are sure to hear all the clocks ticking, even over the music. They are known to have extremely good hearing. Let's try a central location here, in the lot. Are you sure you know how to set a timer?"

"No, but that's why we're having a practice run. By the way, I like your choice of names. I like that-vamps." Mikael wrapped the blasting cap wires around the bells of the alarm clock. Boris had laid a stack of dynamite sticks near a pile of rusty cans in the center of the lot. Mikael set the clock for 1:05. It was now 1:00 p.m. It gave them five minutes to find a decent hiding place. They both hid behind the abandoned building next to the club.

The dynamite blew, making a tremendous amount of noise, with dirt and cans flying everywhere. "That sure was noisy. Thank God, no one is around" Boris still had his hands over his ears, while he laughed, he was nervous. "But it blew straight up in the air and left a hole in the ground. If it blows like that, we're going to have a lot of vampire pieces lying around, but not necessarily dead vampires, though. We have to burn the club down, too, if we really want to get rid of the vamps"

"Well, what do you suggest we do?"

"If we were at home we would put hay under and over the dynamite. The hay would ignite, when the dynamite went off. It would at least burn some vampires and possibly burn the whole building down."

"Boris, we are not in the country. Where am I suppose to get hay from? What else can we use?"

"I bet tablecloths or curtains would work the same way. If we put the dynamite near the stage curtains, I bet they would ignite when the dynamite sparked. We would blow up everyone standing near the stage or on the stage. By the time the fire department got there, most of the club would be ashes. Should we try one more time?"

"*No! We* were lucky with all the noise from that first explosion. I don't want to push our luck. Plus, we don't want to waste dynamite. I don't know where we would get anymore if we used it all up in practice runs. We know the clock works with the blasting caps. We just have to hope either the stage curtains or tablecloths will burn because we don't have anything to burn right now. I don't think we should tell Petyr about the fire. He may not like the idea that we are burning down his new wife's club." They both laughed and slapped each other's back at that comment.

Chapter 42

As Petyr and Nicci arrived at the food bank, they both noticed Boris, who was helping Samuel pass out boxes of food."Where have you two been all day? Mikael and I had something to show Petyr."

Petyr and Nicci looked at each other with a knowing smile which Boris mistook as a sign that they must have spent the day lovemaking.

****

"This is getting creepy. I know Nicci doesn't die because obviously she still has another volume of diary entries to write. I think Mikael and Boris are crazy. How can they predict that the dynamite will only kill vampires If I didn't know better I'd of sworn Boris stole the dynamite idea from a modern day soap opera. But in the 1930's, they didn't have TVs, much less soap operas. I hate to think they could possibly ruin one of Nicci's fabulous dresses either.

****

It was the night before the wedding. Petyr was feeling rather sexy. They hadn't been able to really enjoy sex for nearly a month. With all the wedding planning and the dynamite planning, they hadn't been able to really enjoy each other.

They were finally alone. Nicci had given both Samuel and Remi the night off. Remi had set a bottle of 'Red Chardonnay' and two goblets for them. As they sat on the sofa, Petyr said. "It's the night before the wedding. I don't have a bachelor's party to go to. I'm tired of talking about; blowing things up, wedding gowns, tuxedos, invitations and food. Can we just sit here and make slow passionate love with the only conversation being moans, sighs and groans?"

"I would love that. I, too, never thought I would tire of talking about food and clothing but I have." I began playing with the curls around the nape of Petyr's neck. I heard him sigh as I gradually rubbed his earlobes and blew little puffs of air inside his ears.

Petyr slid my skirt up and unsnapped the garters holding my stockings. I caught my breath each time one snapped. When he slid my silk stockings over my knees, I felt him nibbling at my neck. With every nibble, little sparks of electricity appeared. I heard myself moan. With my stockings completely removed, (we had slipped our shoes off earlier) his hands rose further up my skirt, reaching for my undergarments. With vampire speed my panties were torn away. His right hand was inching its way to my breasts. I felt myself panting and growing wet. I had to slow him down. He was still pretty new to sex and was going to make me have an orgasm within the first ten minutes. I didn't want to hurry.

I moved his hand from under my skirt with kisses to his palms. While placing his hand around my waist, I voraciously kissed him. I felt our tongues twisting around in his mouth and a groan escaped from him. While he was focused on our kisses, I rapidly removed his shirt and pants. To increase the intensity of the moment, I began massaging his thighs and occasionally brushing his member. I could see it growing and I'm sure he felt it.

Suddenly, I felt him bite my neck. "Don't let the blood drip on my blouse, Petyr. We don't want to be sloppy."

I sounded as if I could barely breathe as I whispered. "Take my blouse off." With the removal of my blouse and camisole, he bit my breast. I could feel the blood drip to my nipple as he began licking it up. My moans were growing closer together.

Rapidly, I mounted him. I could feel his thrusts throughout my entire body. I matched his thrusts and whispered in his ear. "I'm coming." The whisper went to a near scream. "Petyr, are you ready? I can't hold on any longer!" I was beginning to see a red haze before my eyes from the sheen coming off his body. I'd never seen that before because vampires don't normally sweat. The friction of our lovemaking had created a type of red steam, not just electricity.

Suddenly, he screamed and continued to whimper. I knew with the little moans he was making, he was spent. We collapsed upon each other.

Petyr whispered into my chest. "I've never felt anything like that before in my life."

I agreed. "That *was* pretty exciting. I've never seen that red haze before. And I've had many lovers over the years. Not one has ever created a red haze before."

Petyr smiled and poured us each a goblet of Chardonnay. We both gulped it down and quickly poured another glass. "I'm spent but I guess we should polish this bottle off and get dressed. I just realize we have to get to the club and put the finishing touches on the tables and anything else you may think of when we get there."

My smile turned into laughter. "Do we really have to move? Can't we just lie here for the moment and enjoy the beauty of our sexual activities?"

Petyr slapped my bottom. "Get up! Get dressed! We are getting married tomorrow night! Think! And I don't mean about sex. Do we have enough 'red' champagne? Do we need to check the stock? I'm sure there is going to be a large crowd at the reception. Every vampire in town will be there." He started laughing again. "We need to take a silverware and plate count. I'm sure we'll also have a lot of sticky fingers at the reception. Your silverware and plates are going to be worth a lot on the Black market. Remember we won't be there in the morning to make sure the humans set up right. We have to count on Samuel and Johnny to make sure everything is right. I'm counting on SuChi and WuYi to do the final check."

I just smiled at Petyr. I thought to myself. "He worries like an old lady." Out loud I said. "I'm sure the girls will make sure everything is perfect."

Chapter 43

Finally, it was the night of the wedding. I arrived immediately after sundown. The Savoy looked incredible. Everything was beautiful. We had never held a wedding at the club before and it had been transformed. Martha and Samuel had blended the Catholic Church and the Greek Orthodox Church inside the club. It reminded me of St. Mark's in Venice. The only reason we weren't getting married in a church was because no priest would marry us from two different religions. They kept telling us we weren't 'equally yoked'. Of course, they had to throw in, they didn't want to do an evening wedding. 'It just wasn't proper.' The club turned out even more beautiful than I could have imagined.

All the tables had bouquets of small white roses and lilies instead of carnations. Someone had laid a 4 foot wide strip of white linen paper from the door to the stage. The ceiling held netting full of white balloons and red glitter to be dropped at midnight. The center table (the bridal party table) had six bouquets of small red roses and red lilies at two foot intervals. The corner of the table held a four-tier white wedding cake. Each layer had deep red edible roses sprinkled over them. The top tier held real red rubies shaped as two bells and baby white roses instead of the customary bride and groom dolls. Red and white rose petals were scattered across the table. The whole thing was breath-taking.

I didn't think I would be so excited about this impromptu wedding. I didn't think I really loved Petyr, even if he was good in bed. Yet, he was a quick learner, so the sex was improving by leaps and bounds, so to speak. At the rate he was learning he was going to surpass Heinrich in technique.

I could hardly wait to put my wedding gown on. Samuel had picked it up. He even stopped by the shoemaker to pick up my white lace up boots.

Enough looking around! I had to go get dressed. I couldn't wait to see Petyr in his white tuxedo.

****

Boris and Mikael had been at the club earlier that day. Supposedly they were reviewing the last minute instructions Petyr had given them for the wedding. "Mikael, where do you think we should hide the dynamite and the clock? We can't have the ticking of the clock be heard, either. I think we should use the stage. We definitely want the stage curtains to catch fire."

"Boris, if you make the bundle look like a piece of the decorations, no one will look twice at it. I found this large white vase that we can put the dynamite in the bottom with the alarm clock. We can then cover it with some old tablecloths I found. When the dynamite explodes, the sparks will cause the tablecloths to ignite. The pieces from the vase will make the explosion bigger due to the flying pieces of ceramic. I decorated the vase with red and white roses, just like what she has in the club. Between the music and the ceramic vase, the ticking of the alarm clock should be covered. Placing it on the side by the drapes from the stage should cause a flash fire."

"That's a great idea, Mikael. The wedding is set for 8p.m. If we set the alarm for midnight, it will ring and explode when the balloons drop. During the confusion of the balloons dropping, people dancing, and loud music most of the guests won't even realize the dynamite has exploded until it's too late. I heard they convinced Cab Calloway to come and sing 'Minnie the Moocher' at midnight. No one will even notice what's happening." Boris was laughing. "What a great way to get rid of vampires. It will be like a celebration only we're celebrating the destruction of a vampire coven."

"Boris, aren't you even a little bit concerned over the killing of non-vamps?"

"Mikael, if we hurt a few humans during the explosion it can't be helped. Humans can heal. The vamps will turn to ashes. Anyways, it's too late to worry now. We have already hidden the dynamite on the stage. The alarm clock is set to go off at midnight."

Chapter 44

"Oh, my gosh! I'm beautiful!" My wedding dress was all silk with small red sequins sewn around the waistline and neckline. They looked like red rubies. Miss Zelma had cut a huge V down the back. Since it *was* a wedding, it was filled in with white lace. Naturally, because I'm old fashioned and a romantic, the lace went all the way up to my chin. It was sheer, but not overtly sexy and still beautiful. My sleeves were made from the same lace and trimmed with the red sequins. My 8 foot long veil also had red sequins around the edges. It covered my face. Because Petyr was Greek Orthodox, we had to wear these crowns when we exchanged vows. I hadn't seen the crowns yet, but I'm sure they were gold from the old country.

I believed in starting on time, so the wedding started promptly at 8 p.m. I marched (really I strolled, quite delicately) to 'Embraceable You' by George Gershwin. I'm not sure why but it was one of my favorite songs at the time. It seemed fitting. I walked down the white linen paper and met Petyr at the steps leading up to the stage.

(The entire stage had been decorated to look like the altar inside of St Marks in Venice. It made me want to cry. Suddenly I was homesick for Italy and all my friends I had left in Venice, especially Martinique. She was my best friend over the years. She had been executed for not following the rules of the vampire community.)

Petyr stood at the foot of the stairs. He looked so elegant in his white tuxedo. When he reached for my hand all those sad memories disappeared. We joined hands and climbed the stage steps together. At the top, stood a Catholic priest and a Greek Orthodox priest. (Spread enough money around and you can get a priest of any religion to go anywhere.) The Greek Orthodox priest placed the gold crowns on our heads.

Each priest, alternating turns, spoke our vows, both in English and Romanian. Just before we were pronounced man and wife, the Greek Orthodox priest walked around the makeshift altar three times, with us following. (I guessed it was some part of the Greek Orthodox marriage ritual.) After this, they spoke in unison, with big smiles."I now pronounce you, husband and wife."

Father Murphy raised his arms and spoke to the crowd. "Please greet; Mr. and Mrs. Petyr and Dominique Apostal."

With that, we turned and smiled at our wedding guests. An explosion of glitter and rice hit us.

****

I can't believe she did it. She actually married Petyr. I <u>really</u> can't believe those two dummies, Boris and Mikael, who call themselves vampire hunters/killers haven't realized that Petyr and Nicci were vampires, by now. I mean, come on, how many times can Petyr not be available before sundown? Even I would have figured something was up.

I wonder if Sally was jealous. She hadn't spoken about him in a while. Where in the hell is Heinrich. He usually shows up when you least expect it. He's just like she said. 'A bad penny turning up when you least expect it.'

I hope only a few people get hurt in the explosion. I'm not convinced Boris and Mikael knew what they were doing with the dynamite

****

I feel like I have been sitting for at least two days, reading this journal. I'm hot, hungry and I ran out of water. I guess that's my cue to go home and start again tomorrow I think the excitement level is due to go up a notch. I have a strong feeling the reception is going to be exciting!

Chapter 45

I can't believe I really went through with a wedding! I've been alive over 100 years, had many lovers, but never married one. I didn't even marry Franco. I'm still not sure I love him. Since I made him a vampire, I have plenty of time to fall in love with him. Besides, I had another master plan. The only problem is, I haven't quite figured out the whole plan. Part one; blow up two vampire killers, then? I haven't figured out part two yet. Although, this is the perfect plan to get rid of a couple of vampire killers. They have no idea that I know about the dynamite and the alarm clock. They have no clue I changed the time on the alarm clock. They set it for midnight and I changed it to 12:30. By the time they figure out why the dynamite didn't go off, most of the important guests and vampires will be at an after party at the Cotton Club. I'm hoping when they go to check the dynamite, it'll blow them up. I hate to sacrifice my club, but it can be rebuilt.

****

We had just been pronounced Mr. and Mrs. Apostal and turned to greet our guests. Guess who was standing in the midst of the guests with a champagne goblet in his hand? Heinrich! Where in the world did he come from? And he had a white tuxedo on as if he was the bridegroom. I knew there was going to be trouble. The dynamite going off was going to be the least of our problems. He had a look on his face that said anger. His beautiful blue eyes were solid black. I had never seen so much rage on his face. He couldn't have really believed that I would never marry anyone but him. I mean he only stayed with me till another war was declared.

Petyr had never seen Heinrich before so he didn't sense the tension that was building in the room. Petyr was caught up in the moment. He was gripping my chin with one hand for a quick kiss, before we descended the stairs. I quickly glanced at Heinrich and thought I saw flames shooting off him. Heinrich began pushing and shoving, knocking people over, while he attempted to get closer to us.

"Nicci!" He was shouting. "I know you didn't just marry this man! You are mine! You will always be mine!"

Petyr looked confused and angry. "What is he talking about? Who the hell is he?" He, too, was shouting, now.

A hush had fallen over the room. Even the band had stopped playing. I froze. "Heinrich, what are you doing here? I thought you were off fighting some war? You weren't even invited. How did you find out about my wedding?"

"Nicci, just because you don't physically see me doesn't mean I don't know what you are doing!" By this time, he had worked his way up to Petyr. He immediately punched Petyr in the nose. Of course, his nose began to bleed all over his white tuxedo.

Gasps could be heard all around the room.

"You punched me! You punched me! Did you just really punch me? I don't even know who you are or what you want?"

Heinrich was fuming. "I'm Nicci's lover! She's been mine for years. Can't a man going away to war and come back to his woman?"

"What are you talking about? World War 1 ended a long time ago. It ended in 1918. Where have you been all these years, if you're really Nicci's lover?" Petyr was trying to talk and hold his nose at the same time.

Just then Heinrich punched him in the gut. With the whoosh of air Petyr released, blood flew from his nose to spatter Heinrich's white tuxedo. "You got blood on my tuxedo! This is borrowed. How am I supposed to get the blood out?" Heinrich was yelling.

(Heinrich had no idea that I had turned Petyr. Petyr had fed before the wedding so his color was very natural looking. Petyr knew

Heinrich had to be a vampire because he said he had been my lover forever.)

What a mess! I screamed. "What are you doing Heinrich? I gave up on you a long time ago. When you didn't appear after I found out about Jack's death, I moved on. I fell in love with Petyr. Did you really think I would wait forever?"

Suddenly, Petyr clobbered Heinrich with a chair. Sally and Samuel appeared at the edge of the crowd, trying to shove their way in. People began shoving back. Boris and Mikael had been standing out in front of the club pretending to smoke. They heard the commotion and as they turned around they saw Petyr hit a man with a chair. The band began packing their instruments to get out of the club.

Boris overheard someone say. "There's a party at the Cotton Club. Let's get out of here before we get hurt or arrested!"

I was furious. People were shoving their way to the front door, to get out of the way of the two men now rolling around on the floor. They were actually brawling at my wedding! Dishes were shattering as they bumped the tables. My beautiful bouquets were being crushed as the tables fell over. Heinrich and Petyr were in the middle of the dance floor tussling.

Eventually, Sally, Samuel, and Robert were able to get the two apart. By now, all five of them were filthy. Petyr and Heinrich had blood and black smudges from kicking, on their tuxedos. Even my dress had been ripped. It was ruined. What was I going to wear to the Cotton Club! How was I to keep from crying over my ruined dress? If I cried everyone would see my bloody tears which would drip on my torn dress. What a mess! Heinrich did it again. I used to think he was the love of my life but he had a knack for going away to some war, then suddenly reappearing when I was about to make a significant life decision. Maybe I should kill Heinrich, myself.

Sally and a few other vampires began laughing. "Didn't Heinrich do this when you were starting to get close to Jack?"

Martha and Tracy, both, put their arms around me. "It's not funny. Look at her dress. They ruined it. Look at the club! Come on Nicci, let's get you changed. Once you're calmer we'll head down to the Cotton Club for your after party. Sally, you and Samuel clean up this mess,"

"What a mess! What a mess!"

Chapter 46

The two fighting men had finally calmed down. I was in the female dancers' dressing room changing clothes. I was finally calm enough to go to the Cotton Club for the after party. The party was a little earlier than planned so I decided to take the cake down to the Cotton Club. Thank god the cake hadn't been touched during the fight. To be on the safe side, I felt it would be better to cut it at the Cotton Club. I sent Martha with a message to Sally; to have Samuel transport the cake, in the food bank truck, to the Cotton Club and I would cut it there. I didn't trust Heinrich to not start another fight.

WuYi and SuChi were helping the men put the club back together. Petyr and Heinrich, both, had ice on their noses to stop the nosebleeds. (Thank god, I had made all the vampires invited, to make sure they fed before they came to the wedding. I didn't want any hunger accidents.)

"Petyr, I'm sorry I ruined your tuxedo and the wedding. Sometimes, when I see Nicci with other men, I lose control. I'm Heinrich, by the way. I'm sure Nicci has told you about our great love affair. It has stood the test of time."

Petyr was laughing so hard, he was snorting, which caused more blood to splatter. "I'm sorry about your tuxedo, too. But I've never heard of you. Nicci has never said a word."

Heinrich's eyes were dilating to black, in anger again. He bent over and straightened a table, tablecloth and bouquet, as he spoke. "You're just teasing me, right? I'm sure she's said many wonderful things about me. I bet she's even compared the two of us, sexually?"

"No, I'm really sorry. I'm not teasing you. I have no clue what type of relationship you had with Nicci. It doesn't really matter, though, because she's my wife."

I had slipped on a red sequined flapper dress. It was perfect to dance the Charleston in. I came in on the tail end of this conversation. "He's right, Heinrich. I'm now his wife. At some point in the future, I'll tell him about you. But not now, it's my wedding night and reception. It's about 10:00. Why doesn't everyone chip in and help get the club back in some sort of order so that we can go on with *my wedding reception.* I'll have Sally, WuYi and SuChi bring out the food that didn't get ruined from overcooking. Johnny, can you start filling the glasses with 'red' wine, white wine and the pink champagne. I have convinced Duke Ellington and a few of his band members to stay, if you promise not to start fighting again. I had the cake sent to the Cotton Club. I don't trust you two men."

Everyone, that remained, shouted various things. "Sure! We'll be glad to help, for food!"

I smiled, almost allowing my fangs to drop down, due to the smell of fresh blood on both men's jackets. "Great! It shouldn't take long. WuYi, could you get a mop and get this blood up? Robert, do you or one of the other guys have jackets these gentlemen, and I use the term loosely, can change into?"

WuYi hid a smile in his sleeve and left to get a mop. Robert came back with two silver sequined jackets.

Petyr and Heinrich moaned together. "Do we really have to wear that?"

"Yes, now hush and get to work. Please put my club back together. Try to salvage some of the dishes and flowers."

It took about twenty minutes to clean up and another fifteen before everyone was served. I now felt like I was having a reception. We had good music, food, and lots of laughter. Even Boris and Mikael were enjoying themselves and not watching the time. They thought everything was back on track. I kept glancing at the clock.

By 11:20 a lot of the guests were drunk. Since Lucky Luciano and Mayor LaGuardia were guests, Johnny had to pay off a large

number of cops to allow for all this drinking and protection. After
all, Prohibition was still going on. No one was going to arrest the
Mayor or Mr. Luciano without a major fight. At 11:30, Johnny
stood and made one last toast before we headed towards the Cotton
Club to party some more and cut cake. He began tapping his wine
goblet:

"Please, everyone raise you glasses!

Dominique Santa Maria and Petyr Apostal are

now man and wife. They are two of my best friends.

I pray they have a long life, marriage and lots of children

(lots of laughter here)

God bless you both, Mr. and Mrs. Apostal.

There was hooting, hollering, lots of laughter and cheers. "Here,
here!" It could be heard throughout the room into the street.

After the toast, Duke Ellington quickly packed what was left of
his band. "We'll see you at the Cotton Club. We have to leave now,
to allow time to set up."

Boris noticed it was near 11:50 and people were leaving. They
were streaming out of the club in small groups. "Mikael, what do we
do? You didn't say there was to be another party at another club. We
should have put dynamite there, too. Or at least set the alarm clock to
go off earlier than midnight." He was whispering when he looked at
his pocket watch and saw it was 11:59. He was getting frantic. They
had to get out of there.

I grabbed Petyr to kiss him, at midnight. I whispered in his ear."
I changed the alarm clock on the dynamite to 12:30, so that almost
everyone could get out of here by midnight. But I suggest we get out of
here now before Mikael and Boris figure out that I changed the time."

Mikael was whispering and beginning to sweat. "Are you sure
you set the alarm clock for midnight? It should have gone off by now.
I think you should be the one to check, since you put it in place."

"But you set the alarm clock and wrapped the blasting caps around the bells of the clock!"

They stood at the door arguing for approximately fifteen minutes and the dynamite still hadn't gone off. The club was almost completely empty. Robert was picking up an extra jacket for Nicci when he saw Mikael.

"Why are you still here? I thought you would have left with Petyr?"

"Boris left his gift near the stage and he wanted to make sure we take it to the Cotton Club with us. He was just going to get it."

"I'll wait for you. We can all walk up to the Cotton Club together."

Boris was really rattled. He whispered to Mikael. "It's probably not going to go off, if it hasn't by now. The club is empty now. We might as well go get the dynamite now, No one will know we had it in that big vase on the stage."

"You're right. It's okay if Robert sees you. He's in on the getting rid of the vampires. We'll just have to practice one more time to see what we did wrong."

Both men were sweating and Boris' hands were shaking.

Mikael said. "Relax Boris, if it hasn't gone off by now it won't." It was 12:28 a.m.

By the time Mikael fished the dynamite out, the second hand was making its final sweep to 12:30. "Boris, I was wrong. It can still go off." With those final words . . . , the alarm clock detonated.

****

Nicci and Petyr were sitting in Petyr' wedding gift. Through the window of his new Model T you could see the blood tinged tears roll down both their faces.

Petyr spoke first. "I know their job was to kill vampires and we had to stop them. Mikael was my best friend from childhood to our trip to America. I'll miss him."

I wept for Petyr's loss. I, too, like Mikael. Neither one of us knew Robert had still been in the club,

****

'The New Yorker' read the next morning;

THE SAVOY BOMBED.
Last night after the nuptial of Dominique Santa Maria and Petyr
Apostal,
the club was destroyed.
The new Mrs. Apostal, the owner of the Savoy,
said the club had just closed for the night to
continue the wedding reception at the Cotton Club.
(Mayor LaGuardia and Lucky Luciano are reported to have been
attendees.)
It is unclear if the bombing was politically motivated.
It appears that the pieces of three men, Boris Yemnov, Mikael
Dragomir and Robert Manchester
have been found. The police are pretty certain the two men planted
the bomb
and something went wrong.
The explosion could be felt for two city blocks.

Part 2
The Reopening of the Savoy

Chapter 47

When all the damage had been assessed, we realized the Savoy only had to be gutted from the inside. The main structure of the building had been saved. It was the perfect excuse to redesign and redecorate the club. I redesigned a newer and classier look. It was set to open Dec. 5th, 1933. That was the day Prohibition was to be repealed.

****

Pieces of Boris and Mikael had been shipped to Romania. We still hadn't figured out Robert's role in the killing of so many vampires or why he was still in the club. We thought he had left with the rest of the dancers. At least, Boris and Mikael were gone. It was a very sad time, but Nicci and Petyr knew the truth. Boris and Mikael had tried to slaughter a large number of vampires. Now that Robert was gone, too, we would have to worry about anyone informing vampire killers who the vampires were. Al least for now.

Upon receiving the bodies, the Order of St. Gerome sent a telegram to us:

We are unable to replace Boris or Mikael at this time.

Stop

Please work with your new wife in the execution

of your duties. Stop

The Order of St. Gerome

Petyr and I read the telegram twice. Neither one of us could stop laughing. "I wonder what they would think if they knew they were asking two vampires to become vampire killers!"

"Nicci, we can't let them find out. As funny as it is, what are we going to do? We can't kill our friends or let people know we are vampires. It's a bigger mess than you realize."

"But Petyr, how will they know if we haven't killed anyone? It's not like we have to send pictures."

"Nicci, they monitor obituaries and newspapers to follow local deaths."

"Don't worry Petyr. I have a mortician friend that supplies us with fresh blood. We can use one of his bodies and have it die a second time. We can decapitate it or stake it. I'm sure that will work till they find replacements."

Petyr leaned over and kissed me. "That's why I love you. I knew you would think of something.

****

As I said before, we reopened the Savoy on Dec 5, 1933. Prohibition was over and it was the Christmas season. I was looking forward to an exciting Christmas. Alcohol was legal! Bloody Marys were legal! Scotch, rum, and whiskey were now legal! Everyone was going to get drunk at our big Christmas party.

At least, Petyr and I didn't have to kill any vampires, for now. The Order of St. Gerome seemed to be happy with the number of reported vampire deaths we had been sending them.

We had two clubs to get ready for Christmas; the Savoy and The Cotton Club. Since Prohibition was over, we needed to throw a big shindig. I could have Cab Calloway perform at the Cotton Club and use Duke Ellington at the Savoy. I heard he had a new singer named

Ella Fitzgerald. She was only seventeen and supposedly could sing anything Cole Porter wrote.

We bought a ten foot tall evergreen tree. We wrapped it with tinsel and this silver stuff they call icicles. Everyone attached their favorite ornament. When we finished hanging stuff, Martha covered it with this white stuff called angel hair. I don't know what it was made of but it itched like crazy if you got any on you.

Everyone that was somebody, including those in the mob, would be at both clubs. Owney Madden still ran the Cotton Club. I didn't have time to send individual invitations so we made flyers to post around the neighborhood. *Everyone* was invited. Of course, I did have a little bit of class about myself, so I had Remi call the important people. Even though I didn't send individual invitations, I didn't want my important guests to read a flyer. This was to be the first year since the start of the Depression that food and alcohol would be abundant.

Sally was planning a dinner with duck, turkey, and a side of beef. Naturally, it couldn't be a party without Sally's famous 'blood stew', alias beef burgundy. We'd eat dinner with wine and drinks at the Savoy and have after dinner champagne at the Cotton Club. If we got enough people drunk enough, we could have 'warm blood' for dessert.

Chapter 48

It was two days before Christmas, Dec.23ʳᵈ. We'd been planning the party for weeks now. Lately, Johnny had begun to talk about becoming a vampire. I just realized Johnny was running out of time. His time as a human was drawing to an end. He had been human for almost twenty five years. I'd known him for twenty. His sabbatical had only been for twenty, originally. Somehow he had gotten to stay longer. The time was coming for him to return to being a faerie.

I didn't know how to tell him that I didn't know how to turn him. His blood wasn't like a human's and couldn't drink it. We couldn't do a blood exchange. It wasn't enough for him to just drink vampire blood. He needed to be bitten.

I was standing at the bar when WuYi came in with a box of red long stem roses. A Christmas bow of gold ribbon was wrapped around the box. "What's this?"

"Ma'am, a delivery boy from Frannie's Florist brought this box. He said it was for you. The card is inside. May I ask? Who would send you flowers?"

"I don't know, WuYi. I am just as surprised as you are. The roses appear to be blood red. Do you think a vampire sent them? Jack is gone. Who do I know that is that romantic? I don't think they're from Petyr."

"Ma'am, open them up and look at the card."

While I was pulling the card from the box, Tracy and Linda appeared from nowhere. With their vampire enhanced senses, they could smell the roses across the room. Martha trailed behind them.

Linda spoke first. "Who sent flowers? Are they from Petyr? He's such a romantic guy."

Martha said. "He's not that romantic. I bet they're from a secret lover. Hurry up, Nicci. Read the card!"

"Hold your horses! Do you really think I have a secret lover? Maybe Petyr really did send me roses. That's so sweet. Let me read the card!" I was so excited I could barely get the card out of the envelope. As I pulled the card out, I glimpsed the name before I even read the message.

"Unbelievable! This is worse than leprosy. When I wanted him I couldn't find him. Now, he won't go away and stay away." I plopped on a bar stool. The card fluttered to the floor.

"What's wrong, Nicci? Who in the world are you talking about? Nicci, I'd swear you just got paler even though I know that's not possible." Tracy said. She put her hand on mine and picked up the card. When she read it she let it flutter back to the floor and put her hand over her mouth. Martha bent over and picked up the card. She read it next.

"You've got to be kidding. Is that really Heinrich's name? The same Heinrich, that hit Jack and went away to fight in the Austrian Army? You couldn't have been lucky enough for him to get killed instead of Jack? That's not the same Heinrich, which almost destroyed your wedding now trying to apologize?"

"Yep! Don't talk like that, Martha. He used to be the love of my life."

"The key is, Nicci, he *used* to be the love of your life. He's the knife in your side. He's a lying, cheating, womanizer who happens to be a vampire. W here did he come from this time?"

"Martha, you have to admit the flowers *are* beautiful. I'm glad Heinrich is back. At least he's alive. I know he is safe and not hurt. I wonder if these flowers are to say I'm sorry for the way he acted before he left for Austria and the way he acted at my wedding."

****

Just before WW1, Heinrich, who I hadn't seen for nearly one hundred years, reappeared one night at the Savoy. He proceeded to get into a fight with Jack. He was the previous owner. I had spent the night with Heinrich, with the hopes of rekindling our long lost love. He was, after all, my maker. Not only was he my maker but I thought he was my eternal soul mate. When he turned me, I was a virgin living in a convent. I had yet to have experienced any type of love or male companionship.

He left me after nearly a decade to return to fight in the Austrian Army. I should point out he was in the army when I first laid eyes on him. He left. I never saw him again until one night he showed up at the Savoy. I had been heartbroken when he left but over the years I had moved on. I found many new lovers but foolishly compared every man to Heinrich.

One night, he showed up at the Savoy. I didn't even know he was in the United States. When I first arrived in New York I saw his name in the big books on Ellis Island but I could never find him. That night he gave me an excuse as to why our paths hadn't crossed over all those years. To make a long story short, he got into a fight with Jack and eventually left again for war in Europe. I thought I was through with him.

Now he's back again, with roses. I bet its some sort of peace offering.

****

Heinrich had been in New York City again, for about a month. He had been at the Savoy for Nicci's wedding and the bombing. He felt in his heart the wedding was merely a cover not true love. She must have been planning to get rid of the vampire hunters/killers. It was obvious that she had married a vampire hunter/killer. His partners were killed in the bombing. He wondered if the two killed knew their partner was a vampire.

He didn't want to marry Nicci but she was an incredible sex partner. He thought back to when he first met her and she was still a virgin. Over his long life time he had rarely taken a partner's virginity. In the beginning, he thought he loved her. He grew to realize, he loved the act of fighting in a war more than playing husband.

He had sent a dozen blood red roses to her club. He was definitely planning to go to the Christmas party. He had to find out more about this new husband of hers, The only thing he knew about Petyr was that he had been a vampire killer. He didn't know how long Petyr had been a vampire but it was long enough for him to have fangs.

He had written his phone number on the front of the card he enclosed with the roses. He was hoping she would call. The card said:

Hello Nicci, I hope you've forgiven me for the way
I acted at the wedding. I miss you.
I still love you!

212-555-6793

Heinrich

****

Nicci read the card twice. She couldn't believe, what with all that had happened he had the nerve to send a card expressing his love. She read it one more time and ripped it in half. She threw it in the trash.

Martha stood there laughing. "He *didn't really just express his love?* Where has he been all these months? Jack's been dead for over a year. He didn't even come to the funeral. Sally's here. You've married Petyr. Just where does he see himself fitting in? Oh yeah, don't forget the fight he caused at the wedding."

"I'm not sure, Martha. But . . . I'm married to Petyr. Heinrich had his chance many years ago and he left me for; first, the Austrian Army, then another woman, then WW1 with the Austrian Army. No matter how old I get, I just can't sit around waiting for him. I think he believes I'll call him. In two days is the big Christmas party and I don't want any complications."

Chapter 49

It was Christmas Eve, the night of the biggest party Harlem had ever seen. Not only was Prohibition over but it felt like the Depression had been put on hold. Even, if it was for only one night. There would be more than enough food to go around. People started arriving promptly at 7 p.m. WuYi and SuChi had barely finished putting the food out. The women were wearing evening gowns of every style imaginable. They had more than red and green gowns on. I saw gold, silver, sequins and even velveteen. All the men had either black or white tails on with top hats. Every man seemed to have a scarf on that matched his date. For those who couldn't afford tails or gowns, they had their best 'Sunday come to meeting' clothes on. It was a sight to behold. No one felt out of place.

I arrived at 8:30, fashionably late. Secretly, I was hoping Heinrich would appear to see how fabulous I looked with Petyr on my arm. My gown was a silver strapless number made from satin. Over my shoulders, I had a silver shawl made of some sort of sheer netting, Mr. Zuiggi, my new designer, had imported from Spain. My new seamstress, Ms. Cravens worked with him to create my fabulous gown. No evening gown was complete without my ruby choker. Petyr had black tails with a silver satin scarf around his neck. Prior to my arrival, Ricardo had been at the door, greeting the guests, Sally was in the kitchen preparing food.

The first show was at 10 p.m. The dance troupe had prepared a couple of new dance numbers. I had found another new young singer, Lena Horne, to work with the dancers. We were all excited. She was only seventeen and the Cotton Club had let us borrow her. We had never combined singing and dancing at the same time, I had decided not to replace Anita or Robert for now.

****

Heinrich had been dressing ever since he got up. He had chosen black tails. For once, he didn't want to stand out. He needed to observe the relationship between Petyr and Nicci before he made his move.

Heinrich knew nothing about Johnny. Prior to the war, he had focused all his anger and attention on Jack. He had no idea that Johnny was a faerie or that Anita had been killed by the vampire hunters. He didn't even know Petyr's history as a vampire hunter. He was nearly in total darkness when it came to what was really going on at the Savoy. He was overly focused on Nicci. He thought Sally was in Harlem because of the notoriety he had created with his food. He was totally unaware that Sally had had a sexual relationship with Nicci, too.

Heinrich was still extremely egotistical and couldn't believe that Nicci would pick another man over her. Especially a short, tubby man, even if he did have a nice personality and could cook. He wasn't even worried about Sally. He was convinced Nicci would just pick their relationship up where he had left it before the war. He still carried that love letter she had given him to keep close to his heart, before he left for WWI;

My love Heinrich,
I'm sorry you are going to war again, but
I want you to take a piece of my heart with you.
I know a large passage of time occurred
when you went to war before
with the Austrian Army.
Please don't let it happen again.
I will keep the taste of your blood always on my tongue
and your kisses on my lips.
Wherever you are in war torn Europe, please

keep me in your heart.
Love, Nicci '14

The letter was beginning to fall apart from all the folding and refolding, he had done over the years. Even during the war, he had kept it inside his uniform shirt pocket. He believed he had fallen in love with Nicci all over again. (He had no clue Nicci wrote that just so he could have something near to him in case he got hurt. She had written the almost identical letter to Jack.)

He reopened the letter one more time before he walked into the Savoy. He truly believed she had only married Petyr because she didn't know he was still around. He was surprised, though, to find out Petyr was a vampire.

He was determined to make it through the evening festivities without fighting. He told himself to be on his best behavior. He wanted to avoid standing in the line to get in. He hid in the shadows of the entrance. He knew he couldn't just walk in. Samuel and all the dancers, even Sally, knew him by sight. He saw Nicci and Petyr go by. She looked incredible. He had to get her away from Petyr so that they could talk.

A large crowd of New York socialites, with their escorts, were standing in line, laughing at some joke someone had told. Heinrich joined the laughter and walked in the front door without Ricardo giving him a second look. Once he was through the front door, he slipped into the shadows of the club. He sat at a small table in the back. He knew she would be around greeting her guests. When she got to his table he would make her sit for a few minutes. It was then, he would profess his love for her again.

****

(Heinrich should have known by now that Nicci no longer loved him. It was over one hundred years ago that he turned her and took her virginity. He was using such typical male thinking; because he was her first, she would love him forever. He couldn't accept Nicci had moved on. I don't care how gorgeous he was supposed to be. He was too possessive for me.

I haven't figured out what she is up to yet. I know she doesn't really love Petyr. I don't want to cheat and flip ahead in her diary. He did help her get rid of the vampire killers/hunters, Boris and Mikael.

I wonder if she'll be able to turn Johnny or will he have to go back to being a faerie? I have so many questions. Most of all, I wonder if Heinrich can ever be on his best behavior. I just know this Christmas party is bound to end up in somebody fighting.)

****

Heinrich had found a table near the back wall. He was hidden under the limited lighting. WuYi came up to get his drink order. "Aren't you that man that caused that fight with Mr. Jack and Mr. Petyr? Were you invited to the party? Does Miss Nicci know you are here? I'm going to go tell her, right now. We don't want any trouble tonight. This is a very special night for her. You cause much trouble."

"Sir, you must be mistaken. I love Nicci. I would never cause trouble in her club. Just bring me a Bloody Mary, and mind your own business."

WuYi couldn't be hypnotized or compelled after working with vampires for so long, Heinrich couldn't command him to do anything. He left, though. He rushed away. He had to tell Miss Nicci right away. He knew there was going to be trouble, no matter what the man said.

I was making the rounds as I usually do. The club was packed. Even the bar was three deep with patrons. WuYi came running up to me. He was sputtering something. I could hear his heart racing and he was sweating.

"Miss Nicci! Miss Nicci! I saw that Heinrich man. He's sitting in the back of the club. I *know* you don't want trouble. Every time you see him, trouble follows."

"WuYi, how did he get in? Can we get him out without trouble?"

"I don't know, ma'am. I don't think you can just ask him to leave."

"I'll talk to him and maybe I can get him out of here before Petyr realizes he's here." I added under my breath. "Why can't he just stay away?"

I got his Bloody Mary from the bar, taking a goblet of 'red wine' with me. I slapped him, hard, across the cheek. "Heinrich, why are here? Why did you send me those roses? You didn't really think if you sent me roses I would forgive all? Every time we get together, before the night is out, you start a fight."

He was rubbing his cheek in surprise, as he spoke. "I read the note you sent me, before the war, again. Remember the love letter you sent me before I left for the Big War. It said to keep it near my heart. I don't believe you love Petyr. Not if you wrote that letter to me. That's why I ended up fighting with him. I believe you love me."

"Heinrich, that note was written almost twenty years ago." I was laughing. "Do you really think I still mean that stuff? I mean when I wrote it twenty years ago, I didn't mean it then. I just said that stuff so if you should lie dying somewhere you would think I loved you. Whether I love Petyr or not, is not the point. I *really* don't think I love *you* anymore. I have experienced another lifetime since you left. This is an important night for me and the community. It's a celebration of the end of Prohibition. Please don't ruin it."

Heinrich just looked at the floor. "Okay." Because he was quick tempered and the kind of man that was never true to his word, he knew he was going to end up fighting someone before the night was out. He just wasn't sure it was going to be Petyr.

Chapter 50

The longer he sat in the corner, the angrier he got. He couldn't believe Nicci had slapped him. No woman had ever slapped him. *How dare she!* Did she not know the rules about being a vampire? He was her maker therefore she was his, forever. That means until he or she dies. He knew he had no plans to be recently demised. He felt she was his. How dare she marry, especially another vampire. They could be together, forever. He would have to solve that problem. Also, he noticed Johnny had gotten overly friendly since he had gone to war. Did they not know or appreciate he was a *war hero!*

He was going to have to get rid of Petyr and Johnny. (He had no idea that Johnny was faerie on Sabbatical or that Johnny was running out of time. He couldn't stay human much longer.) He couldn't use vampire killers; first, it might get back that he hired them and second he'd heard Nicci and Petyr were the local acting vampire killers.

The more he thought about it, the crazier his ideas became. He'd put a contract out on Petyr with the condition, his head had to be removed. They could just kill Johnny. He knew he wasn't a vampire and would die easily. He had money. Since people were slowly recovering from the Depression, he could easily offer $5000 per contract. That could go a long way with times being as tough as they were.

He would have to use Owney Madden from the Cotton Club to contact Lucky Luciano. No one could know he was involved. Nicci would never forgive him. It was perfect. He could get rid of both of them without anyone knowing he was involved. *Nicci was his!*

Chapter 51

I knew Heinrich was up to something. He was never that agreeable. I watched him sitting in the dark, drinking Bloody Marys. WuYi said he was just ordering one drink after another, as if he thought he could get drunk.

I had to let it go for now. The club was packed to capacity and the young girl, Lena Horne, they had borrowed from the Cotton Club was getting ready to sing. She sang "It Don't Mean a Thing if it Ain't Got That Swing" with Duke Ellington. It was the first time I had ever seen this young Negro woman sing outside of a church. Her skin color was so fair, like all the girls at the Cotton Club. What a beautiful voice. She reminded me of all the wonderful singers I had heard in Italy.

I had to put all my angry thoughts about Heinrich behind me for now and concentrate on my guests. I asked WuYi to keep an eye on him so that he wouldn't get into any trouble. Tonight had to be a success. We were trying to make a comeback after the destruction of the Savoy. Even Sally was trying new food.

****

Heinrich had to figure out how to meet Mr. Luciano. He sat in the back brooding over his drink. He couldn't ask Johnny because he wanted Johnny dead, too. He would never be able to just walk up to Lucky and ask him to put out a contract on two men. He had to finagle an introduction and then get into a conversation with him about contract killing. He was confident that would work perfectly.

****

Naturally, I had to greet Mr. Luciano first. Not only was he a partner of the Savoy but he was presently head of the mob. Even Johnny was pulling his chair out for him. He was with some woman I didn't recognize. She was probably famous, too. Most of the men in the club appeared to be practically drooling over her. She was rather pretty with her short blonde hair. I knew no woman could out do the sparkle of my gray eyes and lustrous black hair. I didn't feel one bit threatened. Plus, I was a vampire. No one could outdo our beauty. It's just part of being a vampire.

After Mr. Luciano took his seat, the female, took hers. (I had to find out her name.) I noticed two big burly men sat on either side of the couple. I presumed they were his bodyguards. They, too, had dates. This had the makings of a good night if Mr. Luciano felt relaxed enough to let his bodyguards have dates.

As I looked around the club, I saw the mayor, Fiorello LaGuardia and the governor, Herbert Lehman, with their wives. I noticed a few judges and lawyers in the crowd. It was rare for them to mix with the non-law-abiding crowd. No one looked like rift raft tonight. Every woman had their best jewelry on, even if it was paste. The Depression had forced a lot of women to sell their jewelry, just to survive.

Samuel checked everyone that came through the door. We couldn't afford to have any pick pocket artist, thieves or rival gangs with guns in the crowd. This was a celebration to end all celebrations. It was considered neutral ground for the evening.

We had to hire extra staff due to the large amounts of food to be served. I had to make sure the vampire guests were not to touch the staff until the end of the party. I was not going to tolerate staff disappearing and reappearing, slightly drained of blood and woozy. I had contacted both of my mortician friends and they guaranteed there would be enough 'red wine' to go around.

Most of the food had been laid out buffet style but the dishes had to be constantly replenished. Glasses had to be refilled and plates had to be removed. The dishes from the vampires had to be rinsed right away because dried blood was very difficult to get off. Also, I couldn't have the head of the mob, the mayor or the governor standing in a buffet line.

The plan was to eat at the Savoy and finish drinking at the Cotton Club. I was going to have the waiting staff, cigarette girls and dishwashers hang around after the final show at the Savoy. This was my Christmas gift to all the vampires that had help keep the place open when time were hard for the club. I rarely had to slip into my personal savings to keep the club afloat. The vampires were allowed to drink from them but not drain them. I didn't want any bodies turning up on Christmas day.

I oversaw the placement of the food, then headed to Lucky's table. Maybe he'd introduce me to the woman he was sitting with. Heinrich was watching me as I walked to Mr. Luciano's table. I wasn't sure if it was me he was staring at or the woman Lucky was with. She was quite beautiful for a human. As I stood at the table, beginning to extend my greetings to everyone, Heinrich crept up behind me. Suddenly, he pecked me on the cheek. "Hello darling. Who are these good looking people you are talking to? I recognize Mr. Luciano but I don't know anyone else at the table."

Mr. Luciano had a strange look on his face and was staring at me. "Nicci, is he a friend of yours or should I let my gentlemen friends, sitting next to me, have their way?" As he said this, both bodyguards began to rise and slip their hands into their jackets.

I quickly placed my hand on Lucky's shoulder. "He's an old friend of mine. Sometimes he feels the need to meet every good looking man I talk to."

This seemed to appease Lucky for now. He began smiling. "I understand that Nicci. If you were mine, I'd want to know every man you met, too."

"Let me introduce you. This is Heinrich . . . . Schmidt. (I didn't know what last name Heinrich was using this century so I had to make a German sounding last name up.) He is a very old friend of mine. Heinrich, this is Mr. Luciano and his companion. I'm sorry Lucky I don't know your date's name."

"I'm surprised you didn't recognize her, Nicci. She is very famous in the Hollywood crowd. This is Greta Garbo."

"Excuse me, Miss Garbo. Sometimes I'm so busy with the club, I don't get to follow the Hollywood scene. I rarely get out to see any movies. And Heinrich, these are Mr. Luciano's associates. (I had no idea what their names were and I didn't ask.)

"Please to meet all of you. How are you enjoying the food and the show? I was trying to catch Nicci, to see if she had time to dance. If Nicci doesn't have time to dance maybe you'd being willing to share your date for a quick dance?"

****

Heinrich knew Nicci didn't have time to dance. He just wanted to be close enough to hear what Nicci and Mr. Luciano might be discussing. He wanted to get a feel for how close she was to him. In the back of his mind, he also wanted to dance with Greta Garbo. For a human, she was incredibly beautiful and maybe he could compel her to talk about Lucky. He also needed to know how strong the bond was between the two, Nicci and Lucky, before he suggested putting a contract on her husband. He couldn't afford to have Lucky tell Nicci what he was planning. He might have to compel Lucky, too, into believing he was doing the best thing for Nicci's heart.

He knew he couldn't get rid of the bodyguards, so he quickly entranced them for a few minutes. He needed privacy to discuss his plans with Mr. Luciano. He would explain how much he loved Nicci and how Johnny and Petyr had stolen her away. They had taken the love of his life. Heinrich would reinforce the idea that he and Lucky were both Europeans and understood how strong the bond of love could be. He had heard Johnny worked for Mr. Luciano so he had to tread lightly when it came to accusing Johnny of anything. He did add, though, that Petyr was probably a gypsy and had a history of stealing.

(Heinrich had no clue how silly this conversation was going to sound to Lucky. He thought of me as the daughter he never had. Heinrich was so arrogant, that he really believed he could convince anyone of his love for me, with or without compulsion and they would believe it. Lucky truly believed that Petyr and I were in love. He thought this 'stolen love of my life' story was silly. He even questioned Heinrich's sanity.)

****

I was standing near Lucky. "I'll have to bow out of this dance, Heinrich. Mr. Luciano and I have some private business to discuss. Why don't you dance with Miss Garbo? She's Swedish and you're Austrian. They're close enough for you to talk about your homelands. If not, she can talk about Hollywood. She makes talking movies."

I knew he was up to something but for now I needed to have a private conversation with Lucky and get rid of Heinrich.

"What private business do we have to discuss, Nicci that makes you want to get rid of my beautiful date?"

"None, Mr. Luciano. I was trying to get rid of Heinrich. He can be so overprotective. Every man I look at, he thinks I want. He doesn't quite understand or doesn't want to understand that I'm married. He won't accept that I don't want him anymore."

"Nicci, you know I think of you as my daughter. Would you like me to _help_ Heinrich understand or even disappear?"

I started laughing. "Thank you, Lucky. I don't think it would be right to hurt Heinrich. He was a lover once. I'll talk to him but I'll remember your offer."

Just as I leaned over to kiss Lucky on the cheek to say good-bye, Heinrich came back with Miss Garbo. He pulled her chair out and assisted her up to the table.

"Did you enjoy your dance?" Lucky asked both Heinrich and Greta.

Greta smiled at Heinrich saying. "Thank you. It was wonderful, sir."

Heinrich was grinning. "Thank you, too. It was wonderful. You're a marvelous dancer."

I was inching away from the table. "Enjoy your evening, Mr. Luciano, Miss Garbo, gentlemen. I must continue to greet my guests."

"You go, Nicci. I'm going to stay and chat awhile with Mr. Luciano and Miss Garbo."

As I was walking away, I saw Heinrich pulling a chair up to the table. It was too noisy in the club to hear the entire conversation. I was only getting snatches. "Petyr loves her." "I need help." "Can you do it?" I couldn't hear any of Lucky's answers.

Chapter 52

Heinrich was about to sit at Mr. Luciano's table. This was one of those rare moments where he was both scared and nervous. He was glad he didn't sweat. As far as Lucky Luciano could tell, he was calm and collected. He had been standing when he started the conversation. He wanted to be invited to sit.

Lucky asked his bodyguards to leave for a few minutes. Greta excused herself to the ladies' room. He extended his right hand and motioned as if to say, sit down.

After sitting, Heinrich jumped right into the conversation. "Mr. Luciano, I heard you think of Nicci as the daughter you never had. She is my lover that keeps getting away. I need to get Petyr out of the picture. I know he's supposed to be her husband. She only married him because I hadn't returned from the war, yet. She didn't know whether I was dead or alive. I tried to stop the wedding but I was too late. I'll pay good money to have him taken out of the picture. I'll even pay an extra $5000 dollars for his head. I know that sounds gruesome but it's important to me to see his head unattached to his body. They can get rid of the body any way they want. But, I want the head unattached."

"Mr. Schmidt"

"Call me Heinrich."

"Mr. Schmidt, do you think Nicci in love with her new husband and would just forgive you if you had him killed? She spoke to me about your unrelenting love for her. Why are you unable to let her go? Why do you even think she still loves you?"

"Mr. Luciano, may I call you Lucky?"

"No!"

"Well, Mr. Luciano, if I may talk to you, man to man. I was her first love. She was my first true love. I am unable to stop loving her. This Petyr is a road block. He's just a piece of Romanian trash. I know deep in her heart she really loves me. She only married Petyr because Jack was killed and she assumed I was dead. Well, here I am to take my rightful place."

"I'm going to look at this contract as strictly business. I don't want to be involved in breaking Nicci's heart. I won't be responsible for the pain you are about to cause her. Okay, for $5000 dollars I will put the contract out there. I won't tell her you did this, Mr. Schmidt, but you must not bother her again until the deed is done. If she wants to return to you, she will. You may help her through the mourning process but be careful. Do not push her. Let her grieve in her own way."

Heinrich said thank you profusely. He decided not to ask about a contract on Johnny. He didn't think Lucky would support that decision. He had a strong feeling that Lucky didn't like him. He didn't trust Lucky. He would have to watch the shadows to make sure Lucky hadn't put a contract out on him.

****

I wonder if Heinrich has finally lost his mind! I think through the entire first diary Nicci was obsessed with finding him and picking up where they left off. Now, Heinrich is obsessed with her and getting her back. Sometimes I find that life really does move in a circle.

I can't believe Lucky Luciano was dating the great Greta Garbo. I wonder if she knew he was a mobster. She was so beautiful. How did he even meet her?

I want to jump ahead and see who takes out Petyr. $5000 dollars doesn't sound like much money but I guess in the twenties it's a lot. I heard a loaf of bread was only a nickel so $5000 dollars had to be a lot of money.

Chapter 53

It had been a month and Petyr *was still* walking around. Heinrich was wondering if he needed to increase the amount. He had continued to send blood red roses, daily. Petyr hadn't even been hurt yet. Even if he was a vampire, someone should have a least tried to have kill him. He was wondering if people were afraid to cross Nicci.

Finally, as the summer ended he heard that Nicci was complaining that Petyr kept having unusual accidents. Just two weeks ago a flower pot fell from a third floor window and hit him on the head. Then he was walking near a ladder, not even under it, he tripped. While he was trying to untangle himself from the ladder, a single paint can hit him in the head. He was unconscious for two days. He still wasn't dead, though.

****

I was beginning to wonder why Petyr had suddenly become so clumsy or was someone after him? Especially, since he kept getting hit in the head. Without a head, Petyr will be extremely dead.

It was apparent Heinrich had finally grown weary of sending roses. They finally stopped coming to the club. I didn't really care about the flowers. I never called him. I noticed he hadn't even been at the club since Petyr's first accident. I was beginning to wonder if Heinrich was somehow involved in the accidents. I didn't think he was actually causing them but it felt like something he would put someone up to. But what does he gain from Petyr having an accident? He knew Petyr was a vampire and could just heal himself. Petyr couldn't die unless he was beheaded.

****

Heinrich assumed Lucky must have worded the contract wrong. He needed Petyr beheaded not thumped in the head. He had to figure out how to meet with Lucky to fix this mess. He wanted Petyr dead not Nicci nursing him. She was starting to get suspicious.

Saturday night he went to the Savoy, he was hoping he would run into Johnny. He needed him to set up a meeting with Mr. Luciano. This misunderstanding was driving him crazy. Maybe if he offered $10,000 dollars, they would cut off his head and stop fooling around.

Johnny was at the bar talking to Petyr. He couldn't hear the conversation and he didn't really care what they were talking about. It was important that he got Johnny alone. Heinrich signaled for WuYi.

WuYi approached, while Heinrich wrote a brief note on a matchbook cover. "Could you give this to Johnny Vittini for me? He's sitting at the bar with Petyr."

"Yes sir."

The matchbook cover said; Savoy, on the outside. Inside he had written; We need to talk, alone. Heinrich WuYi handed the matchbook to Johnny. Heinrich watch Johnny flip the cover open and quickly read the message. He saw Heinrich watching him. He nodded and whispered to WuYi.

WuYi returned with the message; he said meet him after the next show, in the men's room. The next show would be ending around 12 midnight or near1 a.m. It was the last show of the night.

Heinrich arrived immediately after the last show to make sure no one was in the bathroom. It only had two stalls with two urinals. It was easy to check. He stuck a fake note above the doorknob. It read; out of order. He didn't want anyone coming in while they were talking.

Johnny arrived about five minutes later. "What do you want Heinrich? I won't help you get Nicci, if that's what you think. Don't bother asking."

"No, it has nothing to do with Nicci. (sort of!) I need help setting up a meeting with Lucky Luciano."

"Why would I do that?"

"I have some business to discuss with him. It's a project we're working on and it needs some clarification."

"Can't I just give him a message?"

Heinrich gave it some thought. "No, I think we should meet in person. I need to discuss some finer points with him. Those things can't be relayed in a message."

"Okay, I'll meet with him in the morning and see if we can set something up."

"Can we plan something in the evening because my mornings are pretty busy?"

"Speaking of busy, Heinrich, what *is it you do?* I've never seen you work, yet you always have money. Even with us in the midst of the Depression, you have money."

"Well, you know I'm a Captain in the Austrian Army. They pay quite well. I also teach some medical techniques for the US Army, such as drawing blood and transfusions." Heinrich was laughing to himself. All vampires draw blood!

"Why are you laughing? I was just curious because I've never heard Nicci mention any type of job you did."

"Just arrange the meeting and I'll be grateful."

****

Johnny set up the meeting with Lucky Luciano for the following weekend. Lucky arrived without a date but had four rather large men with him. Heinrich assumed they were bodyguards. He was walking in the center of them. They surrounded him like a box. Lucky was by no means a small man, so they walked with military precision. The bodyguards anticipated every step he took. They met at the Savoy, at a private table in the back.

"Well, what do you want, Mr. Schmidt? Johnny said you had important business to discuss with me. I thought I had said everything that needed to be said the last time we met."

"Er . . . . Mr. Luciano, there seems to be some confusion about the contract. Petyr has been thumped in the head three times already; Twice, with a flower pot and once with a can of paint. Obviously, they didn't kill him. It just made Nicci think he was either extremely clumsy or unlucky. She's had to nurse him twice. That defeats the whole purpose of me trying to get him away from her. When I said I want his head, I meant it literally. He needs to be beheaded. *I want his head chopped off!* That way I know he is really dead. If need be I'll increase the contract amount to $10, 000 dollars. That's a lot of money."

"You're right. That is a lot of money. Can you afford that? I mean you must really want him dead."

"I told you, Mr. Luciano, I needed him completely out of the picture. I want Nicci and I know she's not leaving him anytime soon, without help. These accidents are making them closer."

"Okay, for $10,000 dollars, I'll clear up the confusion. Is there anything else, Mr. Schmidt?"

"No, Mr. Luciano. Thank you for meeting with me." Heinrich extended his hand to shake.

Lucky looked at him, then his hands and frowned. He rose with his bodyguards, turned and left the club.

"*Whew!* He's a strange, powerful man. I'd hate to get on his bad side."

Chapter 54

Petyr had been hit in the head three times last month. He was glad he was a vampire. Even though, it hurt to get hit, he did recover quickly. He didn't understand why he had even been hit, though. He knew he wasn't clumsy. He felt like he'd been hit on purpose.

Nicci told him she'd heard rumors that someone wanted him dead and was willing to pay for it. He didn't believe her when she first told him but after the ladder incident, he knew something was up. Who would want him dead enough to pay for it?

He was going to have to put his feelers out. Petyr was worried someone thought or possibly just found out he was a vampire killer. Only he and Nicci knew he was a vampire and all the reports they had been sending to Romania were faked. Could he have possibly gotten into trouble with the Romanian Council and they wanted him dead? He didn't really think so, but he had to be sure.

"Nicci, do you think the Council is after us? Do you think they figured out we've been faking vampire deaths? Maybe they have ordered my death."

"Don't be silly, Petyr. They would have ordered both our deaths, not just yours. Remember we're both vampires. I haven't had any accidents! But, now that you mention it, you know how much Heinrich hates you. Do you think he'd be mean enough to ask someone to kill you? I'd never forgive him if he did something as mean as that."

"Heinrich is mean enough and jealous enough but I don't think he'd be silly *enough* to have me killed."

****

Little did they know that was exactly what Heinrich had up his sleeve. He'd had enough of sharing Petyr with Nicci. He had been desperate enough to raise the bounty on Petyr's head but that was still taking too long. He was going to have to get rid of him himself.

He'd laid low during Petyr's accidents so he thought now might be a good time to start sending flowers again. He'd make sure they weren't just roses. A nice mixture of wildflowers should do the trick. He could use the excuse that he was hoping Petyr would make a speedy recovery. Maybe, he could stop by Nicci's new home and see how he was doing. Heinrich knew he was playing a dangerous game by going to see Nicci and Petyr but it had been at least a month since he'd seen or spoken to Nicci. She wouldn't answer or return his calls. Anyhow, he loved danger. It was time to make aggressive moves, he thought. He would show up at her door with a summer bouquet and a bottle of 'red wine' for Petyr.

Nicci was now living off 132nd St instead of just at the Waldorf-Astoria. She hadn't let that apartment go because she enjoyed having that as her getaway place when she needed to 'breathe'. She now had Remi working for her. At sundown he was on her doorstep bearing gifts. He rang the doorbell.

Remi answered. "Can I help you? Is that you, Heinrich? What are you doing here? I know you didn't come by to see Nicci. If you did, she is with *her husband, Petyr.* He keeps having these strange accidents and she is trying to console him."

"That's why I'm here. I heard about the ladder incident. I thought it would be nice to make a get well visit and bring a gift. It's 'red wine'. I know he loves this label. It's even a good year." He turned on his best charming smile. "Could you let Nicci and Petyr know I'm here? You can tell her I'll go home if they don't want to see me."

"I'll let her know." Remi shut the door in his face. With his vampire hearing, he could hear her walking to a nearby room. He could hear the conversation but couldn't make out the words clearly.

He heard bits and pieces; "Heinrich" "at door" "red wine". He hadn't moved from his spot in front of the door when Remi returned.

"Nicci said you may come in. She also said before you come in, that you are expected to be on your best behavior. There are to be no comments about their relationship." (Nicci hadn't really said that but Remi couldn't resist putting that in. She knew how Heinrich liked to start fights and Petyr needed his rest.) "Also don't stay too long. Petyr is still recuperating from a serious head injury."

Heinrich knew that Remi knew they were vampires and heal instantly. It took all his strength not to break out laughing. "Yes ma'am. Could you find a vase for these flowers before you bring them to Miss Nicci? Please bring three wine glasses, also. I'll open the bottle when you bring the glasses back."

"Yes sir. Follow me to the sitting room. Petyr is lying on the chaise-lounge, resting."

Heinrich was about to burst open from laughter. Did Nicci really think she could play the human housewife and Petyr the injured patient? As he was ushered into the room, he saw Petyr fooling with a giant white bandage taped to his forehead. "How are you feeling, Petyr? I see you have a large bandage on your head. Does it hurt much?" he snickered.

"No, Heinrich. It seems to be healing quickly and it barely hurts."

Before Heinrich could make a sarcastic rebuttal, Nicci interrupted. "Why are you here? *I mean really here?* You don't even like Petyr."

"Nicci, I promised Remi I would be on my best behavior. I even brought wine, 'red' naturally. I brought it to share with everyone. Would I not bring a bottle if I didn't want to apologize for my atrocious behavior at the wedding? I did say I was sorry to you Nicci. I never apologized to the both of you. I'm sorry! *(No He wasn't.)* I didn't know things would get so out of hand. You know with the explosion and all. But if we hadn't fought, you might have been trapped in the explosion. Plus, I heard about your head injury and I wanted to see for myself, how you were healing."

"You're right, Heinrich. We accept your apology and we won't talk about it again. He's healing rather well, as you can see for yourself. Why don't we drink that 'wine' and then you can leave. Petyr needs his rest."

"Okay." Heinrich was teeming inside. He should have been the one relaxing on that chaise-lounge. He wanted to hit Petyr in the head, himself, with that wine bottle. He couldn't wait for someone to cash in on that contract.

Nicci let him finish one glass and called for Remi to show him to the door. As he left the room, he looked at the front door one last time. Suddenly, he was hit with an idea. He was old enough to remember when Marie Antoinette was beheaded. He thought to himself. "Why not create a guillotine at the front door. When Petyr leans over to pick up a package, it would trigger the blade. Then there would be no more Petyr. How was he going to make a guillotine? He had to really think on that."

Chapter 55

Heinrich finally realized the only way he could get a guillotine installed without anyone know would be to get Nicci, Petyr, and Remi out of the house. While they were gone he could have it built. The more he thought about it, he realized he only had to get Remi out. Nicci and Petyr would be in their coffins during the day and never know what was going on. He had to make sure the carpenter he hired could complete the job in one day. It would be perfect. He loved his plan.

****

The next evening, he went to the Savoy. Nicci was there greeting everyone, thanking them for all the good wishes for Petyr's health. She was reassuring them that Petyr was alright. He even heard laughing about Petyr's clumsiness. Even the vampires joined in on the laughter, though they knew Petyr had never been hurt or in any danger. Most people were asking how one man could be so clumsy.

Heinrich found himself laughing along with the other men. This was the perfect time to ask Samuel if he knew a carpenter. "Nicci, do you think Samuel could put me in contact with a carpenter? I have something that needs to be built. I need a talented carpenter. It should only be one day's worth of work but I'll pay well. Everyone could use money. The Depression isn't over yet."

"Sure, Heinrich. What are you up too?"

"Nothing special. I just need some carpentry work done."

****

Samuel, had a good friend, who was a carpenter. Thomas Peterson came highly recommended. He had only been doing odd jobs since the beginning of the Depression. He had a hard time keeping food on the table for his small family. No one could afford to hire him for an extended period of time. He was even having trouble keeping the electricity on. Samuel tried to think of him whenever he heard about some available carpentry work.

Thomas came by the following Saturday night. "I'm Thomas Peterson. Please to meet you, Mr . . . I didn't catch your last name. Should I call you Heinrich?"

"No, just call me Sir. After this job is done you won't know me. I will not know you. I expect total discretion and possibly I may use you again."

"It's nothing illegal is it?"

"No, No, nothing like that."

"Okay, I can be very discreet, especially for a paying job. What do you want me to build?"

"A guillotine."

Thomas looked very confused. "A what!. What is that?"

"It's a torture device of sorts. It's used to cut a person's head off. I have a sketch here of what it's supposed to look like." Heinrich pulled the sketch out of his overcoat pocket. "Do you think you can build this? I'll pay you $1000 dollars."

"Is that a knife blade at the top? If I may ask, sir, are you really going to cut someone's head off?"

"Thomas, that's not for you to worry about whose head I'm going to cut off. If you must know, though, it's a burglar alarm I'm developing. Can you build it? If you can, I'll have more work for you when it's completed." Heinrich knew he was appealing to his need for money. There was no way he would turn down $1000 dollars. He knew he would change his memory when Thomas had completed the guillotine.

Thomas seemed to be satisfied with that answer. Although, he was still curious about it. No one had ever asked him to construct something so odd. He felt sorry for any burglar that might run into a guillotine. It took one day to construct the guillotine and one day to test it. Thomas never thought to question the odd hours he met Heinrich.

"Sir, I've completed the guillotine and tested it. Where would you like me to set it up?"

Heinrich had come up with the perfect idea. "Thomas, I want the guillotine set up at 148 132nd St., Miss Nicci's new home. You are to tell Remi, her housekeeper, that you are rebuilding the framework on the doorway. When Miss Nicci bought her new place the previous owner had noticed some termite damage. In good faith, he needed to repair it as he had promised. You should be able to do the work in a couple of hours and then be out of her way. You are to make sure she doesn't see the guillotine blade."

"I'm not going to be involved in a murder, am I, Sir?"

"No, Thomas as I said before this is a twentieth century burglar alarm that I have developed. It's meant to scare the burglar, not kill." Heinrich wasn't worried. He had already planned to wipe Thomas's memory when he paid him. He was going to tell him he had built a rocker for me to give to Nicci as a wedding gift. He couldn't take the chance that he would talk to Samuel. Samuel would tell Nicci when Petyr was beheaded, that he'd used Thomas to build a guillotine. She would know right away that he did it. He couldn't risk her anger.

Chapter 56

The doorway was installed. Heinrich had driven by to make sure Thomas had done a good job. He also had wiped Thomas's memory when he paid him. Thomas had even said he hoped Nicci enjoyed the new rocker.

To make sure Nicci didn't accidently get beheaded, he had called her. He said he was leaving a case of 'red wine' at the front door. It was his way of saying he was sorry for all the trouble had been causing. He had said it was probably too heavy for her to carry. He knew she had vampire strength but if the neighbors were watching it would be suspicious if she carried it in.

He had planned to attach clear magician's string to the case. One end would be at the guillotine release mechanism and the other on the wine. When Petyr picked up the case it would release the tension on the blade and it would drop. Voila`, no head for Petyr! In the confusion the bottles would break and the string would be lost.

Heinrich delivered the case personally so that he could set the string up with the blade. He knew they would have just risen and Nicci would be dressing for the club. He placed the case in front of the door. Quickly, he rang the doorbell and hid across the street. He wanted a good view of all the excitement.

****

Petyr heard the doorbell ring. Nicci had told him they were getting a case of 'red wine'. They hadn't had freshly bottled blood in quite a while. This was a real treat. Heinrich had gotten them a whole case. Maybe, he could finally be forgiven.

"Nicci, I'll get the door. I hope it's the wine." He opened the door and the case was there. He yelled. "Nicci, it's the wine!"

As he lifted the box, the blade whooshed down. Before he could call out in surprise, his head was sliced off and rolling toward the bushes. His life's blood was pouring out.

Heinrich had to cover his mouth to keep from laughing, as it came to a stop under a shrub. "Finally, he's really dead! I bet he won't recover from that!"

I heard a thump and a crashing sound of glass shattering. I ran to the front door calling out. "Petyr, what was that? Are you okay? Petyr? Petyr?" As I got closer to the front door, I could see a pool of blood. Blood was flowing down the sidewalk like a small steam. At first, I couldn't see what had happened or where the blood was coming from. I felt as if I was moving in slow motion. Petyr's body was lying in the doorway. Bloody glass was laying around his body and a crushed box was under his body.

"Petyr! Oh no! Petyr, no!" I was screaming. "Your head! Where's your head?"

Heinrich hated watching Nicci being in so much pain. He wanted to rush to her and hold her. With all the blood surrounding the body, she hadn't noticed the blade from the guillotine. He had to get that blade out of there.

I kneeled in the midst of the blood to pick up his body. I held him weeping. Heinrich crossed the street as if he just arrived.

Running up to Nicci, he shouted. "Oh my god! Nicci! What happened? Are you hurt? Where's Petyr? I was just coming to see if you had received my gift."

I could barely speak. "I'm okay. This is Petyr!"

"Is that Petyr? Where's his head? How did this happen? I didn't even see him pick up the box. Was something in the box?"

"I don't know. I don't know what happened. His head is gone."

He had to get that blade from under the box Petyr's body had crushed. Somehow he had managed to fall on it. Nicci was weeping bloody tears and rocking his headless body. Finally, he was able to lift Petyr and brush her hair out of her face. He smeared blood on her face so that no one would be able to tell if the blood on her face was from her tears or his body. She clung to Heinrich's arm as he tried to take Petyr away.

"Let's take him in the house. We don't want the neighbors to see this."

"You're right, Heinrich. Let's put him on the settee. I can always buy another settee. *We have to find his head."*

It was the perfect scenario for Heinrich. He lifted and carried Heinrich's decapitated body to the settee. He couldn't figure out how to arrange him. I placed his shoulders in my lap and wept. "Nicci, you stay here with Petyr. I'll go look for his head."

Upon saying that, I wept even harder and louder. Heinrich knew this was the perfect opportunity to get the blade and hide it. He grabbed a pillowcase for Petyr's head and a brown paper bag for the blade,

"Nicci, I'm going to gently place Petyr's head in this pillowcase. I'll sweep the glass into this paper bag. Should we call the police?"

"Heinrich, how could this have happened? Are there new vampire hunters or killers in town? Petyr and I were the only ones sanctioned by the Romanian Council that I know of. We can't have the police investigating. I don't need them hunting down vampires. Call Sally, Samuel and Johnny. Maybe they can help. Please find his head. I don't like looking at him like this."

"Let me get the glass up first. I'll wash the sidewalk down. I don't want Sally and Johnny to have to walk through all that blood. (He knew he wasn't supposed to mess with the crime scene.) Where is Remi? Why didn't she come running when you screamed?"

"I don't know where she is. Do you think she's dead, too? I don't know if Petyr sent her to run an errand."

"I don't think she's dead. Maybe she's with Samuel on some errand." He knew she wasn't dead because he hadn't killed her. He hadn't taken into consideration where Remi might be. He had just got lucky that she wasn't home. He couldn't worry about that now. He had to get that blade off the front porch and find Petyr's head. He couldn't afford to have anyone find the magician's string or the guillotine blade. He knew Johnny would be asking questions; especially how did he get there so fast.

Petyr's head had come to a stop under a bush in the front yard. The guillotine blade lay in the middle of crushed bottles and blood. Glass was everywhere. Checking to make sure no one could see what he was doing, he scooped the blade up with a pile of glass. He shoved it all into the brown paper bag. He moved the bag onto the back seat of his car. Heinrich found a broom in the kitchen and grabbed a large pot of water. He returned to the front porch and attempted to wash down the sidewalk before anyone arrived.

****

Why was Heinrich being so nice? I was tired of men. In the past ten years alone, I had lost; Jack, Johnny, now Petyr. I seemed to always have bad luck when it comes to love and men. except Sally. Maybe I need to leave men alone.

I would mourn the loss of Petyr. I knew within three days he would be ashes. It was just like taking three days to become a vampire. It takes three days before you fade away in death. There is no burial, just a wake or memorial service.

Samuel and Johnny didn't know Petyr was a vampire but Sally did. Maybe I could pull off a fake cremation or bury an empty coffin. The wedding had been such a big deal, then the bombing of the Savoy, the loss of Mikael, Anita. I knew I had to have a big service and farewell dinner for Petyr. People would ask questions if I didn't do something. Before that, though, I had to find out who did this. I believed there must have been a contract on his life, out there. That was the only explanation for the bumps on the head and now the beheading. Who wanted him dead, besides Heinrich? I had to talk to Lucky.

Chapter 57

Remi walked through the door just as the men arrived. Samuel had driven both Sally and Johnny to my home. They jumped out before Samuel had even parked. Johnny beat Sally to the door and opened it without even knocking.

"Nicci, are you okay? What happened? Heinrich wasn't too clear on the phone. All we gathered from his shouting, was Petyr had been beheaded. I could hear you crying in the background. How in the world did Petyr get beheaded? Why? It couldn't have been the men who beheaded Anita. I thought we solved that problem when the Savoy exploded."

Sally was trying o pry my hands away from Petyr's headless body. "How could this have happened? Did you see anyone or hear anything?"

When Remi saw Petyr's headless body in my lap, she fainted.

Johnny said. "Did she just faint?"

Heinrich frowned and moved to pick her up. He carried her to her bedroom in the back of the house. "We don't need another hysterical woman right now. We need to figure out who could have done this."

Upon Heinrich's return, I tried to explain to Sally, Samuel and Johnny, what happened, in between my hiccups and tears. "No, Petyr went to get a case of 'red wine' at the door. I heard Petyr calling my name and then a crash. I ran to the door and saw his body, headless, lying in a pool a blood."

I let go of Petyr, crying into Sally's shoulder, as he knelt by the settee. Blood was dripping down my face from tears and hands from holding Petyr. "Who would want him dead? I thought we had moved past his vampire killing days . . . . No one has been killed since the Savoy was destroyed and Mikael and Boris were killed in the bombing."

Sally whispered. "I don't know Nicci. Most people didn't even know Petyr was a vampire. But only another vampire or a vampire killer would cut off his head. You don't think Heinrich is mean or mad enough to be involved?"

"Sally, I know Heinrich still loves me but to behead Petyr is unthinkable. Besides, he wasn't here. He arrived after I found Petyr's body."

Johnny came up behind them. "What are you two whispering about? Petyr was a good man. He needs a special funeral. Did Heinrich find his head?"

"Heinrich walked out of the kitchen, drying his hands. "I heard you, Sally. I didn't have anything to do with Petyr's death. Yes, I do still love Nicci. *But to kill Petyr!* How could you think that of me? What have I done to make you think that of me?"

"Well, you did have that big fight with Jack over Nicci, You both resorted to fist-a-cuffs. Then, there was the fight at the wedding. Then . . . ."

"Okay, okay. That's enough. That was different, anyway. What's this about Anita and the vampire killers beheading people?"

"Shh. We'll talk about that later. Johnny didn't know she was a vampire. We changed his memories. Now is not the time to be trying to teach him or reawake his memories."

Johnny and Samuel had come back from Remi's room, making sure she was sleeping. Samuel spoke first. "What are you whispering about?"

Johnny added. "Heinrich, did you at least pick up Petyr's head. We need to clean up his body and head so that it can be laid out for a funeral. Nicci is really suffering."

I started sobbing again.

Samuel said. "I still think we should call the police. We need help to figure out who did this. I mean, we need to know if someone is trying to get revenge, Nicci. Have you made anyone angry, lately? Do you think Lucky Luciano could possibly be trying to send you a message?"

"I doubt it Samuel, Lucky Luciano thinks of me as a daughter. Why would he be sending a warning? I haven't done anything. I'm pretty sure he even liked Petyr."

Sally kissed my forehead. "Nicci, let Johnny and I get you to bed. Heinrich can finish cleaning up. After we get you settled we'll come down and help him. We'll try to make Petyr as presentable as possible."

I let go of Sally. As I climbed the stairs and walked towards the bedroom, I felt the room spinning. I had lost many lovers over the span of my life. I don't understand why the death of Petyr was hitting me so hard. Maybe it was just an accumulation of all the recent deaths. I started to say something to Johnny and I fainted. Sally caught me before I hit the floor.

After placing me on the bed instead of in my coffin, Sally sat next to me, holding my hand. "Nicci, why are you taking this so hard? We've lost many close friends over the years. Why is Petyr so special? You only turned him and married him, to get information about what he, Mikael and Boris were up to."

"Sally, you know how much I love you but somehow because you were always busy in the kitchen I began to look for a substitute to fill my needs. Originally, I was just using Petyr to fill that need and to make Mikael angry while gathering information about the vampire killers. After Heinrich showed up trying to rekindle our love, I realized I cared for Petyr more than I knew."

He kissed me on the corner of my mouth, not wanting to make the kiss to sexual but still intimate.

"Thank you, Sally. I needed to know you are still here."

This time he kissed my forehead and thinking out loud, said. "We should have a memorial service. We won't have a body, because he'll be ashes by then, but we can have people talk about how much they loved him and music. Vampires don't usually have funerals, since we fade so fast. This might be fun. Everyone that came to the wedding can come to the service. We might be able to figure out who killed

Petyr. I'm sure they'll show up. I can even try out some new recipes. You know me, I'm always looking for an excuse to cook or try a new recipe."

I had to laugh. "Sally, that's why I love you."

"There's my girl. You look beautiful, even with those bloody tears on your face. At least, I know you clean up well."

My smile broadened.

"That's a great idea." Johnny added, standing in the doorway. "I don't know anything about vampires but everyone loves a good funeral with lots of food and alcohol. You can almost guarantee the killer will be there, to gloat over his handiwork. Nicci, do you think you can handle that?"

"Of course. By then, I will have come to accept his loss as just one more man in my life that I lost. I think a memorial service is a great idea. We can even have Lena Horne sing. It will be nice to send him off in a blaze of glory, so to speak." I laughed. "Why not! My lovers never get to have a glorious funeral. They tend to just fade away."

That made Sally and I laugh even harder. Johnny asked. "What's the joke? Why are you laughing?

"It's what they call an inside joke. I'll explain it to you later. Let's just plan this memorial. We have to invite everyone. Can the three of you make the calls to invite people and they can spread the word to the community. I'll call Father O'Reilly to officiate. We're going to do this with class."

Chapter 58

The memorial service for Petyr was to be held at Saint Rocco's Chapel in Brooklyn. It was on 27th Street. Petyr and Mikael used to attend Mass there, when they lived in Brooklyn. Father O'Reilly was the pastor and going to give Eulogy. Petyr was killed Wednesday so the service was to be that Saturday night. Naturally, the coffin was closed. He was probably ashes by now. Only a few of my select group even knew Petyr was a vampire.

Duke Ellington's band was going to play the processional and Lena Horne was going to sing 'Ave Maria'. I'm sure everyone would remember her from our wedding. I was praying there would be no explosions at St. Rocco's Chapel. I didn't want a repeat of the wedding bombing. Both the Cotton Club and the Savoy were closed, out of respect for Nicci. Everyone knew she was involved in both clubs. Everyone was sad at her loss.

I wanted this to be a good old fashioned party with everyone sharing stories about Petyr. Prohibition was over, that meant alcohol would be flowing. Sally wanted to cook and Petyr's favorite meal was beef stew. A couple of vats of stew could feed a large crowd. Everyone would eat well.

****

Sally called the Savoy and spoke to Martha. "Martha I have some terrible news. Petyr was murdered tonight. Nicci won't be in because she's too distraught over the murder. She just can't work. Can you or one of the men play host or hostess? Also spread the word; Petyr is dead and his memorial service will be at Saint Rocco Chapel. He'll be buried at Greenwood Cemetery in Brooklyn. Evidently, that's Petyr and Mikael's old church."

"Oh my gosh! Sure Sally! You can trust us to handle the club. Tell Nicci not to worry about a thing. We send our love. Will Johnny be in to pick up receipts, as usual?"

"Johnny is here with me at Nicci's house. He's going to send Vito. You remember him as Johnny's old partner. I don't think you should have any problems with the money. Johnny will let Lucky know about the change and why he did it. Call here if you have any problems. Her number is 212-555-6025. The service will be open to the public.

****

'The Memorial Service'

Saturday finally came. There was so much to be done before the start of the Memorial Service. I had made arrangements with Father O'Reilly to handle the religious parts of the service. I had to make a sizeable donation to the Church to have Father say a funeral mass in the evening. The service was set to start at 7 p.m. tonight.

The pall bearers were the three male dancers from the Savoy and three male dancers from the Cotton Club. Duke Ellington began playing the processional as they carried the coffin into the church and placed it on a large gold stand. I walked behind the coffin with Sally and Johnny supporting my arms. Naturally, I had to drop to my knees a couple of times as if I couldn't walk. Sally had hired a couple of old Romanian women, draped in black to wail at certain intervals. Petyr would have loved all this pageantry. I even had the pall bears wear white gloves and black top hats, white scarves around their necks with black tuxedos.

I had chosen a black walnut coffin and it was draped with a large black doily. The craftsmanship was incredible. Thomas had done the carpentry work. He had worked, meticulously, night and day to complete the work.

The church was filled to capacity. Father O'Reilly raised his hands to God. "Please be seated. This Mass is being given to give praise to God and to send Petyr on his way to heaven. This Mass and service will be a celebration of Petyr's life."

I heard wailing come from somewhere in the church. I smiled into my hanky while pretending to sniff. That was perfect timing. I thought. "Boy, they're good."

I could hear people whispering:

"Was Petyr that good of a man? I don't remember anything that special about him."

"I heard he was beheaded!"

"She really went all out. I heard they hired real Romanian mourners!"

"Look how beautiful she is! I hope I look that good at my funeral."

I almost broke out laughing. If I knew funerals could be like this I would have had more.

Father O'Reilly stopped praying for a moment. "Please stop all that whispering. This *is the house of the Lord!* If you have any questions please wait until Mass is over."

I couldn't believe he just said that. I didn't think the whispering was that noticeable.

Father O'Reilly read the Gospel and then began his Eulogy. "I've known Petyr since he first arrived in New York City, with his best friend, Mikael. I can compare his life to the story of the Good Samaritan in the Bible. He would give you the shirt off his back . . . ." He spoke for about fifteen minutes then continued Mass.

Near the end of Mass, before the final blessing, he turned to the congregation and said. "Now is your moment to tell your stories and express your love for Petyr, with your stories and memories you want to share."

I didn't move. I looked around the church to see who would come forward. Would you believe it! It was Heinrich, standing, moving towards the podium. H*e didn't even like Petyr much less have a story to share.* I knew whatever Heinrich was about to say would be a lie.

Heinrich began his first story. "I still remember the first time I met Petyr. We were going to school at St. Gerome's. It was run by a group of Brothers in Romania. *(My mouth nearly fell open. I didn't hear him just say he went to school with Petyr? I knew Heinrich was a showoff, but really!)* Petyr was a great prankster. I remember when we were in secondary school, you call it high school. Petyr put a dead snake in Brother Schminsky's desk drawer before Latin class started. When Brother Schminsky reached in to pull out a piece of chalk, he; pulled out the snake. Not only did Brother Schminsky scream but so did all the boys in class. He flipped the snake onto the floor and stomped on it. Petyr and I were doubled over with laughter. Eventually, everyone in class was laughing. When Petyr broke down and told the truth about what he'd done, he got ten lashes from Brother Schminsky's large brown leather belt he wore around his hips. Naturally, that wasn't funny. But still." Heinrich raise his shoulders as if to say that's the price for fun.

Everyone, in church, either laughed or smiled at Heinrich's story. Heinrich went on to say he had even more stories to share, including the ones about the long standing rivalry he had with Petyr for Nicci hand in love. As you can see Petyr won. He said he would tell one of those at the reception.

(I couldn't believe Heinrich had horrendously lied in church. *Competition with Petyr for my hand!* He had never gone to school with Petyr. He didn't even know Mikael. I bet when Heinrich was in high school the Brothers of St. Gerome didn't even exist. Much less, Petyr wasn't even born yet or even a twinkle in his mother's eyes.)

After Heinrich sat down a few of Petyr's real old friends, including Sally and Johnny, spoke. They mostly spoke of how good a friend he'd been. Very few people knew he was a vampire, but he was a very young vampire. Each story was told with great caution.

Finally, Father O'Reilly rose to give the final blessing. "May Petyr have a safe journey to heaven. May the Lord bless his home and all within it, especially his wife, Nicci. We ask you to bless us all. Amen. In the name of the Father, the Son, and the Holy Ghost, Amen."

Everyone said Amen in unison. Mass was over. The coffin was removed and carried to a hearse, to be driven, to the cemetery. I was going to do the whole thing. I know it was unusual to have a burial in the evening but I had explained that Petyr was a man who always thought the evening was the most romantic. I wanted to continue his love of the darkness. No one seemed to question the oddness of the situation. Money will do that. People rarely question money. No one would ever know there was nothing in the coffin but Petyr's ashes.

After I had gotten seated in the limousine, Sally, Johnny and Heinrich piled in after me. Once the limousine pulled off, following the hearse, I confronted Heinrich. "What were you thinking? You never went to school with Petyr! For that matter, how do you even know where he went to school? You told that ridiculous lie in church. How could you!"

"Nicci, don't be so stuffy. I knew he was from the Brothers of St. Gerome. Most vampires know that's where they train vampire killers. So what if I embellished. I *could* have gone to high school with him. I *could* have seen him put a snake in Brother Schminsky's drawer. I'm sure someone has done that to Brother Schminsky at some point. I mean if there is really a Brother Schminsky." Heinrich started laughing. "Don't be such a stick in the mud. It was a harmless story. Funerals can be so boring. I thought that funeral could use a laugh. No one was hurt by my story."

"Heinrich, it wasn't that anyone was hurt by your story. You gave the impression that you had been friends since high school. You didn't even like Petyr."

Sally interrupted, laughing. "She's right Heinrich, you hated Petyr. He wasn't even a twinkle in someone's eye when you were created."

"It wasn't that I didn't like Petyr, he was in the way of my being with you. I didn't like that."

"Did you kill him, Heinrich? I bet you did! I don't know how but I bet you did."

"Now Nicci, would I do something so horrific to hurt you? I love you but I would want to see you happy with me."

"Humph"

****

It seemed like the five minute ride to Greenwood Cemetery took forever. I had bought a plot of land. The head stone was already in place. It read:

Petyr Apostal 1900-1939

Husband of Dominique Santa Maria

Liver of Life

I stood there stoically, as they lowered the coffin in the ground. I couldn't cry without bloody tears streaming down my face, so I just sniffled. I held it in until later. Lena Horne sang 'Ave Maria' and I heard more wailing. I could hear sniffling throughout the crowd. Roses had been passed to all the mourners. After Miss Horne's solo, I dropped a white rose on his coffin. Everyone else had been given a yellow rose. They were tossed into the coffin one by one as each mourner left.

Sally, Johnny and Heinrich returned to the limousine, as I said my final good-byes. I had planned a memorial reception back at the Savoy.

Chapter 59

My limousine was the last to arrive at the Savoy. The celebration was already in full swing. WuYi and SuChi were passing flutes of champagne out to the large crowd of guests. There were so many people. I could hardly get in the club. It seemed like there was a large number of people I didn't even know. I wasn't sure if they were friends of Petyr's or just funeral crashers.

Thank goodness, Sally had prepared a large amount of food the night before. Having never been to a funeral I wasn't sure how much they would eat. I went into the kitchen to check on Sally and his crew. I wasn't sure he needed help but I needed a shoulder to cry on for a brief moment. I knew it wouldn't matter to him if I shed bloody tears.

Sally was at the sink washing his hands as I walked up to him. "Sally, I'm not sure how much I miss Petyr, but I feel the need to cry and be held."

"Come here! Let's go into my office and you can put your head on my shoulder for a moment."

Upon getting seated, in his office, on an old torn sofa, I kissed him. "You know we used to be good together, before Petyr. What happened?"

"Vampire killers changed our lives, Nicci. Plus, a faerie caused mass confusion."

He kissed me and suddenly, I felt the old sparks of electricity we used to generate when we made love. "Did you feel that! That was electricity!"

Sally smiled. "I remember when every time we kissed, we either steamed up a room or almost set fire to it with the electricity we generated."

"Sally, I don't know why or how but I still love you. It took the loss of Petyr to make me see how much I missed you. But Heinrich's back. He brings trouble every time. I know he killed Petyr or had something to do with it. I can't prove it though."

Sally reached up and put his fingers over my mouth. "I had forgotten how when you get nervous or stressed, you can't stop talking. Hush! Just kiss me."

While kissing me, he carried me to the door to lock it and pull the shade. "They won't miss you for a few minutes. They may not even notice you've gone."

I laughed. "You're probably right." I didn't even remove my dress. I was so well practiced at making love in a hurry. I slid my dress up and his pants down. We came together with a burst of electricity that cause the trashcan by the desk to burst into flames.

We broke apart, laughing as Sally tried to smother the flames from the fire.

"*That's what love is like!* Nicci, you haven't laughed like that in a long time."

"I know and it feels good." I smoothed my dress and straightened the seams to my silk stockings. I said. "Meet me when the last guest goes. I don't want to be alone tonight. I want you to share my coffin tonight, if you don't mind.

****

By 10 p.m. most of the human mourners were drunk. The vampires seemed to be unusually happy, also. Some were excited over the willingness of all the mourners allowing them to drink their blood. Heinrich continued to make up stories regarding all the years he had known Petyr. He even had nerve to talk about the rivalry he had with Petyr over me.

I stood on the edge of a group of young women gathered around Heinrich. I had forgotten how dashing he looked in his dress uniform. He was ranting about what kind of lover Petyr had been before he'd married. He made Petyr sound like some sort of lady's man. I knew Petyr had been a virgin when I met him. I was shocked at Heinrich's blatant lies.

"Heinrich, may I talk to you alone, for a minute?" I said as I pushed my way through the women surrounding him. "We need to check on the amount of champagne I have in stock."

"Sure, Nicci. You've never asked me to look at the liquor count before, but I'd be glad to do anything for you, in this time of need."

I had never taken a non-employee to the lower level of the club. I just had to get Heinrich to shut up for a while about his friendship with Petyr. I felt myself getting angry.

"Heinrich, why do you insist on telling stories, like Petyr was your best friend? Remember, you beat him up at our wedding?"

"Nicci, these young women love my stories. They don't care if they're true. I'm not sure they even know who Petyr is. They are worshiping me. I think they came for the food and alcohol. I'm looking forward to drinking some of that young blood. Did you really want me to help with the liquor count or were you just trying to get me alone?"

"Heinrich, you're still so arrogant."

He laughed. "But that's why you still love me. *Why are we really down here?*" He grabbed my wrist, pulling me forward. He planted a wet kiss on my lips. I was tempted to resist.

Just that quickly, memories of my first kiss and the loss of my virginity with Heinrich flashed through my mind. Why not! Petyr's dead. This may be the perfect way to find out what Heinrich is really up to. I may even find out if he had anything to do with Petyr's death. He seems to be trying to get comfortable in my life again.

I kissed Heinrich on the neck, while sliding his jacket off. With vampire speed, I had his trousers down, including underwear. I simply readjusted my clothes, leaned Heinrich against some cases of whiskey and climbed on board. Heinrich was always ready for sex, especially after talking to a young group of women. I won't deny it, I still love having sex with Heinrich

He stirred up memories of our past one hundred years. I remembered Mardi Gras in Venice, strolls in the Campo. I remembered sleeping nude in his coffin with him. Those were the good old days.

We couldn't have been gone more than fifteen minutes. I had to play hostess again. Time to mingle and circulate through the mourners, again. I finally had to throw them out at 3 a.m.

WWII
1940-1945

Chapter 60

We had gotten word that Europe was involved in another war. Mussolini had taken over Italy. Hitler was on the rampage in Poland. Johnny had gotten word to return to Ireland. We still hadn't figured out who beheaded Petyr, but there weren't any more deaths. The police had moved it to their dead cases.

Everything seemed to be upside down. Not only did Heinrich want to leave and join another war but Samuel wanted to join, too. Samuel had to be at least fifty years old by now. I hate wars. I lose more men to wars. Now, I've even lost my chauffeur.

"Don't worry, Miss Nicci. I'll find a replacement for you. I know a young man named Elijah Cornwall. I'm sure Elijah will be glad to take over for me."

Naturally, with another war in Europe and the possibility the United States would join, Heinrich was ready to leave. I expected Heinrich to leave, but not Samuel. Now, Johnny said this was the perfect cover for him to return to Ireland. His Sabbatical had been extended long enough. He'd seen so many wonderful things. He had a friendship with me to hold onto. He tried to reassure me since he was immortal that they would meet again in another lifetime. The three of them were leaving from the New York Port of Embarkation in Brooklyn.

Elijah

Chapter 61

Samuel had promised before he left he would find her a replacement. He wanted the replacement to be a young, responsible, and most of all a respectful man. He knew quite a few men like that in Harlem. Elijah Cornwall stood out his mind. Elijah looked to be about 6'5" tall. He was what was called a high-yellow Creole. Samuel though he would look very distinguished in his chauffeur's uniform. He had good manners and knew his place. Also he was only twenty-four and strong. He would be able to handle Miss Nicci's heavy gowns and boxes. Samuel believed Miss Nicci would be safe with him.

Tomorrow after he left for the Army Induction Center in Harlem, he would go to Elijah's house. Elijah still lived with his mother in Harlem. Due to lack of jobs and food during the Depression, he had moved back in with his mother to help her survive. Samuel knew Elijah would be thrilled to get this job offer.

****

It was a beautiful Spring morning when Samuel left the induction center. Samuel felt so sure of himself. He was going to the Army, at his age, with Heinrich and Johnny. They were both two prominent white men. He was convinced this would reflect highly on his character. He was hoping after boot camp, he would get a good military job. Not that he minded being a chauffeur but he always dreamed of being a soldier for his country.

He had telephoned Elijah before going to the Induction Center. He was expected.

Elijah stuck his head out of the window. "Samuel, come on up. My mom has some coffee on and she just made her famous butter pound cake. We're celebrating my new job."

Samuel broke into a smile as he climbed the stairs, to their second floor apartment. He loved Mrs. Cornwall's pound cake. She rarely made it because she couldn't always afford to buy extra butter and sugar. The Cornwalls had a small apartment but Elijah's mom kept it spotless. Samuel was glad he was able to help Elijah.

After fixing his coffee and grabbing a slice of pound cake, he sat at the table with Elijah to discuss his duties as a chauffeur.

"You're not just her driver." He said. "She'll expect you to run errands and do shopping. You are to be at her beck-n-call practically twenty four hours a day. She often goes out at the wee hours of the morning and needs a ride. The most important thing is that you can't ask questions. She will trust you implicitly with her secrets. You can't ask questions about anything or reveal any secrets that she may decide to confide in you. Please, remember, that is very important to her. She has to trust you. Please don't disappoint me."

"Samuel, I'm so grateful for the job. I won't mess up. You can trust me and so can she."

****

The next day, Samuel brought the limousine to Elijah's apartment. The days of the Model T and boxcar Ford were over. Samuel gave him a quick driving lesson. He even took time to show Elijah how Miss Nicci likes her car to sparkle. Naturally, she rode in a ruby red limousine. He explained how Miss Nicci loved rubies and elegance.

He reminded Elijah, the only time he was to touch her was when he assisted her into the car or the door. He said he was not to comment to her or others about her beauty or youthful appearance. Samuel had been with her for nearly twenty years and she was still as beautiful as the day he met her.

Elijah laughed. "You're an old man, Samuel. What do you know about beauty?"

"Trust me, Elijah. Her beauty is remarkable. Many men fall in love with her, just because of her beauty. Do not over step your boundaries. You are a black man and she is white. Times may have changed due to the war, but not that much."

Elijah just laughed and shook his head at Samuel. "Why would I care about an old white lady? Don't worry, though, I will take good care of her and remember to say; yes, ma'am, no ma'am."

****

Samuel shipped out the next day and left the limousine parked in front of Elijah's stoop. He had already given Miss Nicci Elijah's phone number. He left the keys with the instructions that Miss Nicci would call that night. He had explained that his days would be free most of the time. She usually only used the car, in the evening and early mornings, when the club opened and closed. He left the address to the Savoy, with the keys to the club. He was sure Elijah had been at the club before. Everyone partied at either the Savoy or the Cotton Club.

She called, just like Samuel said she would. It was 7 p.m. and he had to pick her up at the Waldorf-Astoria. Samuel had neglected to tell him she lived at the most expensive hotel in New York City.

As I came out the entry way, he thought. "Oh my God! She's beautiful. Samuel had underestimated her beauty." He felt himself getting excited. Thank goodness, his chauffeur's suit jacket was long. He would have been so embarrassed hiding the bulge, while he opened the door for her.

"Good evening, Miss Nicci. My name is Elijah Cornwall. I am Samuel's replacement."

"Well, Elijah, Samuel never greeted me with a bulge in his pants, before." I couldn't stop laughing.

"I'm sorry Miss Nicci. I didn't expect you to be as beautiful as you are. You look like you're only in your twenties. I expected and old wrinkled woman. Although, Samuel did warn me you were incredibly beautiful"

I gave him my best smile. "I'm not sure if I should say thank you or not." I got into the car. "Please take me to the Savoy. Did Samuel tell you how to get there?"

"Yes, ma'am. He gave me complete instructions regarding how to help you and take care of the limousine."

"I'm not much of a talker so can you just take me to the club?"

Elijah was dying to get into a conversation with her. Her beauty was unbelievable. Samuel didn't do her justice. She looked like a goddess. Even though she was pale, her skin looked as it had been freshly tanned. She had the most glorious dark brown/black hair with what looked like strands of silver running through it. Not that old lady silver but almost gold. It was piled on top of her head with ruby stickpins scattered through it. Little wisps of dark brown hair framed her face. What a face! It looked like a work of art. When she smiled her whole face lit up. He kept peaking at her in the rearview mirror.

I noticed he was looking at me more than the road. Finally, I said. "Mr. Cornwall, I don't know how to drive but I'm sure you're supposed to watch the road and not me."

"I'm sorry ma'am. I just can't get over how pretty you are. If I'm not overstepping my boundaries, why don't you have a husband?"

"You are overstepping your boundaries. But my husband passed away."

"Again, I'm sorry, ma'am."

Eventually, we made it to the Savoy. "Thank you, Mr. Cornwall. The club closes at 2 a.m. Please be here by 3 a.m. to take me back to the hotel. I gave up my house when my last husband died. I moved back into the hotel. I couldn't stand being in the house my husband died in."

"Yes, ma'am." On that note, he smoothly parked the limousine in front of the Savoy.

****

Things had been very quiet at the club since Petyr died. It seemed like the only thing people talked about was how they had suffered from the Depression, WWI and now are men were leaving again. WWI was supposed to be the war to end all wars and yet here we are at another World War. The US hadn't officially joined yet but our young men were still leaving. I had expected Heinrich to go. He went to every major war he could. I was truly surprised when I found out that Samuel had enlisted, too. He had to be at least fifty years old. I know he never talked about his family but I was sure he had grandchildren, by now.

I was happy he'd found a replacement for himself. This Elijah kid, was a good-looking young man. He was beautiful, too, with coffee-milk colored skin. By being Creole, he even spoke a little French. It was fun to hear a foreign tongue when he was flustered. I was a little nervous about the way he kept trying to steal glances. I was hoping I wouldn't have to deal with another love-sick man.

I had given him a list of errands to run. I wanted to test his reliability. I gave him a list, just like I had with Samuel when I first hired him:

1. Pick up wine at the grocery store
2. Pick up summer gowns from the seamstress
3. Get fitted for new chauffer's uniform
4. Make bank deposit

Chapter 62

Elijah returned to the hotel to pick up Remi, just as Samuel had picked up Marie. She was Nicci's new assistant and he need her help to run some of the errands.

Elijah picked up 12 bottles of 'red wine' from Small's Food and Liquor. This was a local grocery store. (Elijah didn't know this was the latest way Nicci was getting her blood from the mortician.) He was surprised that Nicci got her wine from Small's. He figured it must have been a left over habit from the Prohibition since Small's didn't used to have the sign with Food and Liquor on it. He was dying to taste it and ask why she would buy fine wine from a local grocer. He was nosy enough to ask was it moonshine. Before they tackled the next item on the list, Remi insisted they take the wine home to the refrigerator.

He was excited. He'd never been inside the Waldorf-Astoria, much less been in a suite of rooms. He'd, also, never ridden in an elevator. Upon entering the elevator, his arms were full of bags with the 'wine' in them.

"Hi, I'm Elijah. I'm Miss Nicci's new chauffeur."

"Please to meet you. I'm Alphonso, the elevator porter. Martino is my relief on the weekends. (Alphonso was new to the Waldorf-Astoria, but he knew about Nicci's habit of bringing different men to the suite and to never ask questions. Jimmy had filled him in when he retired.) How do you like my box? Most people get nervous when they hear the doors close shut. They seemed to compare it to being put in a coffin and buried in the ground." He started laughing. "You seemed to be taking it well." Alphonso loved to see people get sick in the elevator.

"I've been in an elevator before. I've been to the top of the Empire State Building. That's a really big elevator. It goes all the way to the top. You know that the tallest building in the world! This is still exciting, though. I'm going to Miss Nicci's suite on the twelfth floor."

"I've never been to the Empire State Building. I work too much in an elevator to want to ride in one on my day off, even if it is the tallest building in the world. Well, here we are. This is Miss Nicci's floor."

"Thanks."

Remi said. "Follow me, Mr. Cornwall. I'll let you in and you can place the bags on the table. Can you put a couple of bottles in the refrigerator and I'll put the rest in our wine cabinet in the study."

"Sure. "Elijah took two bottles into the kitchen. He was surprised, when he opened the refrigerator, at how little was in it. Finishing quickly, he said. "Do you need help carrying the bottles?"

"No, I'm fine. I just have to make room."

****

While Remi was in the study, Elijah looked around. He began to quietly open drawers and rifling through them. A large roll top desk sat in the corner. Some large painting hung above it. He started picking through the cubbyholes. One such spot held two bank passbooks; one was from The First National Bank of New York City. He noticed most of the pages were full. He knew better than to look but he flipped to the last page anyway. He had to check the balance. It read; $20,659,000.32. He dropped the book and almost choked.

"Are you okay, Mr. Cornwall? I'll be out in a few minutes. I just had to make room for these new bottles."

"I'm fine. I was looking at the paintings and bumped into the sofa. I was just wondering who the artist was?"

"I think most of them are by Van Gogh. That's Miss Nicci's favorite artist."

Elijah didn't hear a word she said. He had just noticed the other passbook was written in a foreign language. He knew Nicci was

Italian so he figured it was a bank book from an Italian bank. It read 15,028,105 lira. He didn't know what that was in American dollars but it had to be at least $15 million dollars.

He whispered. "Oh my god! This woman is filthy rich. And I think I love her. I've never known anyone with that kind of money, much less work for them. I didn't think it was possible to have that kind of money." He shoved the books back into the cubbyhole just as Remi returned to the sitting room and he sat down.

"Miss Remi, could you get me a glass of water?"

When Remi left the room, he rushed back to the desk to see what else he could find. He started pulling drawers open. In the bottom drawer he found a soft brown, leather bound book. The cover said 'Diary'. The first page read; "my diary by Dominique Santa Maria." He thought what a beautiful name for such a beautiful page. As he flipped the pages, he noticed it was written in Italian. He was able to quickly pick out a few words that appeared similar to French. He saw:

Padre-father - *pere(fr)*
Mamma-mother - *mere(fr)*
Di colore-colored (Negro/colored) *personne de couleur (fr)*
Bianco-white - *blanc(fr)*

He thought about it. Slowly it dawned on him that Nicci was talking about her father being colored and her mother was white. That meant she was a mulatto. Oh no! That meant she was passing. She had been married to a white man.

Didn't she know it was against the law in the United States? He didn't know what the law was in Italy but we had anti-miscegenation laws. She could go to jail. Worse, she could be lynched. If anyone finds out about the money and her background, they'll seize the money and lynch her.

He had to tell someone. That was too much information for Elijah to keep to himself. Elijah had no idea what to do with all this information. Samuel was his best friend, but he had already shipped out. Maybe he could tell his mother. He wasn't sure she could keep a secret. Here he had only known Nicci two days and he loved her, plus, knew her deepest secrets.

Remi came from the kitchen with his water. By now, he was sitting on the couch in a state of shock. He was overwhelmed with all this knowledge.

"Are you okay? You look a little pale. Do you feel sick or something? Do you need to eat?"

"I'm fine. I think I'm hungry and tried. I was so excited about my job, I don't remember if I ate today. I'm not used to working at night *and* trying to work during the day without sleep. I should probably go home and rest. Thank you for the water, though. I know we have a few more errands to run but maybe I should go home and take a nap and come back." He felt himself babbling but he was so nervous he couldn't stop. He had to get out of there. "I know, we still need to go to the seamstress to get Miss Nicci's gowns and I have to get fitted for my own chauffeur's uniform."

"Why don't you just go home. We can get the gowns tomorrow or later this evening, if you are more rested. Remember, Miss Nicci will want you by 7p.m. to take her to the club."

(Little did he know, I was sleeping the sleep of the dead, in the next room.)

Chapter 63

Elijah was back at 7 to pick Nicci up. He was much calmer after the initial shock. He was dying to share his knowledge, though. As she climbed into the back seat, he kept stealing glances of her in the rearview mirror.

"Elijah, is there something you want to say or ask me? I've noticed you keep looking at me like something is on your mind."

As he pulled away from the curb, he couldn't hold it in any longer. "I don't know if it would be presumptuous to say. I may be speaking out of place."

"Samuel recommended you. I trusted him for years. What could you say that would be out of place?"

"Okay, here goes. I love you." Elijah felt himself beginning to stutter.

"How could you love me? You don't even know me. You just started working for me yesterday."I tried not to laugh.

"I know it sounds crazy, but I do love you. *And* I know you're a mulatto, so it will be okay."

First, I felt like the floor just fell from under me. Then I got angry. "How do you know if I'm a mulatto?" I remembered the last man that accused me of being a mulatto. He was dead. I snapped his neck after I drained his blood. He had the nerve to think he was going to blackmail me.

"What do you want, Elijah?"

"Nothing, ma'am. I'm just saying, I love you. I know you have money but I'm not after it. Do you think you could learn to love me?" Elijah felt himself nearly begging.

I started laughing. "You're kidding, aren't you?"

"No, ma'am."

"Why don't you just take me to the club? We can talk about this when I close the club. I'll even invite you back to my suite for a drink."

"Yes, ma'am." Elijah could barely drive.

****

I thought all night about what Elijah said. I had so many questions that needed answering. How did he find out she was a mulatto? Did he know I was a vampire? How did he find out about my money? Did he just make an assumption about her money because she owned the club? I was lonely again, since Petyr died. Heinrich and Samuel had left for the war. Johnny had gone back to being a faerie *What was I to do?* He was a Negro, even if they called him a Creole. That meant nothing to me.

I knew I could trust Remi. Remi would never divulge that kind of information, willingly. How in the world did he find out? Suddenly, it dawned on me that I had been writing in my diary and left it in the bottom drawer of the desk. I hadn't felt like putting it away this morning because I was tired. He must have gone through my desk. How dare he!

It had been a quiet night. Since it was a work night for most of her guests, very few had come out tonight. Now that the Depression was over, more people were able to work instead trying to meet people that could possible send them business. I was glad when the evening was finally over. WuYi had closed the Savoy down by 2 a.m. Elijah was waiting at the door. I hated to admit that he cut quite a handsome figure in his black chauffeur's uniform. I just stood at the front door of the club watching him as he stood at attention, waiting for her.

As I moved away from the door and the shadows, Elijah caught sight of me and opened the door. As I brushed by him, he caught a whiff of Spring roses. He'd never noticed her fragrance before. He felt his heart rate pick up and I heard it. He thought. "How was he going to make this work? They were from different sides of the tracks."

"Good evening, Miss Nicci. I hope you had a good night?"

"Why thank you, Elijah."

Elijah produced his arm and assisted her into the car. As he bent down to help her get seated, he stole a kiss.

I began sputtering and then just slapped him. "What do you think you are doing? You have no right to kiss me."

"I'm sorry, Miss Nicci! I just couldn't resist. You smell like Spring time. Your beauty drives me insane. I promise I won't do it again. May I ask if you feel okay, though. Your cheek is awfully cool."

"I'm fine, Elijah. I was working in the cooler before I came out." It was then I realized he didn't know I was a vampire. That much was in her favor. Obviously, he hadn't read her whole diary. But now, I had to find out how much he *did* know. I was still so angry that he had the nerve to kiss me.

Chapter 64

Elijah pulled up to the Waldorf-Astoria. A doorman reached for the handle. "Elijah, why don't you go park the car. I'll wait for you at the back entrance. We can take the elevator up to my floor. We need to talk."

"Yes, ma'am." Elijah drove the limousine to the back of the hotel and went through the back entrance. He knew, even as a chauffeur, he wasn't allowed through the front door. "I've been to your apartment already, so I'm not afraid to ride the elevator. Remi had me bring the wine upstairs, earlier."

They boarded the elevator together. He stepped behind her, once they had entered the elevator. He could hold doors for her, but he knew he wasn't her equal. Therefore, he couldn't stand next to her, not even in the elevator.

Before they entered my suite, I looked to make sure we were alone in the hall. I couldn't afford to have a nosy neighbor watch me bring a strange Negro man into my apartment, even if he did have a chauffeur's uniform on. After all, I was a widow. No doors were cracked as I invited Elijah in.

"Elijah, have a seat and let me change into more comfortable clothes."

While Elijah was driving, I had played with the idea of having sex with him. Even though, it had been rather presumptuous of him to kiss her, she could make that work to her advantage. It had been a while since she'd had sex and had no prospects on the near horizon. It might open up the situation to find out what he was really up to.

I re-entered the room in a ruby red negligee. Under a sheer lace robe, I wore a red bra and red panties. Elijah couldn't stop staring. He felt his mouth hanging open and himself starting to drool. He'd never seen anything like it before in real life or on a real person.

"Miss Nicci, *what have you got on?*"

"I told you I was changing into something more comfortable. Do you like it? I just had it made."

"I love it but do you think you should be wearing it in front of me?"

"Why not? Aren't you a close friend?" I knew I was taunting him, but I couldn't resist. I hadn't flirted with a man since Petyr died. I knew Elijah would like it. What harm could I create?

"Miss Nicci, you know I love you. Why are you teasing me?"

I sat on the sofa, with my negligee draped seductively over my bare legs. "Elijah, you can't love me. First, you barely know me and second, we must be realistic. There is a color issue."

"Miss Nicci, as I told you before, I know you're not white. I would never tell anyone, though."

"Elijah, I don't know what you really want from me. You can't possibly love me or even know me in this short period of time. Is it money you're after? Are you trying to blackmail me? The last time someone tried to blackmail me, it didn't end well for them."

"I'm not trying to blackmail you. *I really do love you.*"

"You realize, if what you say about my color is true, and I'm not saying it is, I will be destroyed. People may even try to lynch me. Do you want to see that happen to me?"

"No ma'am. We could run away together! If you don't want to do that, I can keep a secret."

"That's silly. Won't people wonder why I'm seeing such a young Negro man? How would I answer the questions? You know it's not socially acceptable. Please tell me know one knows my secret? I won't be safe after all these years." I pretended to start crying.

"Don't cry Miss Nicci. I promise, I haven't told anyone. I haven't known you long enough for anyone to even believe that I love you."

I smiled, thinking maybe I could play with him for a little while then disappear. I had learned many years ago, men were not to be trusted with such important secrets. I could use him as a sexual toy for a while. I would just have to be careful because sometimes real love can be stronger than compulsion. Times have changed. A new war had started in Europe with rumors of the United States actually joining in. Race laws had changed. Segregation was on the rise. If anyone knew her true color she would definitely be lynched. For now, if I showed him a side of sex he'd never known, just maybe he'd keep her secret just a little longer.

"Elijah, come sit near me." It was time to be seductive.

He had been sitting in one of my Victorian chairs, I brought from Rome, so long ago. He almost fell flat on his face, moving so fast. As he sat near me, I could feel his heart rate pick up speed. When I grabbed his right hand, I heard him gasp. Next, I began kissing his fingertips. After each kiss, I licked the tip of his fingers. With all the moaning and gasping he was doing, I wasn't sure he wasn't going to faint.

From his fingers, I moved to his forehead, while simultaneously unbuttoning his shirt, one by one. With a kiss to each cheek then lips, his shirt was completely unbuttoned. Due to the heat, he had a simple white tee shirt on under his dress shirt, having left his chauffeur's jacket draped around the back of the chair.

I licked his shoulders as I slid his shirt off, then his tee shirt. His muscles were extraordinary. His pale brown, hairless chest was well defined and smooth as a baby's bottom. I alternated between kissing and licking his muscles. I pulled him back towards my lap as I played with his nipples. He closed his eyes and moaned. "Miss Nicci, what are you doing to me? I can hardly breathe."

"Relax Elijah. Just close your eyes and I'll transport you to another level of lovemaking. And stop calling me Miss Nicci."

"Miss Nicci, I have to tell you something. I mean, Nicci."

"Shh, Elijah!"

"Miss Nicci, I'm a virgin." He whispered.

I smiled. "Okay. We'll have to fix that Miss Nicci stuff. Don't worry, I won't hurt you. I'm what they call a worldly woman. I'm about to introduce you to the world. I can be gentle with a virgin." I unbuckled his black trousers and slid them down his hips. His member had been bulging through the fly of his pants.

"I see you don't wear boxers?"

"No, Miss Nicci, I mean Nicci. It's too hot to wear them in the summer."

"Well, let's get your pants off. You are about to give me your virginity" As I helped him slide his pants off, I licked his member from every direction I could reach. While he was gasping for air, I slid my panties off.

"Lay here, Elijah. You're going to feel some pressure and my weight as you enter me. Just relax and enjoy the moment."

The moment I climbed on him, he had an orgasm. He was unable to control himself. "I'm sorry Miss Nicci. I didn't expect it to be so wonderful. I couldn't help it."

"It's okay. But please stop calling me Miss Nicci, at least in private. I'm not your damn teacher. Excuse my language, but you're driving me crazy with that Miss Nicci."

"Yes, Miss Nicci."He laughed. "I'm sorry, Nicci."

I laughed, too. "That's better. Now just lay her for a few minutes and we'll try it again. *Only practice makes perfect!"*

Chapter 65

I sent Elijah home at 5 a.m., just before sunrise. "Elijah a girl has to get some sleep. You go home and I'll see you this evening. Remember, I'm not as young as you, so I need more than a few hours of sleep."

"You'd never know it, Nicci. I had a fantastic evening. I hope we can do it again another night."

"Remember, keep my secret and we can."

As Elijah dressed, he said. "Yes, Miss Nicci." He laughed as he headed out the door. He was practically ready to explode with his secret. It was more than Miss Nicci was a mulatto. She had taken his virginity. Who would believe that he just lost his virginity and to an older woman? None of his friends ever spoke about sex being so fantastic. Nicci was so patient with him. She didn't even get angry when he came so fast.

Oh my god! They'd made love all through the night. How'd she do that? He felt like he could barely walk and could sleep for days. He was utterly exhausted.

How could he keep this experience a secret? It had to be written all over his face. Samuel had warned him of her beauty, but not her sexual prowess. He bet Samuel had never even had sex with her. Samuel would never have gone off to war if he'd had sex with Miss Nicci. She was incredible. That left him with very few trustworthy friends.

He'd tell Jackson. They had been friends since they were two. He remembered play dates, grade school, even high school together. Jackson never kept secrets from him. He remembered when Jackson stole chemicals from the chemistry lab, to try and make whiskey during Prohibition. It was the nastiest stuff he had ever tasted, ever. They both had gotten really sick. He never told where Jackson got the chemicals. He knew Jackson would keep his secret.

Elijah went home to try and get a couple hours of shut eye, before he had to pick Nicci up to go to the club. It was 6 a.m. Although he was tired, he was overflowing with energy.

When he walked into his mother's apartment, as soon as he opened the door, she hit him with a broom. "Where have you been all night? I've been worried sick. Did you forget how to call and tell me you'd be late or not coming home?" She hit him with the broom again.

"Ma, stop! I'm sorry! It was late when I dropped Miss Nicci off and I fell asleep on her couch. She woke me up to make me go home." (That was the best story he could think of, that still had an element of truth in it.)

"Are you sure all you did was sleep on her couch? You look awfully happy, for so early in the morning. Isn't she an old lady?"

"Well sort of. Ma'am, all I did was lay on her couch all evening." His face lit up, just at the thought of laying on her couch. He caught himself grinning as he relived part of laying on that couch with Nicci."

"What are you grinning about, boy? Are you sure that's all you did."

"Momma, please don't call me boy. I'm a grown man. I told you I laid on her couch. I fell asleep, that's why I'm just now getting home. Stop questioning me."

"Okay, Okay! I know that white lady didn't feed you. Come sit at the table while I fix you some breakfast; sausage, eggs, grits, and biscuits, okay. You're way too skinny."

It was then he realized, he was starved. "Yes, ma'am, All that food is going to make me sleepy. I have things to do today, momma. I can't be sleeping the day away." Elijah was slowly pulling the chair out from under the table.

"Don't worry, I'll wake you by noon. You'll still have time, before you have to pick up that lady. Now sit down."

"Yes, ma'am."

****

After a brief nap he was rejuvenated. The secret was bubbling just under the surface. He couldn't hold it any longer. He called Jackson, to meet him at the park on the corner.

Chapter 66

Jackson saw Elijah turn the corner and called out to him. "I'm over here, Elijah. What's so pressing and secretive that we had to meet in the park?"

Elijah ran across the street, hugged Jackson and whispered into his ear. "I have an explosive secret to share. Let's find a bench that's not in earshot of anyone else. You're not gonna believe it."

They walked deeper into the park, finding a bench near the back exit of the park.

"You're not gonna believe what happened last night." Elijah's eyes began to sparkle as he laughed. "Have you seen how beautiful my boss is? You know, Miss Nicci, at the Savoy? I've never seen a more beautiful woman. Her skin color—it looks as if she just stepped out of the sun. Her eyes are grey but I felt like they looked like storm clouds about to let rain or thunder loose. I mean that's how dramatic they are."

Jackson started laughing. "Man, I think you're in love or you hit your head on something. Isn't she too old for you? Didn't I hear her last husband got his head chopped off, somehow? I also heard she's a friend of Lucky Luciano. Do you really want to get involved with her? I mean, doesn't that sound like maybe she's dangerous."

"That's just it, Jackson. Somehow, I really think I'm in love." Lowering his voice, he added. "I lost my virginity to her last night. Can you believe it?"

"You're kidding, right! I didn't even know you were still a virgin!"

"I know. I am twenty-one. The opportunity to be *deflowered* just never arose." Elijah started laughing, too.

"Did you just say *'deflowered'*?"

"Yes, I mean, I lost my virginity to the most incredible and beautiful woman, I have ever met. I would call it being deflowered considering the way we made love. But hush! That's not the whole secret. I promised her I wouldn't tell a soul, but you are my best friend so I don't think telling you counts. You *can* keep a secret, right?"

"Who would I tell? My mother—she doesn't care about your virginity. What is it already?"

Elijah spoke in a barely audible voice. "Miss Nicci is a mulatto, passing."

"Are you *kidding?* How do you know? She sure looks white!"

"I found her diary. It was in Italian, but you know I understand some broken French, being Creole and all. Some of the words were similar. I figure her dad must have been a foreign Negro of some sort. Her mother was some foreign white. People around here would have a hissy fit if they knew a mulatto owned the Savoy and had been passing for white. You can't tell anyone!"

"You're not kidding, are you?"

"No, Jackson! She would kill me if she even knew I told you! It's getting late. I have to go get ready for work. I have a few errands to run for Miss Nicci before I pick her up. I didn't have a chance to finish the list she gave me. Promise me, you'll keep my secret!"

"Don't worry Elijah. I won't tell a soul!"

With that, they rose, shook hands and headed towards their individual homes. As soon as Jackson could no longer see Elijah, he took off running towards his home. The secret was burning a hole in his brain.

Chapter 67

Jackson nearly broke the front door down, after running up four flights of stairs. He lived with his mother and father, on the second floor. He thought if he gave his father this information, he might be able to get a better job at the Savoy. He hated that his father was only a janitor at the police station. It was common knowledge that everyone who worked at the Savoy or the Cotton Club made good money. There was also the prestige that went with working at one of the clubs. He was tired of watching his parents struggle. The Depression was over but they still never seemed to have enough money after rent was paid.

Jackson burst through the door yelling. "Mom, dad, you're not going to believe what I just heard."

Mrs. Todds spoke first. "What is it Jackson? What's got you so excited? This must be some really good news."

"You both have to sit down. You're not gonna believe what Elijah told me. Of course, it was in the strictest confidence. We can't let anyone know that Elijah told us. It would cost him his job. He found that woman's, I think they call her Nicci, diary. You'd never believe what he translated. He said it was in Italian. He was able to pick out a few words."

"Are you sure you should be telling us something Elijah found or read. I mean it was the woman's diary. That's considered private."

"Mom, when I tell you what he translated, you won't care. I think it can help dad get a better job."

"Son, what kind of information, from some woman's diary, could get me a better job?" Mr. Todds was frowning. He thought Elijah and Jackson were probably just gossiping like two old women.

"He said, she's a mulatto and she's passing! Her father was some kind of Negro in Europe and her mother was white."

"And just how do you think this information will get me a better job?"

"Dad, if you let this Nicci woman know that you know her secret, she would hire you to keep her secret."

"Do you really believe that? How do you know she won't have me killed? I've heard Lucky Luciano was one of her partners. Do you really think the mob would give me a chance to even use the secret? We must be very careful with this information. Don't even discuss it with Elijah. Let me think if there is a way I can use this information."

Jackson's dad was angry that not only was a Negro woman passing, but was wealthy, too. He never believed she was an Italian. How dare she be wealthy. He'd heard her husband, that died, was wealthy, too. She must be really something if she survived Prohibition and the Depression. She even has a chauffeur. He really got angry when he thought, how could Samuel gave his job to that young punk, Elijah? Why didn't Samuel give him the job? He thought they were friends. He'd watched Samuel work his way from a porter at the Waldorf-Astoria to the chauffeur for this rich white woman, who he just found was passing.

He was going to put a stop to this, somehow. Somehow, he was going to let the police know. He knew it was against the law to pass. He wasn't going to blackmail her. He was going to break her and she would never know that he had done it.

Chapter 68

Mr. Todds worked nights at the Harlem Police Department off 7th Avenue. The night shift was a skeleton crew and the cops were more relaxed. Many nights went by with Mr. Todds sitting around talking about old cases with the on duty cops, after he'd completed his cleaning the offices. He would mention to one of the older cops-they tended to be more bigoted-he'd heard a rumor. Cops love rumors. It would spread like wildfire in the office. Men were worse than women. By the morning, the story would no longer be a rumor but a fact. She could possibly be arrested before the week was out. They couldn't take her money but they could freeze it in the banks until they found a real white relative to give it to. Everyone would be fired. They'd shut her club down. Serve her right! He hated uppity Negroes.

Jackson forgot all about the conversation with his parents. Elijah had faith in their friendship and trusted Jackson wouldn't share his secret with anyone. Little did he know, Mr. Todd was about to destroy everything.

****

Mr. Todds worked the 11p.m. to 7a.m. shift that very night, at the Harlem Police Station. He left home early so that he could get to the station before shift change. He wanted to grab a cup of coffee and have a brief chat with Sgt. O'Hannon. He covered the front desk until the shift, of cops, changed at midnight. He knew O'Hannon was one of the biggest gossips at the station. Telling him a secret or a rumor was like turning on the faucet; it just flowed everywhere. You were guaranteed he'd tell anyone and everyone.

Sure enough, Sgt. O'Hannon was sitting at the front desk, reading the paper, when he walked in. "You're early, Tony. What'cha doing here? You don't start for another hour."

"Sergeant, I just thought I'd grab a cup of coffee early and sit around and shoot the crap with you. I've heard some really juicy gossip." Mr. Todds grabbed his coffee and pulled a chair next to the opening in the back of the front desk.

Sgt. O'Hannon went to refresh his cup of coffee. As he climbed onto his stool and got comfortable, he said. "Okay, Tony, let's have it. You looked like you swallowed a canary. What have you heard?"

"Now Sarge, I don't know how true it is, remember. It's just a rumor, I heard. So I don't know who started it. But anyhow, have you ever been to that club called the Savoy?"

"Normally, I can't afford it, but I did go when they had that big Christmas party at the end of Prohibition. It seemed like a nice place for the hoity-toity. Like I said, I can't afford it on my pay. What about it?"

"Well, I'm sure you've seen that beautiful woman, with the rubies. I think her name is Nicci. I heard she's supposedly connected to the mob. She's like a daughter to Lucky Luciano. He's protects her business, even from jail." Suddenly he whispered, conspiratorially. "She's passing. Her father was some foreign Negro."

"Did you just whisper, she's passing?" (He didn't even care about the Lucky Luciano comment. His mind went straight to the color issue.)

"Now Sarge, I said it was a rumor. You can't tell anyone. This conversation is in the strictest confidence." Tony knew nothing would keep the Sarge from spreading this rumor throughout the precinct. Everyone knew it was against the law to pass. They'd have to arrest her unless the mob already knew and had paid them off. From O'Hannon's expression, he didn't think they'd been paid off.

So as not to appear too obvious, the Sarge asked about her connection to the Mafia again. "Prohibition is over Tony. She doesn't have to buy illegal alcohol. What could she possibly need the mob for anymore?"

"I don't know. Well, my shift is going to start, so I'll have to talk to you later." As Tony got up, he knew he had planted the seed for trouble for Nicci. There was no way the Sarge would let the night go by without telling the rest of the cops.

****

Tony went to the back, to the janitor's closet and began getting his equipment ready for the night. As he selected his mops and brooms, he heard two cops rush by the door. He could hear the sergeant's loud booming voice floating down the hall. He could hear vulgar name calling. He heard someone say "Negro", "passing" then "who does she think she is?"

He heard the Sergeant calling his name. He stayed in his janitor's closet, as if he couldn't hear anything. Finally, he heard a tapping on the door and someone calling his name.

"Tony, I know you're in there. We've looked all over the building. No one has seen you, so you have to be in the closet. Come on out! We want to know more about this rumor."

"Is that you, Marc? What rumor? I don't know anything." He said, as he slowly opened the door.

"Tony, the Sarge said you heard a rumor about that beautiful woman at the Savoy. He said, you heard she was passing. She's too beautiful and too smart to be passing. Plus, her dead husband was a white man. I realize she's from somewhere in Europe but she's been in the US of A long enough to know colors don't mix."

"Mr. Marc, sir, I don't know if she is really passing. It's just a rumor I heard. But look at all the money she has. I've never seen a Negro woman with all that money. You know how colored folks talk. I think I overheard my wife's church's coffee and tea clutch women's group talking. But I heard she used to work with Lucky Luciano, too. Maybe you can bring her in and get some information on the Mafia or the mob, whatever. Can't you make her prove she's not passing? Doesn't she only have to show her birth certificate? I mean it will show her parents race. I got work to do sir. I can't stand here talking all night." Laughing, he said. "That hall won't mop itself and I'm behind schedule."

Marc laughed, too. "You're right, Tony. If she's white, let her prove it. Don't worry. I won't let anyone know I heard the rumor from you. I didn't mean to hold you up." With that, he heard Marc walk away mumbling to himself.

Tony knew he had the ball rolling, so to speak. She was finished now. Mr. Todds knew you only had to have a few drops of Negro blood and you were considered a Negro. Every room he walked by, he stood outside the door with his mop as if mopping, listening. He could hear various policemen discussing the beautiful Nicci Santa Maria, the beautiful host and owner of the Savoy. In every room the conversation was the same. "Could it be possible? Is she really passing? She's so beautiful."

One office he heard someone say. "I even saw her taking pictures with Greta Garbo. Nicci's one of my favorite pin-up girls. It would break my heart to think I was in love with a Negro."

He laughed to himself as he mopped down the hall. He hated what he considered uppity Negroes. He felt she deserved it. How dare Samuel, his friend, not get him a job with her. He was hoping she'd never get her money back.

Chapter 69

His plan didn't go quite the way Tony had hoped. Before the week was out, every cop in Harlem was talking about whether Nicci was a Negro or white. Within two weeks, word had gotten back to Elijah and I. Elijah swore he hadn't told anyone. I knew he was lying but there was nothing I could do about it, now. Elijah knew he had told Jackson, but couldn't figure out who in the world Jackson could have told. This was a disaster.

People were coming to the club, asking questions all night long. I couldn't run the club. By the end of the week I had posted a sign announcing the temporary closing of the Savoy. The sign said:

Closed for Remodeling

Everyone knew she wasn't remodeling. I just couldn't take any more questions.

It was May 28, 1940. The 'New York Times' had a huge article in the socialite column:

A Negro Passes

The Savoy closed. Dominique Santa Maria (Nicci)
Was found to be a Negro. Her father was a Negro from Europe.
She is purported to be an Italian. Her mother is a
White European. In the US of A, that makes you a Negro.
She is accused of miscegenation.

Her husband was Petyr Apostal. Questions are being asked,
did she behead her husband for his money.
She is being charged with:

1. Paying Negroes exorbitant amounts of money to drive her
around.
2. Getting illegal alcohol from Lucky Luciano (the Mobster)
during Prohibition. (The statue of limitations has not expired).
3. Working for the mob.
She is being held at the 43rd Precinct in Brooklyn.
Miss Santa Maria has reportedly pleaded 'not guilty' to all charges.
Her trial will be open to the public beginning
June 15, 1940

****

I had been arrested. It was unbelievable. What had that fool done?
I was arrested for passing, not being a vampire. No one was allowed
to see me. I couldn't even get a word to the vampire council. Every
night, for the past two weeks, I could hear Sally's voice drifting back
to the cells. He was not allowed in. This was a total unexpected turn
of events.

She had been a vampire for nearly one hundred fifty years.
Throughout those years, I had stopped worrying about being a
mulatto. I'd almost forgotten until Elijah found my diary and then
fell in love with me. Every time I play with a human I get in some
sort of trouble. I definitely needed help to get out of this situation.

The night before opening statements in my trial, I could hear
loud, angry voices in the front office of the jail. I was being held in
a small local jail until trial. If found guilty, I would be moved to a
women's prison. The voices were getting louder, when suddenly the
door separating the two sections, banged open. I was praying it was a
group of vampires coming to rescue me. I was wrong. It was a group
of angry white men with sheets over their heads and clothes. I was
frightened. I rarely get frightened, but I was truly frightened. I knew
as long as they didn't cut off my head, I would be okay. At least, no
one knew I was a vampire.

There were only five men. I could have easily killed them with my vampire strength. But, how would I explain five dead men in the jail, though? I was going to have to let them take me and see what happens. The worse they could do was kill her. They obviously didn't know the tricks to killing a vampire. They hadn't even bound me with anything stronger than rope.

I decided not to scream. It seemed safer to see what they were go to do instead of taking her chances with the court. I had no desire to go to jail for something as simple as passing and all the other trumped charges they had read her. If convicted it, I wouldn't die in jail. I would be there forever.

I did cry, to make it more dramatic. Naturally, they were fake tears. "What is it you want? I go to court tomorrow. Can't you wait till they throw me in prison?"

Someone slapped me. "Shut up, trash. We hate uppity Niggers. You think you're better than us, with that phony accent. I bet you're really from Mississippi."

"No, sir. I'm from Siena. That's in Italy, outside Rome. I'll admit I was born in Portugal but I grew up in Italy. My accent is real."

I heard a deeper voice. "He said shut up. I don't know where no Portugal is. Is that in the US of A. I bet he's right. I bet you're really from some small place down south, where you thought you wouldn't be recognized. You're known to hire Creoles from Louisiana. Can you deny that?"

"It's true, I hired two people from Louisiana, but I don't know what a Creole is."

"There you go, trying to be uppity again." They were dragging her out the door. Someone shoved her into a car.

"Where are we going? What are you doing?" Now, I was really scared.

They drove to Harlem and dragged her out of the car. She noticed, they had arrived at the Savoy. It was completely dark. The sign was still on the door saying: Closed for remodeling. "Why are we here? Please answer me."

No one said anything. Suddenly, I felt a rope slip over my head, and around my neck. I knew then what was about to happen. I'd heard about lynchings in the South. I always thought it was just propaganda in the papers to keep the newly relocated Negroes in line.

I felt myself being dragged to the lamppost that sat on the corner of Lennox and 132nd Street. A rope was thrown over the pole that extended from the lantern. It was attached to the rope around my neck. I believed it was called a noose. Internally, I sighed. Even if they did hang me and break my neck, I'll survive. *I am a vampire!* I just couldn't be hanging there when the sun came up.

I felt the noose tighten and my feet were swinging off the ground. All I could do was hang there 'dead', praying someone would cut me down before sun-up.

****

Elijah had been sitting outside the precinct every night since her arrest, hoping for a chance to speak to her. He felt horrible for what he had done. He thought Jackson was his best friend. He still couldn't figure out who Jackson could have told to get Miss Nicci arrested.

He had been sitting in the shadows crying, again, when the five men pulled up. He knew there was going to be trouble. He watched them pull white sheets over their heads before entering the police station. He heard the crunch of the door being kicked in and Nicci yelling; what was going on? He watched them drag Nicci out. Elijah wanted to intervene but he was scared. Plus, he was only one man.

He followed the car after they threw Nicci in the back seat. Upon their arrival at the Savoy, he watched in horror when they threw the rope over her neck. Elijah knew this was the end of his love. He watched them laughing as her body swung from the lamppost. It seemed like barely five minutes had passed and her body stopped moving. One man placed a placard at the base of the lamppost.

The five men stood there laughing and drinking a bottle of whiskey. One of them was passing it around. He watched them climb into a car and drove off. They just left her hanging there.

Elijah waited until he was sure they were gone. It was then he read the placard. It said: We hate Upity Niggers. They couldn't even spell. He ripped it into as many pieces as he could. Then he tossed the pieces into the trash bin outside the club. Next he cut Nicci down.

As he lowered her to the ground, he began to sob. "Nicci, I'm so sorry. I finally find love and it was gone in an instant. I opened my big mouth after I promised you I could keep a secret." His tears dripped down on her face and clothes. As far he was concerned, she was dead. Her neck was broken. Her head lolled from side to side, like a rag doll.

Eventually, he stopped crying. He didn't know what to do. He couldn't leave her in the street. He carried her to her limousine and laid her across the back seat. How was he going to explain her death to Samuel, if he should return? He promised Samuel he would take care of her. Look at the mess he'd made. He put his head down on the steering wheel an began to cry again.

Finally, he realized he couldn't sit in front of the Savoy crying. He remembered picking up a package one day from a local mortician. He had no idea what the package was, though and it didn't matter anymore. He knew Nicci had done many favors for the local, neighborhood business.

The mortician was two blocks down the road, near the 1st Pentecostal Church of Harlem. He drove there and banged on the back door. He knew the mortician lived over the mortuary. Finally, the back door cracked open. After all, it was midnight.

"Who is it? What kind of dead body can't wait until the morning, at a reasonable hour?"

"Mr. Reynolds, its Elijah. I have Dominique Santa Maria. You know, Nicci! Five white men lynched her tonight. I cut her down. It was too late, though. She's dead. I don't know what to do with her body. I can't let the police have her. I can't afford to pay for a casket or a funeral. What should I do?"

Mr. Reynolds was looking everywhere to make sure Elijah hadn't been followed. "Okay, bring her in. We'll figure out what to do with her. We can't let those white folks have her body. They may burn her for all we know."

"Thank you, Mr. Reynolds. I'm so scared. I don't know what I was thinking when I cut her down. She deserves a big fancy funeral, but people are so angry with her right now. I think her neck broken. She's really dead." Elijah starts sobbing again, when her head rolled off his shoulder.

"Young man, she's definitely dead. We can bury her in Potter's Field in an unmarked grave. It'll be up to you to remember what the plot number is. When the drama dies down you can tell her friends and they can give her a proper burial."

"That's an excellent idea. I can tell Samuel when he returns from Europe and we can dig her up."

"I'll give you the plot number tomorrow, after I return from Potter's Field."

****

That was June 14, 1940. Mr. Reynolds had gone back to bed. He figured he would embalm Nicci in the morning. She was 'dead', where could she go. When he arose at 7a.m. the body was gone. He thought Elijah had reconsidered and returned for her body.

Elijah spent the rest of the early morning crying and mourning the loss of his great love. While doing this, he got drunk and forgot to return to Mr. Reynolds home for the plot number. Three days later, sober, he returned to Mr. Reynolds home for the plot number. Mr. Reynolds had no idea what he was talking about. *Where was Nicci?*

The End

Chloe's final thoughts

One more diary to go. I certainly didn't see that coming. I sure hope Elijah gets to become a vampire and not some sad drunk? I think it's finally time to take that long potty break before I start the final diary. Where in the hell did she go?

Dedication

*Thanks to Jacques McKissick and Jason Cruz, whose never tiring ears
listened to my crazy love stories.*
*Special thanks to Alphonso S. Crawford, whose late night talks allowed
some of my characters to become three dimensional.*
Finally, to Frank B. Santos, for the gift of writing.
P.S a teen mom can succeed with help.